M000105654

Francis M. Nevins:

-Million Dollar Mouse

120-Hour Clock

rupt and Ensnare

blish and Perish

ALSO BY

The Ninet
The
Co
P

INTO THE SAME RIVER TWICE

Francis M. Nevins

Carroll & Graf Publishers, Inc.
New York

COPYRIGHT © 1996 BY FRANCIS M. NEVINS

ALL RIGHTS RESERVED.

FIRST EDITION 1996

CARROLL & GRAF PUBLISHERS, INC.
260 FIFTH AVENUE
NEW YORK, NY 10001

ISBN 0-7867-0314-8

LIBRARY OF CONGRESS CATALOGING-IN-PUBLICATION DATA
IS AVAILABLE.

MANUFACTURED IN THE UNITED STATES OF AMERICA.

For David and Cain Linzee

INTO THE
SAME RIVER
TWICE

One

HE LAY IN THE DARK on the cool, passionless bed and waited
for the Valium to draw him into the caves of sleep and
while he waited he thought of death and the river. The
river was twenty-seven stories below. Its night sounds
drifted up to him through the open bedroom window, the
intimate little splashes of waves, the hollow hooting of
boat horns. After eight months in New York and this
apartment he had come to find the noises soothing but he
still needed the Valium each night to give him rest and
shut down the thoughts that filled him whenever he was
alone in darkness.

*If there's nothing to live for it's better to die. What have
I done with my life? Taught gunfighters how to maim people better. Trained whores.* He was a law professor. When
he was younger he had believed that what he did had a
purpose, he had had faith that slowly and turbulently he
was helping to make the world better, freer, more caring.
In middle age, he believed nothing and hoped nothing and
loved less and less. The life of the law had not been his
unfettered choice but it had grown into him and he had
believed that beneath the system's injustice and rot and
corruption and all the contemptible outrages its core was
sound and good. No more. Now he saw it as a malignant
thug or a blundering mad beast, cruel as life, trampling and
crushing whatever it touched. Yet he continued to live as
he had and work as he had, preparing young men and
women to serve the beast, keeping buried within him the
dark knowledge that turned his heart to stone. He knew no
other way to live.

THE TELEPHONE BELL ripped through his dream like a knife through flesh.

He was dreaming he was back in law school, first semester, living out in fear the months before his baptism of fire in the end-of-term examinations. He was sitting in a barn-like classroom full of first-year law students listening to Professor Hirschberg, who was tall and gawky and whippet-lean with bifocals that seemed to hang by a thread from the end of his nose and hands that flashed in the air like fireworks as he peppered his Introduction to Jurisprudence lectures with Chestertonian paradoxes (so many paradoxes that Loren had to read Chesterton's novels and short stories to get a grip on where Hirschberg was coming from) and Yiddish slang and philosophic puzzles. "Heraclitus tells us we can't step into the same river twice. What does that mean to you, Mr. Mensing? If there is no continuity to experience, how can one case be like another, how should the same rule of law apply to both? Will you tell me Heraclitus was a schmuck?" The canny old jurisprude was pressing him for an answer just as the ringing tore through the fabric of the dream.

He jerked awake in his bed. Sunday morning in New York. The only sounds were a distant fire truck siren and the whisper of cello music from the nightstand radio and the ringing. Even without his glasses he could read the bright red numbers of the digital clock display. 4:06. In peacetime there is no sound more terrifying than the scream of a phone at four in the morning. Loren fought a shudder as he groped for the handset in the dark.

"Loren, I have to see you." The woman's voice broke into his tentative hello and through his sleep haze he sensed her fright. There was a pause then, as if she were afraid she'd dialed the wrong number. "This . . . this is Loren, isn't it? Loren Mensing?"

"Yes." Neutral, noncommittal. He knew that she must know him and thought he remembered her voice but

2

couldn't tie it to a name. Former student? "I'm sorry," he said. "I'm not really awake yet. Who is this, please?"

"Kim!" Whoever it was seemed surprised he hadn't known her at once. "Kimberly. Kimberly . . . Hale." As if for a moment she were unsure of her name.

He knew then, and his thoughts flew madly in all directions. "Princess?" *My God,* he asked himself, *how long has it been?* Since his first semester in law school. Fall of 1964. Dream time.

"It's me, Loren." *Remember when I was your love?* she seemed to be saying. "I have to see you this morning, it's so important. I need to . . ."

"Kim, where are you?" he broke in. "Where in God's name have you been?"

"Can you meet me at the South Ferry terminal down at the Battery, say at nine-thirty? If I'm not there take the first boat to Staten Island and wait for me at the St. George end. I swear I'll be there. Please come? Oh, Loren, please do this for me." *Remember when I was your love?* "There are people trying to shut me up or kill me and no one else will believe me but maybe you will."

He was awake now. The quiet terror in her voice had cut through the mists of Valium and sleep. "Where are you calling from? How did you know where to find me? Why can't you come to me right now if it's so important, or why can't I come to you?"

"No," she said. "We can't do it that way, it's not safe, they might be anywhere . . . Oh, dear God, I think someone's watching me from across the street! Loren, if anything happens to me find Joyce Clarke, she lives in the West Village on Jane Street, and ask how her father died."

"Kim, where are you?" He barked the question into the mouthpiece like a prosecutor cross-examining a hostile witness.

"Loren, I can't talk anymore, I haven't slept in two nights and that car across the street is . . . I'll get to you in the morning somehow, Loren. Think of me a little till then, okay? Please, love." And the next moment the line went dead. She hadn't told him where she was, hadn't even

3

said good night. Was that because terror and exhaustion had been tearing her apart, or had she been cut off?

Loren cradled his own receiver and slid between the blankets and tried to turn off his mind and find sleep again but kept hearing the echo of her voice. He was wide awake and gray-faced with worry when morning light crept into his bedroom.

———————

YEARS LATER, when the affair is a blur of memory, what do you owe your love?

When Loren Mensing started law school in the fall of 1964, the first-year class was divided into three roughly equal sections of about a hundred students apiece who would take all the mandatory freshman courses together: Contracts, Torts, Civil Procedure, Property, Legal Research and Writing. Loren's section contained exactly five women, all white, and two black men, whom in those days one still called Negroes. At the time there seemed nothing outrageous in those figures. Indeed for those who thought of themselves as liberals it was a source of quiet pride. Loren was more interested in the figures of the five women. One especially.

Kimberly Hale happened to be assigned to a seat in the classroom amphitheater that was one place to Loren's right in the row directly behind him. It was natural for him to swivel his chair around and chat casually with her in the few minutes of hubbub before and after each class. At first they talked about the cases they had studied for the day's lectures but soon they were saying to each other almost anything that came into their heads.

As Loren lay sleepless in the milky light with the muted sounds of Schubert's *Death and the Maiden* drifting from the nightstand radio, he relived how it had been between them. She was about five feet two with soft chestnut hair worn long and loose and a neat oval face and a ski-jump nose and a body made to be adored. Several times he had caught a puzzled, searching look in her eyes when she didn't know he was watching her. One afternoon in the third week of fall semester he screwed up his courage and invited her for coffee at an off-campus deli and they talked. It didn't take her long to turn the conversation to herself.

"I honestly don't know if I belong here," she had confessed. "I don't understand half of what the professors are saying, I can't keep up with the reading, and even if a miracle happens and I graduate I don't want to be a lawyer anyway. God, why am I telling this to somebody I'm competing with for grades?"

"I'm not competing with you or anybody for anything," Loren told her.

"Easy for you to say, you're a genius with a full scholarship and book learning's always been a snap for you. Next year you'll make Law Review and when you graduate your father will take you into his firm and you'll tap into his political connections and probably be a judge before you're forty."

"Don't bet on it," Loren said, wondering, *Where has she learned so much about me? And why?* "Look, Kim, I'm just as unsure of myself and scared of the future as you are but I do think you need someone to sit down and talk things out with. Maybe your parents or a girlfriend, or one of the professors."

"I was adopted," she said. "Mother and Dad Hale died in a plane crash in California seven years ago. The airline settled out of court with the victims' families and I used the money for college and then I was a secretary for a while and saved up for law school tuition. The Hales had no kids of their own and I'm new in this area like you so I don't have any real friends in school yet and those professors are just so damn cold and unapproachable! I've always kept problems bottled up inside anyway."

Like me, Loren thought. "Until now?" he asked.

"Loren, I've never talked like this even to guys I was dating seriously. There's something . . . something different about you. I didn't really mean what I said about you competing with me."

"It's these." He tapped his glasses with a fingernail and

laughed. "They make me look ten years older than the other men in class." *And safe like a big brother,* he added to himself ruefully.

Her eyes had changed then, seemed to gleam with a bold brightness not there before, as if the look of her and the atmosphere around her had become electrified. She hadn't moved a muscle nor said a word but Loren somehow imagined that she had shed her blouse and sweater and sport skirt and whatever she had on underneath and was offering herself and he wondered if he'd gone over the edge.

"They're not glued to your ears as far as I can see," she said quietly, and their hands reached for each other under the Formica table. Both of them were woefully unprepared for class the next day.

———————

IN THE EARLY YEARS of the sexual revolution an unmarried man and woman did not advertise that they were living together. Once Loren and Kim reached the ivy-draped law school building each morning, they would put up the barriers and pretend to the rest of the world that they had no more than a chatting acquaintance. They would grab a quick sandwich together now and then in the university cafeteria or coffee shop and they would study together occasionally in the law library but more often than not except for the classes they took together they would see almost nothing of each other until six or seven in the evening, when they would meet by prearrangement at his tiny apartment above a secondhand bookstore or at hers in a dark brick three-story building half a mile away. There would be a hasty supper which they took turns cooking, several hours of studying quietly together, perhaps a movie at one of the university town's revival theaters, or a late walk (the streets in those days being still safe after dark) and afterward a nightcap and bed. Neither of them seemed to need anyone else in the world except the other.

As December approached with its dreaded final exams, their sexual desires dwindled. Those were the longest nights, when they would pore over casebooks and course outlines and class notes in frantic silence, each of them wrapped in a cocoon of concentration until one or two or three in the morning. Then they would stumble into bed and try to snatch a few hours of uneasy sleep before the next day's early class. When they did turn in at a sensible hour she didn't want sex but only to be held close and cuddled and reassured. Loren understood just enough not to pressure her for more.

The night before their first exam they tried to unwind by slamming the casebooks shut and taking in the Alec Guinness double bill at the student center. Afterward at his place he scrawled a few notes in the diary he kept in those years and then they tried to make love and couldn't and tried to fall asleep and couldn't so they clung together in bed and kissed lightly and held each other close and tried to take each other's minds off the morning.

"You know what I think I'd like to do if I graduate with good enough grades?" he asked her somewhere in the depth of the night.

"Take over your father's firm." She squeezed his hand and gave him one of the silly grins that mention of Stephen Mensing always precipitated. By this time he had become one of their private jokes. She knew that it was paternal pressure and not personal choice that had taken Loren into the study of law but she was unspeakably glad it had happened that way because it had brought the two of them together.

"Teach in a law school myself," he said, and waited for her reaction. "Think I'd make a good prof?"

If he had thought for hours about the best way to break her tension and make her laugh he could have come up with nothing better. She all but exploded with mirth at the notion. "Oh, Loren, you'd be absolutely *awful* as a law professor! You're no good at pretending you're God, you wouldn't know how to humiliate the kids, and you have too much common sense to stand up in front of a class and say that things really are the way the law says they are." She held out her arms to embrace him.

7

"No, I'm serious," he insisted. "I don't think teaching law has to be that way. I wouldn't have to be that kind of person. Old Hirschberg isn't that way. And anyhow, it's better than working for my father. . . . How about you? What'll you do with your degree?" As if all the exams were already behind them and forgotten.

"You'd laugh like I just did."

"Try me." He kissed her neck gently.

"Well, it goes back to something I've never told you about myself," she began. "Did you—did you know you've been bedding royalty this semester?"

"If you mean you're a treat fit for a king you won't get a dissenting opinion from me."

"No, seriously." She half sat up, propped the pillows behind her shoulders. "The Hales told me all they knew about my real parents on my fourteenth birthday. They thought I had a right to know."

"They told you you were *royalty*?" Loren struggled to hold back the laughter he knew she would hate him for.

"Well, not quite. They told me I was the daughter of someone who was part of an incredibly wealthy family, one of the richest in America, and they said that someday if everything worked out all right, one or both of my real parents would come forward and reveal themselves to me. That's all they knew about where I came from, the adoption was arranged by lawyers when I was an infant. But ever since the Hales told me who I was, I've been sort of, well, sort of preparing myself. I think that's really why I came to law school, to learn all I could about adoption rights, maybe someday start tracing myself back in time and—you know—meet my parents halfway."

"Kim," Loren said, "the Hales were your parents in every sense of the word that means anything. They raised you, loved you—"

"And I'll always love and remember them," she broke in. *"But they weren't my parents."* The tautness of her voice frightened Loren a little. "You know me, you know I'm a very patient person. Someday I'll find them and find out who I am."

"Nothing in the Hales's records gave any clues?"

"The executors went through all the papers in the house after the plane crash. They didn't find a thing except the formal adoption documents. And the adoption agency's files about where I came from are kept sealed by law. But ever since I learned I was adopted I've sort of fantasized what my real family must be like, the way you have fantasies about being a law professor with a white hat. They are very kind people, rich with old money that wasn't gotten in any dirty way." Her voice fell to almost a whisper as if she were reciting a prayer in the darkness. "My parents were very young when they got involved with each other so they'd be in their early forties now. Just about everyone was in uniform twenty years ago. Sometimes I think my father must have been killed in the war, otherwise he'd have come back to my mother and me. Then sometimes I think it was my mother who died having me, and my father's still alive out there somewhere, and when I think that way I look twice at every man I pass on the street who looks the right age and I ask myself could he be the one, or that man, or the next?"

No wonder she went for the oldest-looking guy in class, Loren thought. "Or they could both be alive and well," he pointed out. "Or they could both be dead. You don't even know whether the money or the royal blood or whatever it is is on your mother's side or your father's."

"I'm entitled to my dreams too," she said, and kissed him on the lips as softly as a child. "Good night, love. Good luck in the morning."

From then on, Loren began to call her Princess.

IN MID-DECEMBER when exams were behind them, Loren went home for a tense and joyless Christmas with his father while Kim flew back to San Francisco where the Hales had raised her. The night before their flights they made love with the wild uncontrollable urgency of their first time together. They promised to phone each other on

Christmas Eve and to meet for dinner at the University Steak House on the tenth of January when they came back to law school for the spring semester.

He phoned her San Francisco number on the evening of December 24 and there was no answer. Every fifteen minutes until long after midnight Pacific time he dialed and no one answered. It was the most wretched Christmas he had ever known. He tried again in the morning of Christmas Day, and at noon and in the afternoon and the evening, and on the day after Christmas and the day after that, and there was never an answer. Three times he called the airline and made a reservation on a flight to San Francisco. Each time he canceled. He had never been to San Francisco and despaired of being able to find her. He was terrified that by some quirk of chance he would find her and that she would be in the arms of another man who reminded her of her invisible father. Throughout the vacation weeks he stayed close to the phone, praying that she would call him. She didn't. When he flew back to school he felt a sick emptiness inside him, a sense of loss more acute than any he'd known before.

She didn't keep their dinner date on the tenth. She didn't even register for the term. The seat just to Loren's right in the row behind him was taken over by a young man, a pudgy carrot-thatched transfer student who belched. During the first week of spring semester he tried the San Francisco number again, and an emotionless phone operator voice informed him that the number was no longer in service. By then he knew he had lost her. He still wondered in an abstract way how she'd done on her exams.

He never saw or heard from her again until the call in the middle of the night almost a quarter century later.

SO MANY OF THOSE intervening years were full of so much pain. When Loren began law school Vietnam was a barely familiar name. By the time he had graduated magna cum laude and returned home to study for the bar, it had become the national nightmare. By fiat of a president gone mad with dreams of power, the military had set out to destroy a tiny country in Southeast Asia in order to save it, and had accomplished little beyond rending the home front apart. Hundreds of thousands of the radicalized young took to the streets, burned draft cards, lay down before troop trains, chose exile in Canada or Sweden or prison rather than submit to taking part in the slaughter. The agony of those endless war years changed Loren's life, drove him out of the world of theories and concepts and civilized dialogue in which he would have preferred to live, dragged him into the world of blood and filth and screams.

After the bar he succumbed to his father's pressure and went to work as a junior associate in Stephen Mensing's firm. He despised his job. He expected to receive his draft notice any day. Every spare minute he spent reading, about Southeast Asia, about the Third Reich. Would he run to Canada, or refuse induction and take a jail sentence and the revocation of his license to practice law? Would he knuckle under as he had to his father, let himself be drafted and ask Stephen to use his political connections to arrange a legal clerk's slot stateside? Loren's weight dropped and he slept only in snatches as he made himself face the horrors and uncertainties of each new day.

And then the miracle happened, or rather the thing happened that almost seemed miraculous to him until he thought about all the poor devils whom chance hadn't kissed. The draft board classified him 4-F. It was his eyes that saved him. Four years of college and three more of law school, seven years of reading closely printed text for six to ten hours a day, had damaged his sight to the point where he was deemed unqualified to butcher infants. In any event that was how Loren interpreted the ruling. The night after the news reached him, he did something he had never done before and would almost never do again. He drank himself into a stupor.

And while the war in Asia dragged on, Loren's life went

into an upward spiral. After another few months at his father's firm he resigned to become Judge Ben Richmond's clerk on the regional division of the intermediate state court of appeals. In time he left the chambers of the wise and gentle judge to become an assistant professor at City University School of Law. While negotiating a corporate merger Stephen Mensing suffered a myocardial infarction and died instantly, leaving his rebel son suddenly blessed and burdened by so much inherited money that, if he chose, he need never work again. The result was that he worked harder than ever. For by then Loren was aflame with causes. He lectured, he wrote, he served on committees, he came near burning himself out on behalf of the values that were his religion. "To remake the world!" he scrawled in his diary on one particularly enthusiastic morning. "But decently, decently, and with love."

Then his life changed course again. The underdog mayoral candidate won a stunning upset at the polls, and during his first week in office the shaggy-haired young municipal executive invited Loren to serve part-time as deputy legal adviser to the police department. Loren leapt with joy at the offer, which would involve not only keeping the PD up to date on all existing restrictions on police power but also working to create new ones. Too many of his friends of both sexes had been beaten, gouged, kicked during demonstrations. Now, Loren exulted, the club would be in the victims' hands.

It turned out to be the most frustrating job he had ever held. The force resisted his modest reforms as he and his comrades had resisted the authorities before. Their right to search, harass and maim at will was under siege. Loren was the enemy. More than once during his bizarre tenure with the department there were hints that he too might be found beaten to death in an alley in the black ghetto. But then the word began to spread through the ranks that this pointyhead with his glasses and bearish build and heart full of mush for the oppressed was one of the most valuable weapons in the department's arsenal.

It happened almost by accident. A murder that defied solution by normal procedure somehow crossed Loren's desk. He made a hesitant suggestion to the detective sergeant in charge of the case and within four hours the killer confessed. A fluke, everyone said. Never happen again in a million years. In fact it did happen again less than a month later. Without even trying, Loren soon developed an underground reputation as the metro area's detective of last resort. His relationship with the police took on a new dimension of ambiguity.

At the time he was having a casual affair with the director of publicity at the city art museum. One night, with the Shostakovich Second Violin Concerto drifting into the bedroom from the stereo speakers and a bottle of chilled Montrachet and two glasses teetering on the spread between them, he tried to explain the police attitude toward him with an analogy from the history of art. "Well, Michelangelo was a libertine and a homosexual and the pope hated his guts but wouldn't kick him out of the Sistine Chapel while he was painting the ceilings because the guy was making such an incredible contribution to the world."

"I'm glad you're not," she said.

"Not making a contribution to the world?" He was puzzled and wondering what he'd said or done to make her want to insult him.

"Guess again." She smiled, set the bottle and glasses on the floor and rubbed her body against him.

Before long, consulting on major criminal cases became his primary function, and the mayor had to find another young Turk for the role of deputy legal adviser. The plainclothesmen who weren't afraid to ask for help when they needed it started dropping in on Loren unannounced at the law school. The bolder ones would phone him at home after hours. Usually his suggestions brought results, thanks partly to his native brilliance and partly, he was convinced, to pure dumb luck, which kept him uncomfortable about taking credit for any success.

Like the murder of the male chauvinist.

13

IT WAS THE WEEK after examinations and Loren was hunched over the desk in his book-crammed office above the law library, reading and grading the term papers of the students in his seminar, Recent Developments in Civil Rights Law. Late-spring sun filled the room with light and made him think of peace and contentment. And of Gael Irwin, who had just dropped off her paper on his desk, ten days over-due. With her bird-bright personality, her perky vulnerable face beneath dark tangled curls, her lovely body inside old shirt and blue jeans, her childlike naturalness and lack of awe before anything and anyone including himself, she was one of his favorites. He was daydreaming about her when the phone rang. He lifted the handset and spoke his name into the mouthpiece.

"Charley Hough," the voice on the other end said. "Major Case Squad. I don't know if you remember me, Professor, I was one of the guys on the stolen python case last year that you cracked for us."

"Of course, the snake-napping at the zoo! What can I do for you, Sergeant?"

"Well, a sort of a funny homicide just got dumped on me and, ah, could you come down to Headquarters after work tonight and sort of talk it over with me?"

"Funny how?"

"The dead guy left a message and it's got something to do with all this Women's Liberation stuff. Say, do you know a memo came down this month that says we can't use Mrs. or Miss anymore in reports when we're writing about a dame. We've got to put M-S-period in front of her name no matter she's married or single or whatever. That's the in thing right now with these crazy broads. Drives me up the goddamn wall."

"It's the fashion of 1974. Most of my female students sign their names that way but it's nothing to get upset about. Anyway, who was murdered?"

"Alvin Apgar. You know, he does the midday talk show

14

on the local station. Until today he did. Before he got into TV he used to write those word game and puzzle books."

"I may have caught his program once or twice when I was home sick or over the summer," Loren said. "When was he killed?"

"Sometime this morning at his house. He lived out in the Stone Canyon area, forty miles from downtown. Hell of a commute every day. I'm calling from there now. It's a beautiful isolated house, fifteen rooms, heated indoor pool, private movie theater, no neighbors for half a mile. Someone cracked his skull this morning with a bronze nude statuette he kept in his den. Body was found just before noon by Sam White, the guy who manages some rental property Apgar bought. Preliminary medical report says he died between ten-thirty and noon."

"Hold it," Loren cut in. "Doesn't his TV show come on at 11:30 A.M.? What time was Apgar due at the station this morning? What time did he usually leave his house?"

"He only had to be on four days a week, someone else covered for him on Fridays, so that doesn't help us at all. But we did get a beautiful break elsewhere. Apgar was separated from his wife and sleeping with every chick in sight. Mrs. A was about ready to file for divorce and hired a local private snoop by the name of Jerry Lusky to keep the Stone Canyon house under surveillance for female visitors. Lusky was staked out in the hills above the house and had the place covered with binoculars all morning. When he saw the cop cars lining up at the front door he figured something had happened and came down and spilled everything he knew. In the time the killing could have been done Apgar had four visitors, two female and two male. Lusky got all their license numbers.

"Now before I get to the four parties let me tell you about this message Apgar left. We know he couldn't have lived more than a few seconds after he got whacked with the nude, but he lived long enough to grab a pen and write two letters on a blank scrap of paper on his desk. Then he crumpled the paper into a ball and rolled over on top of it. We figure the killer was still in the house and Apgar was afraid he'd come back into the den and find his name written out and in plain view."

"Well, if you've got the killer's name, Sergeant," Loren asked, sweetly reasonable, "what do you want me for?"

"Apgar never finished the name. All he left us, like I said, was two letters. M, as in maximum, and S, as in Santa. See where the Women's Lib angle comes in?

"Now for the four visitors. At 10:42 A.M. Lusky clocked in a car which turned out to belong to Mike Stanley, a local writer. He tells us he was ghosting a book for Apgar called *The Women's Lib Joke Book*. He says he went out to Stone Canyon to talk about some problems with the book, but he swears he left Apgar alive and well around 11:00 A.M. Lusky confirms that was the time the first visitor left.

"The second visitor drove up at 11:10 and left at 11:16. By her license number she turned out to be Monica St. Vincent, the gal that does the weather forecasts on the evening news, the same station as Apgar's show. She admits she'd been having an affair with him but says he broke it off last month. She fell hard. Says she came out this morning to beg him to take her back but her key wouldn't work because he'd changed all the locks. She claims she left in tears without catching a glimpse of him. The key she showed us won't go into Apgar's new locks but of course he could have opened the door and let her in and she could have killed him if he did.

"The third visitor drove up at 11:34 in a beat-up old station wagon. Her name's Elizabeth Nunda, she's built like a Mack truck and runs the state chapter of Women United Now. She says she'd heard rumors about the Lib joke book and came out to demand that Apgar drop the project. Claims she pounded on the door for several minutes but Apgar wouldn't let her in, he was afraid of her righteous wrath. Imagine, a Duke Wayne type like Apgar scared of a fat broad like Nunda! Anyway she says she got disgusted after a while, left a note under the door calling him a chauvinist pig and took off. We found the note but she could have written it after she brained him."

"Does Lusky confirm that she never got in the house?" Loren asked.

"He can't. There's a roofed outer vestibule before you reach the front door, and from Lusky's stakeout position on the hill he couldn't tell one way or the other. We haven't found her prints inside or any other trace of her except that note but we think the killer wore gloves anyway.

"The fourth visitor of course was White, the property manager. He got there just before noon for a lunch conference with Apgar. Says he found the front door unlocked, walked in, saw Apgar dead in the den, called us right away. What do you think, Professor?"

Loren leaned back in his creaky swivel chair. "I think you've got more MS's on your hands than I do," he said. "Let's go over the possibilities. MS could mean Mike Stanley, the ghost writer, or Monica St. Vincent, the weather lady. Or, if Apgar simply meant the feminist abbreviation for being female, it could point to Elizabeth Nunda. Or—come to think of it, the message might have nothing to do with either initials or feminism! Weren't Apgar and Stanley working on a book? I gather it's not published or even finished yet."

"It isn't," the sergeant grumpily agreed. "So what?"

"What's a book called when it's not published or finished?" Loren tactfully waited a minute for Hough to supply the answer.

"Uhhh—manuscript?" he hazarded dubiously.

"Right! Now, what's the standard abbreviation writers and editors use in referring to a manuscript?" This time he was certain Hough wouldn't know and volunteered the answer at once. "MS," he said, and took off his glasses and rubbed his aching eyes while Hough wrestled with the implications.

"Let me make sure I read you, Professor," the plainclothesman said at last. "You think we should look for the killer in the manuscript of this Women's Lib joke book?"

"Possibly," Loren replied, although after another moment's consideration he found the notion ridiculous.

"But if Apgar wanted us to look at the manuscript," Hough objected, "why the fuck didn't he say so in English?"

That was what had occurred to Loren a few seconds earlier. "Good point," he mumbled, and listened to the silence for another minute. This time he seemed to hear something worth his attention.

"Word games! Word games!" he barked suddenly into the handset. "Sergeant, what's Mrs. Apgar's first name?"

"I've got Lusky right here, let me ask him." After a flurry of whispers Hough came back on the line. "It's Claudia," he reported. "What difference does *that* make?"

"Alvin Apgar used to do word game and puzzle books," Loren explained. "Suppose he was afraid he wouldn't live long enough to write out his wife's full name? If he'd died before completing the word Claudia he might inadvertently throw suspicion on someone completely innocent named, oh, Clark Kent or something. So instead of setting out to write the name Claudia, he wrote down a word game that would point unerringly to her and her alone! M 8. Mate. Wife. But he died before he finished the 8 and it winds up looking like an S!

"If you look at the situation apart from the dying clue, Claudia Apgar has to be the murderer. You'll recall that the third visitor, Elizabeth Nunda, found the front door locked, while the fourth visitor, Sam White, found it unlocked. How can we explain this discrepancy? Well, suppose there was one more visitor who came between the two, a visitor Lusky didn't bother to report to you because he sees a golden chance to blackmail his client later?"

This time the silence stretched out for minutes. It was broken when Hough apologetically cleared his throat.

"Uhhh, have you got any other suggestions, Professor? I mean, well, my God, if you don't mind my saying so, that one's got holes like a Swiss cheese. Mrs. Apgar's the one person who knew the house was being watched, so I can't see her killing her husband while Lusky had the place under surveillance. Then again, even if Apgar did mean to write M 8 for mate, that doesn't point to just his wife, because like I told you, Apgar was sleeping with every chick in sight, and M 8 for mate could mean any one of them, which is a piss-poor way to tell us who clobbered him. And another thing. If Apgar was trying to make an 8 and died in the middle, I'd expect the pen line to just trail off down the page. But if you'll come out here and look at it, you'll see it's a clean break. I'll bet my pension he finished the figure he was writing. He meant that to be an s. M S. Miz. Uhhh, can you meet me back at Headquarters, say about seven, so we can bat it around some more?"

Loren felt as if he'd been caught unprepared in class by one of his weaker students. "Okay," he muttered absently. "Seven it is." He hung up without remembering to wish the sergeant luck, planted his elbows on the desk, lowered his chin into the nest of his joined palms and stared listlessly at the jumble of books and papers spread out at all angles in front of him. Advance sheets. Examination bluebooks. Reprints of law review articles. Pads of yellow legal paper. The pile of student papers from the civil rights seminar.

Gael's paper, still upside down as she'd laid it on Loren's desk what seemed like hours ago.

MS. GAEL T. IRWIN

BY

VIOLATION?
PREFERRED TITLE: NEW CIVIL RIGHTS
REFUSAL TO REFER TO WOMEN BY THEIR

Ten minutes later he picked up the handset, called Headquarters, and held the phone until his ear stung, waiting for someone in the bureaucracy to authorize giving him Apgar's unlisted number. Finally he was told the number and dialed it and, when Sergeant Hough picked up on the other end, gave him the name of the murderer.

"I can tell you already you're right," Hough said. "Right

after we finished talking the first time, my men found a pair of bloody gloves in the ravine behind the house. Traced them to the guy with one call to the clothing store. He confessed as soon as we started questioning him again. He was juggling the books and Apgar was getting suspicious and he hit the panic button and killed him. He couldn't admit Apgar let him into the house so he claimed the door wasn't locked. Once we knew who did it the MS part was easy. How did you work it out, Professor?"

"Just sitting here and thinking." Loren tried not to sound too smug. "Wondering whether the Women's Liberation angle hadn't flustered you to the point where you were reading Sam White's initials upside down and didn't know it . . . . No, you go ahead and take the credit. What do I need it for?"

He gave Gael a C+ on her paper, which was beset with analytical weaknesses despite the fact that it had helped solve a murder.

Brilliance plus pure dumb luck.

AND NOW IN THE SPRING of 1987 and almost a quarter century after Kim Hale had slipped out of his life she was back and he would see her again that morning. He lay sleepless in the bed and listened to the hooting of barges and tugs on the river and the high thin wail of sirens in the avenues and felt an uneasy excitement rise in him with the rising sun.

Whoever was the first real love in a man's life, whatever time and chance do to split her from him, a tiny secret part of him dreams that someday she'll come back. Once in a thousand times, it happens.

That year Loren was a visiting professor at New York University School of Law, more than a thousand miles from his usual haunts. His home for the academic year was a one-bedroom highrise in the Waterside Plaza complex on the edge of the East River, an apartment whose regular occupant was an NYU law faculty member on sabbatical in Europe. How had Kim known where to call him? That Loren was living here was no secret but the phone was still listed under the other professor's name. Could she have been given the number by someone he knew in New York? Not the Joyce Clarke she'd mentioned; as far as he could remember he'd met no one in the city by that name and certainly hadn't given any such person his number. Then who?

When the radio newsreader came on with the seven o'clock headlines, Loren lurched out of bed and started his morning routines, a shower and shave, coffee and juice and apartment-tidying. As he straightened the bedroom he caught himself looking more often than was his custom at his image in the dresser mirror. How badly had he aged in twenty-three years? His weight was about the same, he still had most of his hair and only the temples had gone gray, the lines at the corners of his eyes were camouflaged by the thick rims of his glasses. The up side of having looked older than his years when he was young, he told himself, was that he didn't have to worry so much about aging when he was in his forties. Then on impulse he opened the bottom dresser drawer and tugged out a cardboard box of odds and ends that he'd taken to New York with him for no particular reason and rummaged through the trivia of his life until he found the laminated student ID card with the photograph of him in his early twenties and suddenly he knew he'd grown very old indeed. If Kim was relying on the pictures of him that she'd taken in the fall of 1964, she'd never know him today.

There were no photos of Kim in the cardboard box. The ones he'd taken of her were mounted on a slide carousel in a box in the bedroom closet of his condo back home. In his mind he kept a picture of her more vivid than any photograph. He saw the sweet oval face, the lean, taut body. He recalled precise details of their lovemaking and where she had liked to be touched. He could hear her cries of ecstasy from twenty-three years in the past. Why had she dropped out of his life like that? What was bringing her back?

21

HE STEPPED OUT of the elevator into the cramped downstairs lobby, nodded to the yawning security guard, crossed the deserted quadrangle that connects the highrise towers of Waterside Plaza and headed west along Twenty-third Street. At eight on a Sunday morning New York is a ghost city. Wind gusts whipped through the lifeless street, stung his cheeks, drove the cobwebs from his mind. At Park Avenue South he went down into the subway station and paced the littered platform for what seemed hours before a local roared to a halt in front of him. He came up out of the ground at Bowling Green and trotted across Battery Park to South Ferry. Inside the terminal he rode the escalator to the barnlike upper level and dropped a quarter into the fare slot. A schedule in a transparent box on the wall told him that the first boat to Staten Island would leave at nine-thirty, fifteen minutes yet. Loren had not bothered with breakfast. He bought a cake doughnut and a styrofoam cup of coffee at the refreshment stand and took them to the waiting-room area. Fans mounted halfway to the high ceiling whirred stale air on the fifty-odd people shuffling impatiently in front of the double access doors with eyes on the electric clock or the NEXT BOAT sign overhead. Two or three dozen others sat or sprawled or stretched on the hard narrow benches along the walls and down the center of the room. Night-shift workers mostly, Loren guessed, homeward bound to drab little cages on Staten Island. The few who were bundled in newspapers or sleeping bags had no homes at all. A pigeon trapped overnight in the building hovered forlorn above the steel doors, waiting for access to the sky. Loren munched his doughnut and sipped the scalding coffee and covered the room with his eyes, studying each woman in the crowd for a few seconds. Some were old and swollen-ankled and reeling with fatigue, the rest were very young and vivacious and Hispanic or Asian or black. None of them could possibly be Kim.

Sound penetrated hollowly from the dock. Through the

smeared glass panels in the access doors Loren saw a stream of exiting passengers flow across the gangway to the outside. He was too far away to make out any of their faces. Could one of them be Kim? Could she have spent last night on the Island, phoned him from there? Then she'd have to reenter the terminal downstairs, deposit another quarter to join him up here. It sounded crazy but not impossible.

When the entrance doors slid open and the rest of the crowd in the waiting room poured through, Loren hung back, staring across the now-deserted barn to the head of the escalator, willing her to appear. She didn't. A few stragglers loped across the room and through the gaping doorway. The electric clock showed 9:28. Loren dared not miss the ferry. Fighting back panic, he crossed the echoing gangplank and stood on the curved concrete apron that made up the vessel's front deck, eyes fixed on the walkway. *Where are you? When will I see you?* The engines throbbed and the boat horn hooted and the huge ferry glided out of the slip, water churning in its wake. Loren wrapped his fleece-lined raincoat about himself more snugly. The wind had driven all the passengers inside except for him and a handful of Japanese tourists who grinned bravely in the lashing cold and took turns snapping photos of each other against the backdrop of the lower Manhattan skyline.

Freezing out here on the exposed deck made no sense. If she wasn't aboard now, she wouldn't be until the ferry docked at St. George twenty minutes from now. He tossed his empty coffee cup and paper napkin into a waste can and dropped onto a yellow plastic seat inside the vessel. A greasy-haired man in his thirties with Yasir Arafat stubble and a violin under his chin was butchering the melody of a Verdi aria, the padded instrument case open at his sneakered feet with a few bills and coins scattered across it, hinting. *Most New York street musicians are a lot better than this guy,* Loren thought to himself for a split second, then he shut out the sounds and sank deeper into his own solitude. Maybe she'd missed the first boat. Maybe she'd be waiting for him at the other end, waiting to fly

23

into his arms. He decided that he wouldn't go straight back to Manhattan. He'd get off at Staten Island, hang around the St. George terminal for a while as he had at South Ferry, let this boat make the return run to the Battery without him, catch the next ferry instead. If she didn't show, he had no choice but to go back to Waterside Plaza and wait for her to call again, if ever. He almost wondered if he had imagined her voice in the night.

The vessel eased against the St. George dock with a clash of steel on steel. Workmen slung thick ropes about the mooring posts and pulled back the waist-high barrier gate and the passengers piled out. Fares were not collected at this end. Anyone who paid a quarter at South Ferry could ride across and back without leaving the boat. The Japanese with their cameras stayed clustered on the rear deck. Loren crossed the main cabin and followed the herd of passengers into the Staten Island terminal, which was smaller than its Manhattan counterpart but just as depressing. He stood inside the entranceway and swept his eyes along the benches, scrutinizing the women among the travelers waiting the signal to board. There were a few chattering Asian girls in their teens with cassette players and earplugs, and one old lady dressed as if for church. They and the males bound for the city passed through the entranceway onto the ferry. Except for the server at the refreshment stand and a homeless man snoring on one of the hard benches, the room in front of Loren seemed to be empty.

Then he saw someone. Her.

She had just come through one of the long line of doors at the terminal's other end and she was wearing a hooded all-weather coat but the hood was down and he could see her face twenty or maybe twenty-five yards across the room and he knew. She was moving toward him, first slowly and deliberately as if she were wading through water or performing a ritual, then quickly, urgently, almost at a run. He thought he saw her lips move and her arms open as he ran across the terminal to meet her.

Suddenly he couldn't see her anymore. Two figures converged on her from opposite sides, one coming out from behind a support pillar halfway across the room, the other from behind a bank of pay phones. All Loren could see of them was their backs as they cut off his vision of the woman. One wore a nondescript mackinaw, the other a Navy pea jacket. Loren shouted something, darted toward them, out of control. He thought he heard a thin wail of fright. He did hear something behind him, footsteps, pounding lightly. Something slammed against the back of his head. For an awful moment he thought he was on fire. Pain stabbed through him. He dropped to the unswept linoleum. His glasses crunched under him. He felt stickiness roll down his forehead into his eyes. His hand groped along the floor for support and found something of smooth wood, curved, with strings. *The violin?* Its bridge cracked under his weight as he lurched to his feet. "Help me, somebody help me!" he cried out. No one approached him. The woman behind the refreshment counter had ducked out of sight, the homeless man snored on the long bench. Loren forced himself upright. His glasses were shattered but he could make out a uniformed man running across the room toward him with pistol drawn. Loren didn't wait. He raced across the terminal, through one of the line of doors to the outer corridor where a panorama of archways faced him. An exit to the parking lot, another to the SIRTOA rapid transit platform, several to bus platforms. He chose SIRTOA, rushed through that doorway. On the other side he saw a cashier's cage and a long concrete apron with a line of train cars vanishing in the distance.

The henna-haired black woman inside the cage stared at him transfixed. Loren saw her shoulders move, guessed she had hit a silent alarm button beneath her counter. "A woman," he croaked. "About five one, five two. Early forties. Attractive. Tan all-weather coat. With two men." He remembered the stubble-faced guy who had hit him from behind with the violin. "No, three. Were they . . . ?" He gestured toward the empty platform stretching in front of them for fifty yards into the cold bright morning. "Please," he whispered.

"I—I didn't see . . ." she stammered.

"Police! Freeze!" Male voice behind him, pitched high. The cop who'd been on his heels? Loren half turned. "I said freeze!" the voice screamed.

Loren's knees went out from under him and he fell forward to the cold concrete and tasted blood on his lips and wept. Through the haze he heard the crackle of a walkie-talkie and the mumble of the cop into the transmitter.

After twenty-three years he had heard her voice from somewhere in the night and then the next morning he had caught a glimpse of her across a bleak and empty waiting room and then nothing.

Gone from him. Gone again into nowhere.

Two

THEY CARED ABOUT HIM or were afraid he might sue them; maybe both. They escorted him to a drab square room with linoleum flooring, cheap pine kitchen cabinets, a midget refrigerator, a battered microwave and a few ancient chairs and couches and card tables. Loren guessed it was a break room for ferry workers but this Sunday morning it was empty. A paramedic in white uniform bandaged the cut on his scalp and asked if he wanted to be checked out at the hospital for possible concussion. "I'm all right," Loren muttered through cracked lips. "I could use some aspirin." They brought him three tablets on a plastic tray with a styrofoam cup of tepid water and a pair of rocklike jelly doughnuts and another styrofoam cup full of steaming coffee. He washed down the aspirin with the water and left the other items untouched. His head throbbed.

The beat cop who came in to take his statement helped himself to the doughnuts. Loren sprawled on the lumpy couch, unable to stand or stir. He wondered if dying would be like this. The cop's bored questions and his answers were punctuated by the distant gonging of church bells. The cop slipped away and time slipped away. A tall slender young man with close-cropped butter-colored hair knocked softly on the door, came in, and carefully undid the button of his tan silk sport jacket so that it draped about him with the proper elegance as he lowered himself onto the edge of the couch and set on his knees the brown leather briefcase he'd carried under his arm.

"Professor Mensing?" His voice was buoyant with the enthusiasm of a born salesman and go-getter. If he were a

27

doctor and had to tell you that you were dying of inoper-
able cancer, he would do it with the same verve and
bounce. "Ted Domjan." He thrust a shield case in front of
Loren's eyes. "Detective Sergeant," he added when he saw
Loren wasn't focusing on the badge. "The name's Hungarian but I get my coloring from my mom. Uh, I understand there's been a little problem here this morning.
Mind telling me what went down?" He unzipped his briefcase and pulled out a full-size spiral notepad. Loren
squinted at the logo on the pad cover and thought he saw
FORDHAM LAW SCHOOL upside down and wondered if
his headache was going away or getting worse. "You're a
. . . law student?" he croaked.

"Yes, sir. Evening division. One more semester and I
graduate and sit for the bar. I've, uh, heard of you, sir. I
know about some of those cases you helped solve and my
Constitutional Rights professor assigned a couple of your
law review articles as required reading. That's why I came
over myself when the report came in about you being
mugged."

"It wasn't a mugging." Loren's voice was stronger now.

"Tell me," Domjan said, gold pen poised over notepad.

Slowly Loren repeated the story, going back to when the
call from Kim had roused him at four in the morning.
Domjan's pen flew across the lined pages, and Loren wondered if he transcribed his professors' lectures verbatim
too. While he talked, the sergeant sipped uninvited from
the cup of cold coffee on the tray and kept making delicate
up-and-down nods as if he were approving Loren's every
word. At the end of the recital Loren leaned back and
massaged his temples, hoping he hadn't forgotten anything. His head was pounding again.

"So," Domjan said. "The lady vanishes, only this time
she does it twice! You, uh, see my point, sir?"

Loren stared dully at the blur that sat where the bright-
eyed young sergeant had been sitting a few minutes before.

"The Hitchcock classic!" he explained in a tone still
brimming with enthusiasm. "Michael Redgrave, Margaret
Lockwood, Paul Lukas, Dame May Whitty! The woman

disappeared from the train and everyone swore she never existed, remember? Uh, you know, you're sort of in that situation today, sir."

"No." Loren said the word angrily as if the thought terrified him. "I saw her. She came in through the street door and started across the terminal and . . ."

"I know, sir. I took it all down the first time. But there's a problem, sir. No one else in the terminal saw her. The security guard didn't, the lunch counter attendant didn't, the poor guy snoozing on the bench didn't, the Rapid Transit ticket clerk didn't. Believe me, sir, I talked to all of them before I saw you. They're not lying and they're not in any conspiracy together."

"She called me. She asked me to come out here and meet her. Why do you think I'd come out to Staten Island on a Sunday morning? For the cultural attractions? For the view?"

"Oh, it's not so bad here, sir," Domjan said. "Lots of rehabbing going on along the waterfront . . ."

"Damn it!" he shouted. "I did not imagine that phone call! Why don't you check with the company, they'll have a record of it, won't they?" He gave Domjan the number at the Waterside Plaza apartment. "She called me!"

"*Someone* called you," the sergeant corrected him. "That is, assuming a call was made at all."

"We didn't have that long an affair and we kept it to ourselves. People did back then. I don't think anyone besides us knew about it. The woman who called me knew about it. Therefore she was Kim." He paused, thought. "That logic stinks. Just take my word. It was Kim."

"So." Domjan slapped his notepad shut, slipped it into his briefcase and zipped the case shut. "But, sir, you can't possibly be sure that the woman you say came into the terminal this morning was this same woman. Right? After all, you hadn't seen her since—since 1964 you said, right? God, I was in second grade then!"

"Who else could it have been?" Loren thundered. "You think it was just some weird coincidence that . . ."

"Let's put that question on the back burner, sir, if you

29

don't mind." Domjan reached for the styrofoam coffee cup, saw it was empty, and with a gesture of disappointment set it down. "Now I'll concede that your story isn't impossible. Because of your background I want to believe you. The security guard might have been facing the wrong way to notice the woman. The woman behind the lunch counter ducked out of sight as soon as the ruckus started. The poor homeless guy was asleep. If your two or three men took the lady out to the parking lot and into a waiting car instead of onto the Rapid Transit platform, well, they might have made it out of the terminal area without attracting any attention. I'll have uniforms check the neighborhood this afternoon, see if anyone noticed, but Sunday's awful slow around St. George between ferries."

"You might do better," Loren said, "tracing the one that did the Isaac Stern imitation."

"Yes, sir, that is our best lead. Six feet tall, skinny, dark greasy hair, three days' growth of beard, and he came over on the ferry with you and into the terminal behind you and crowned you on the noggin with his violin and took off without even trying to grab your wallet. Ruined the violin in the process, and it wasn't an el cheapo either. I'll try to trace it in the morning, and of course I'll be down here myself tomorrow as soon as the boats start running and see if any of the street types who make pocket money strumming on the ferries is missing his instrument."

"That's tomorrow," Loren said. "What about today?"

"A PD artist is on his way here with an Identikit so we can make sketches of the violin guy and Ms. Hale from your descriptions. In a day or two when you're feeling better you can come visit the One-Twenty and look at our mug books. Meanwhile," Domjan said, "I'm going to have your phone records checked for last night."

"They could be killing her," Loren reminded the young sergeant. "You know what they might be doing to her right now while we're marking time?"

"Yes, sir," Domjan replied politely. Loren sensed his skepticism and felt small and helpless as a stunted child. There was a rap on the door and a heavyset black man in

30

tank top and jeans with an artist's portfolio under his arm strode into the room. Domjan thanked him for coming down on his day off and introduced him to Loren and retired to a corner of the room as the artist set up his Identikit and began to question Loren in a soft hoarse voice. The session took most of an hour. Loren watched a charcoal drawing of the violin-wielding assailant emerge from the assortment of interchangeable facial features in the black man's paraphernalia. The sketch of Kim when the artist completed it was vague, unfocused. He had seen her only for a few seconds. Too many old feelings for her were interwoven with his description. Maybe he sensed that the main reason Domjan wanted this drawing was to use it in identifying her body if it was found. Maybe subconsciously he held the insane hope that if he didn't help she might stay alive awhile longer. Finally with a sigh of resignation the artist packed his materials and beckoned Domjan over.

"That could be almost any woman of her size. Looks awful young to have been in law school with you." The sergeant frowned up at Loren from the drawing of Kim. "Won't help much if any unidentified female corpses show up in the metro area." He turned to the sketch of the man who had sawed at the violin. "Much better," he announced, "except none of our regular bad guys looks like that. Maybe you can pick him out of the mug books, sir, when your head's better. Now, there's another ferry leaving in about fifteen minutes. I'm going to ride over to the Battery with you and put you in a cab. Take it easy the rest of the day and trust me to handle things at this end, okay?"

"Do I have a choice?"

"Not really, sir," Domjan smiled. "I'll call around nine this evening and give you an update." He thrust out his hand and helped Loren to his feet and guided him through the maze of corridors to the terminal waiting room. They boarded the ferry together and sat in silence on the upper deck as the vessel skimmed across the glistening waters of Upper New York Bay and into the enfolding shadows of the lower Manhattan skyline. It was well after three when Loren paid the cabdriver and rode the outdoor escalator to the quadrangle that connected Waterside's highrises. The sky gleamed blue, the wind stung his cheeks, river traffic glided past under clouds like cotton candy. Peaceful Sunday in the city. Loren let himself into his apartment, flung off his outer clothing and collapsed on the bed.

HE DREAMED HE HEARD her calling his name from endless miles away. She was crying out for help and he couldn't reach her, couldn't move a muscle. He lay paralyzed on a bed in a room bathed in shadows, unable even to speak. All he could do was feel. Fear and guilt and shame at his helplessness, as if he were an incontinent old man who had wet his bed.

The telephone bell ripped through the dream like a knife through flesh, jerked him upright, gasping, trembling. He heard the pounding of his heart and the fading of his own howl of terror into silence and shook himself into half-wakefulness and groped blindly for the nightstand and knocked over the radio. The room was suspended in a cocoon of deep-gold light. If the sun was sinking he must have been asleep for hours. His searching hand collided with the phone and he lifted the receiver to his ear. "Yes? Yes? Hello?"

"It's me, sir. Ted Domjan." The sergeant's voice still sounded naive and full of awe, as if Loren were a superior being from a distant planet. Law students of the conservative new age tended to speak to their professors in that inanely reverential way. It made Loren sick. "Uh, I'm sorry if I woke you but I said I'd be calling around nine."

"God, is it that late?" Loren muttered, and made himself sit straight on the bed with his back rigid against the headboard.

"Feeling any better?"

Loren's mouth tasted gummy and he was still shaking from the nightmare and with his spare glasses still in a dresser drawer he saw only blurs, but at least his head wasn't coming open. "A little," he said.

"I hope this won't make you worse, sir," Domjan said, "but, uh, no one called you at four o'clock this morning."

"What?" Loren roared. For one awful moment he thought the ringing phone had not awakened him from his nightmare but plunged him into another more terrifying.

"Well, what I mean is, sir, no one called you last night from outside your own 212 area code. New York Telephone has some of the most antiquated switching equipment in the business, but any billable call, in other words any call made to your number from outside the 212 code, the company's computers keep a record of it. Even inside the 212 area they'd have a record if someone called you from a pay phone. And believe me, sir, no one did. At no time last night or this morning."

Loren had no choice but to believe the earnest young sergeant. His mind took the new information and raced with it. "Is Staten Island inside the 212 area?" he asked.

"No, sir. Area code over here is 718."

"So she didn't call me from Staten Island," he said softly as if talking to himself.

"I think we've established that pretty solidly, sir."

"She was over here at four this morning. In Manhattan . . . . That means she went over to Staten Island sometime between then and six hours later. . . . Damn it, that doesn't make sense! If she were over here near me, why didn't she just come by in person last night, or ask me to meet her?"

"I'm sure I don't know, sir," Domjan replied.

The sergeant's inscrutable politeness made Loren furious. He wanted to tear the room apart. "Now, look," he began too loudly, then lowered his volume to a tone that couldn't be heard in the next building. "Sergeant, I did not imagine that phone call and I did not lie to you. I'm—well, I'm trying to see this thing from your point of view and I know you're doing everything you can but . . ."

"But there's still no solid reason to believe that this Ms. Hale of yours exists," Domjan finished for him. "On the other hand, sir, in fairness to you, I don't think you're lying or crazy either. I mean it is physically possible that the woman called you from nearby and then drove to the Island, or was driven, between four and ten A.M. She could have gone out to Brooklyn and over the Verrazano Bridge, or through one of the tunnels to Jersey and over to the Island on the Goethals Bridge or the Bayonne or the Outerbridge from Perth Amboy. But—sir, why would she do that? It's so roundabout. So pointless."

Unless she was setting me up for something, whispered a voice in Loren's head that he didn't want to hear.

"What are you going to do?" he demanded. "Drop the case?"

"No, sir," Domjan replied. "We've still got those sketches and the violin clue, but if they should peter out—well, I don't know what else we can do. Unless of course you can remember something you didn't tell me this morning."

And it was precisely at that instant that Loren did recall something that the blow to his head and his emotional anguish had driven to the back of his mind when Domjan had questioned him in the ferry terminal. He heard Kim's voice again, echoing inside him. "Loren, if anything happens to me, find Joyce Clarke and ask how her father died." He came within a breath of telling Domjan but then he shut his mouth and thought about it and decided No. Not until he understood more of what was going on. "I've tried to remember," he said. "No luck so far. If I think of anything I'll call you right away."

"That'll be fine, sir. Now you take it easy and I'll keep you posted." They exchanged good nights and broke the connection. Even before Loren had replaced the handset in its cradle he was wondering how much of Domjan's overdone deference was a facade, cultivated to get him inside the defenses of crime suspects with a bit of money or fame or power. Loren had worked with the police off and on for most of his professional life but he had never totally lost the distrust of people with badges that was part of his sixties dissident heritage. Until he knew more about Joyce Clarke and the death of her father, he was not going to give Domjan another chance to disbelieve him. *Maybe I'm be-*

ing paranoid, he told himself, *but sometimes paranoia makes sense.*

The room was bathed in a gray haze of dusk. Loren snapped on the bedside table lamp and hunted in the dresser for his spare pair of glasses. In bathrobe and beach slippers he made himself an omelet with Havarti cheese and green pepper and chunks of chicken breast which he washed down with Pouilly Fumé and Debussy's *La Mer* on the CD player. He brewed a pot of decaf and sat at the kitchen counter hunched over the white pages of the phone book. There were enough Clarkes listed to fill a column and a half, but only one with the initial J and an address on Jane Street. On a hunch he checked the Yellow Pages under Lawyers and found no Joyce Clarke anywhere. If she was an attorney, she certainly wasn't practicing in Manhattan. What was her job here then? In the morning he'd check her out in the library.

The digital clock built into the microwave read 9:47 in ruby numerals. He knew he wouldn't sleep again for hours if at all that night. He threw on slacks and a turtleneck which he eased past the bandage on his head with infinite caution and a windbreaker and an Irish walking hat and took the elevator down to the quadrangle and the steep staircase to Twenty-third Street and First Avenue. By New York standards the Sunday evening traffic was light. In five minutes a cruising taxi driver responded to his wave and the cab squealed to a stop. "West Village," Loren instructed. "Jane Street."

The driver made a daredevil turn into Twenty-third and zigzagged so carelessly through pockets of congestion it was almost as if he believed all the other vehicles were made of paper. He couldn't navigate a single block without hitting his horn at least five times. The cab missed sideswiping a crosstown bus by inches. It wasn't until they had burrowed into the rabbit warren of Village streets that the driver slowed to a crawl. Loren caught him scanning a directory on his lap and realized the man had no idea where Jane Street was. Loren wasn't certain either. The cab twisted through narrow streets as the meter clicked merrily away.

"Here we go." The driver caromed off Washington Street in a turn that almost threw Loren onto the taxi floor. "Jane Stritt. What number you want, yes?"

"Just keep on till I say stop. Go slow."

"What you think, I drive the Indy 500 or somezing?" It was a street paved in cobblestones and barely wide enough for three vehicles abreast. The left lane was lined with cars parked bumper to bumper but not many people were in sight. Loren stared intensely out the smeary side window, watched twin rows of old flat-roofed red brick houses slither past, broken here and there by a rehabbed condo building. He tried to focus on house numbers, made out the 67 and the 73. Then it went slipping by him, 79, five stories tall, gray brick with black wrought-iron fencing, light peeping out from behind a few blinds. He was tempted to pay the driver, get out, ring the bell of Joyce's apartment and find out if she was in. Bad idea, he decided. Tomorrow between classes he'd root around, ask some faculty colleagues if they knew anything about the death of Joyce's father, the judge. It wasn't much of a lead but it was all he had.

"You really want we should be here, mister?" the driver demanded. They were near the Hudson River now, in a world of deep shadows and warehouses with truck trailers parked for the night in loading docks. A swarm of hollow-eyed men and women and children filled the steps and doorway of an ancient hotel, rotting away from within, without homes and without hope, the lepers of the city.

"Let's get out of here." Loren turned his eyes away. "Back to where we started."

"Is no need tell me twice," the driver said, and plunged the cab into the northbound sea of traffic on the West Side Highway. Loren got out at Twenty-third and Lexington and walked the rest of the way to Waterside Plaza. He thought back to his walk in the morning breeze along this same street, a little more than twelve hours ago, a lifetime ago. Kim's lifetime. She was dead now. Something inside told him that whatever he did would come too late to save her. Something else told him that he couldn't stop, that he had to find her dead or alive, had to find out why she'd come back to him for a moment and who or what had taken her away. He didn't drop off into sleep until after two in the morning and then he slept so fitfully it was worse than no sleep at all.

In his dream the phone shrilled. He shuddered and lay still and waited and begged for it to stop but it kept shrieking at him until he opened his eyes to shadowed darkness and forced himself to grope blindly along the nightstand for it. The clock radio clattered to the floor under his fumbling. His fingers closed around the handset and guided it to his ear.

"Loren? Loren, is that you?"

First his head and then his whole body went clammy as he sat bolt upright in the bed. The phone almost slipped out of his fingers. It was Kim. Her voice from out of nowhere.

"Kim? Princess?" He thought he heard his heart thundering. "Kim, where are you, what happened to you, why did you . . ."

"Darling, I'm all right, I only have a minute, I had to call and make sure you weren't hurt and tell you I'm safe. Oh, Loren, please forget me, forget I ever tried to come back. Please, for my sake forget it all. Let me go. I'm fine. I'm— very happy. I'll always remember what you tried to do for me. But I can't ever see you or call you again. Please, love, go on with your own life. Just—think of me once in a while."

"Kim, for God's sake tell me where . . ."

"Good-bye, love." The click of the broken connection was soft as a whisper in a garden. Loren stared at the useless and barely visible chunk of plastic in his hand and felt tears begin to trickle from his eyes.

It was only then that he realized he hadn't dreamed it. He was awake, drenched with sweat in the cool spring night, clinging to the phone so tightly his fingers throbbed. He stumbled to his feet to make his way to the bathroom door and the light switch, still believing he might yet be trapped in the dream web.

Until he tripped barefoot over the clock radio on the bedroom floor and sent it crashing into the wall with a smack that jarred him out of the half-world between sleep and waking, and that was when he knew that the call from Kim had been real. That he had heard her voice again.

And that if he talked about it no one would ever believe him.

Three

LOREN'S OFFICE at New York University School of Law was on the fourth floor of Vanderbilt Hall, a red brick fortress on the south side of Washington Square. He stopped there after his 9:00 A.M. class just long enough to toss his lecture notes on the desk. With no more obligations that day until his late-afternoon seminar, he drifted upstairs to the high-ceilinged faculty library and poured a cup of coffee from the silver urn and took it and himself to one of a pair of matching club chairs in an alcove. Ten or twelve professors were scattered about the vast room, each concealed behind a newspaper or a volume of advance sheets or a law review. Two of the women on the faculty were carrying on a hushed conversation over the morning's *Wall Street Journal.* Loren settled back among the soft cushions and, not surprisingly in view of his broken sleep the last two nights, fell into an early nap. Just before dropping off he thought he heard the squeak of boots. When he shook himself awake and focused on his wristwatch it was just short of high noon and the club chair beside his was taken.

"Howdy, pardner," Professor Hideo Okamoto greeted him. "Rough night?"

"I hope you never have a weekend like I did, Tex."

Loren had read of the other's background in a newsletter of the Association of American Law Schools. Okamoto was the son of a Nisei truck farming couple, born in the Manzanar detention camp to which his parents had been forcibly relocated from the West Coast during the second world war. After Hiroshima the family had migrated to west Texas and the restaurant business. Hideo's English had taken on a cowpoke flavor thanks to schoolmates and the endless western films on which the boy had gorged himself, first at Saturday matinees and later on the black-and-white TV screen. He had taught at NYU for fifteen years and was considered a leading authority on the federal court system. If he had any family he had never mentioned them. He wore polished leather cowboy boots everywhere, including class and court, and insisted that colleagues call him Tex.

"Not busy today, I guess?" he asked Loren.

"Just a seminar at three."

"Yeah, I'm loafing too. Finished drafting my exams yesterday. Say, what in the world happened to your head?"

"Got bushwhacked by a varmint," Loren told him, "on the Staten Island ferry."

Okamoto said nothing for a few moments, his face a perfect blank. Then he leaned forward in the club chair and looked more closely into Loren's face. "Looks to me like you might have a hell of a story to tell," he said. "If you want to talk about it, I'll buy you lunch."

A BLACK WAITRESS in a peasant skirt and off-the-shoulder white blouse topped by a serape escorted them to a corner table at the rear of The Old Corral. Okamoto sat Wild Bill Hickok-style with his back to the oak-paneled wall, beneath a fake buffalo head. Without looking at the menu he ordered a pitcher of margaritas, guacamole salad, chicken fajitas and a side of hash browns. Rumor had it that he ate three huge meals a day, never exercised and stayed thin as a lath. Loren and most of the other faculty could have killed him for that. His own lunch order was a ranchburger and a lite beer. He described the ferry incident while Tex wolfed down guacamole on taco chips. Just the bare facts. Nothing about the phantom call from Kim or her disappearance. A simple assault and battery in the St. George terminal by a scruffy street musician grown weary of his violin.

"But he didn't take your wallet or anything?" Okamoto emptied his margarita glass with one swallow and mechanically refilled it from the pitcher.

"Nothing," Loren said.

"Weird hombre. He couldn't be a former student you flunked?"

"I doubt it." Loren was topping his burger with barbecue sauce when something he had noticed in the law school's faculty and staff directory came back to him. "Say, Tex, don't you live in the West Village somewhere?"

"Sure do. Got a co-op over on West Eighth."

"Ever run across a woman who lives on Jane Street? Name of Joyce Clarke?"

Okamoto's features stayed blank. "Well, now," he drawled, "that's a common name in New York, pardner. Would you go to Tokyo and ask around for a Michiko Tanaka and expect to find her?"

Loren tried to prod the other's memory with the one fact he had learned on his own and the one fact, if it was a fact, that Kim had offered. "Unless there's a typo in the phone book, this Clarke spells her name with an E on the end. And there may have been something odd about the way her father died."

"Clarke, Clarke," Okamoto repeated mushily through a mouthful of fajita. "Oh my Lord, Clarke!" His eyes went wide and he gulped another glassful of margarita. "I wonder if . . . Loren, about four, no make that five years ago I gave a lecture at a federal judicial conference and met a district judge from, yeah, from St. Louis I think, by the name of Howard Clarke. I was shooting the shit with him at a reception and he mentioned having a daughter named Joyce who lived in the West Village, and by God he asked me the same question you just did about whether I might know her." Okamoto stared into Loren's glasses as if looking for a reaction he wasn't finding. "Howard Clarke, man, Howard Clarke! Doesn't that ring a bell?" Loren's features stayed without expression. "You might say there was something odd about his death," he went on. "How many federal judges get themselves murdered? With all the detective stuff you've been mixed in, how come this is all news to you?"

Loren blinked in surprise as he realized Tex was right. The murder of a federal judge was something he would and should have known about. "Do you remember when Clarke was killed?"

Okamoto hesitated. "Maybe three years back."

"Okay, that explains it. I was in Europe then, on sabbatical. Either it didn't make the German papers or somehow I missed it. I'll look up the details in the *Times* but tell me what you can."

"He sat in the eastern district of Missouri. Chambers in St. Louis city, home in the county. He was a partner in a firm there before he went on the bench, so with the income from what he made when he sold his share in the firm he wasn't dependent on his salary as a judge. I gather he lived high on the hog."

"What kind of judge was he?"

"If you liked the kind of decisions he made he was a hero, if you didn't he was a beast."

Loren's interests as a law professor were focused on the appellate courts, and he was less familiar with the federal trial judges than perhaps he should have been. "What were his values?"

"Sort of like yours." Okamoto signaled the waitress and ordered flan and coffee. "Friend of those who have no friend. He knew he couldn't be fired or disciplined or held accountable for any decision he made and he exercised his power to the pure-dee limit. Hey, don't you remember *Sampson* v. *State of Missouri?*"

Loren's face made it clear that he'd never heard of the case.

"Gal was denied tenure at the state university and sued for sex discrimination. Clarke ordered every professor who'd voted on her tenure to tell what his or her vote was and why. Two of the faculty said it was a secret ballot and stood on their academic freedom. Clarke held them in contempt and threw them in prison. One was raped and stabbed by a lifer before the ACLU got them released.

Later, the poor fool tried to sue Clarke for violating his constitutional rights. Instant dismissal. I don't have to tell you, Loren, a federal judge is immune from liability for any decision he makes no matter how blatantly unconstitutional it is."

"Oh, God," Loren said softly. "*That* Clarke."

"Hey, hang on a minute, pardner! Don't you *believe* in all that shit? Making up new constitutional rights out of thin air, letting out all the rapists and killers, destroying public school systems with quotas and forced busing?"

Loren felt himself turning red. No more beer with lunch, he told himself sternly. "When did I ever say I believed in that?"

"When did you speak out against it?"

Loren had never failed to be surprised at Okamoto's ideology. Born in an American concentration camp to parents whose livelihood and freedom had been snatched from them because of their race, raised in a redneck environment where schoolmates called him Jap and Slant Eyes to his face, he had become one of the most articulate and highly principled conservatives among scholars of the judiciary, an arch-skeptic about the naked exercise of legislative power by unelected uncontrollable judges. Loren had a sneaking suspicion that Tex had never forgiven the federal bench for turning a blind eye to the rights of Nisei during the war. "Anyway," Okamoto continued between bites of flan, "that's the Clarke you had in mind."

"Who killed him?" Loren asked.

"Could have been any one of hundreds of folks he stomped on, but as best I recall his housekeeper did it. Emptied a six-shooter in his face and called the cops. I don't know if her motive ever came out. Hell, probably he was fucking her or something."

"You know what happened to her?"

Okamoto dug a cherrywood pipe out of the breast pocket of his blazer and a tobacco pouch from a hip pocket. "Either they found her mentally incompetent to stand trial or they tried her and found her not guilty by reason of insanity, I can't remember which. The St. Louis papers must have covered the story."

"I'll check it out," Loren said, although he failed to see how any of it would help. The waitress refilled their coffee cups and discreetly deposited on the tablecloth a tooled saddle-leather folder with the bill in an inner compartment. Tex slipped a twenty from his wallet into the folder and they sauntered out into the street.

"Gorgeous day," Loren remarked. "Too nice to stay cooped up in an office if you ask me. Want to stroll a while?"

"Any place in particular?"

"Just around the Village," Loren replied casually. "Maybe over to the West Side."

"Nothing like a walk," Okamoto said.

They followed Waverly Place into Seventh Avenue, turned off Seventh at Greenwich and headed north and west, keeping up a brisk pace, making pit stops at a tobacconist's for Okamoto and at a music shop where Loren found a CD with a new recording of the Samuel Barber symphonies. At the corner of Greenwich and Jane streets Loren abruptly swung west. "Let's see what's down this way," he suggested.

What he hoped to accomplish he had no idea. Perhaps he fantasized that Joyce Clarke might happen to enter or leave her apartment just as he and Tex were passing by, which of course made no sense since neither man knew what she looked like. Maybe he simply wanted to see the building by daylight. When they walked past number 79 it looked no different to Loren, only a little dingier in the sun, and no one went in or out of the place while they had it in sight. At the end of the block they veered south, taking Christopher Street back to the Washington Square area and the law school.

"Thanks for the grub and information," Loren said at the elevator, and then glanced at his watch. "My God, I'll be late for my seminar!"

"The Old Corral's a fine place to eat," Okamoto said, "but no one cooks Tex-Mex the way my mom used to."

———————————

LOREN'S SEMINAR on Current Problems in Human Rights was supposed to end at five but on this last week of the semester it ran late. With 5:15 showing on the wall clock and the raucous traffic noises from Sixth Avenue penetrating muffledly through the high windows of the seminar room, Loren was still sitting at one end of the long polished mahogany table and trying to moderate and channel the fury. Between three and four a young woman who was an associate editor of the Law Review had presented her paper on affirmative action, ridiculing and decrying what she called the balkanization of opportunity by race, religion, ancestry, gender or sexual preference. Loren had listened intently while trying at the same time to read the body language of the other students in the room. Most of the white males were leaning forward in their seats with expectant faces, seeming to cheer the speaker on as if she were the horse on which they had bet a month's pay. The other white woman, the Hispanic woman, and the black man sat ramrod-stiff and frozen-faced like a family near whose home a tornado has touched down. The brouhaha had started the instant the student had finished. White-hot rhetoric shook the walls of the seminar room. At 5:25 by the electric clock above the chalkboard, a sharp knock sounded and the door flew open, revealing to Loren's startled eyes the trim silk-suited figure of Sergeant Domjan, who mouthed a silent "Excuse me" and shut the door again.

Loren decided that the contention had gone on too long. Cool legal analysis had flown out the windows in the first minute of debate. "Shall we call it a day?" He raised his voice above those of the passionate students. "It's a day, gang, it's a day! Calm down, take off your war paint." The words slipped out automatically, and with the disinterest of a visitor who would shortly be leaving this campus he wondered if any of the students would complain to the dean's office that he had demeaned Native Americans.

45

"Last meeting of the semester's Friday noon right here. If you haven't turned in your papers yet, do it then." Years ago he would have been just as worked up about these issues as his students were; now he couldn't make himself care anymore. He invited the young woman from the Law Review to stay behind for a few minutes and gave her a firm but sympathetic critique of her presentation. As soon as she was gone, Domjan came in and strode down the long narrow room to Loren's side and took a chair.

"At Fordham we're quieter," he said. "At least in the evening division. Maybe everyone's just worn out after a day's work. How's your head, sir?"

"No pain anymore." Loren made a neat stack of his seminar materials and set it in alignment with the table edge. "I'll take off the bandage tonight. If you've come all the way from Staten Island to see me I take it there's news."

"Oh, I don't live on the Island, sir, and anyway I've got a class at Fordham at seven. But yes, I do have news. I found the fellow that owns the violin."

Loren half leapt from his seat as if he'd felt an electric shock. "The guy who hit me yesterday?"

"No, sir." Domjan lifted his palm like a crossing guard. "The guy whose *violin* hit you. I spent this morning down at the ferry terminal interviewing anybody that came aboard carrying a musical instrument. None of them looked like the man you described. But one guy—he was playing the harmonica and kept a padded box at his feet for passengers to toss spare change in—told me an interesting story. He said that what he usually plays on the ferries is an old violin he's had since his teens, but about eight-thirty yesterday morning as he was on his way to catch the first boat to the Battery he was stopped on the street by a man who offered him five hundred dollars in cash to borrow the fiddle for the day."

"Did he get it back that night?"

"He never saw the man again. The thing wasn't worth five hundred bucks so he didn't care all that much."

"So," Loren said. "I assume you asked him to identify what was left of the violin that hit me."

"Right, sir. He said it was his." The sergeant showed perfectly polished teeth in a knowing grin. "I imagine he'll use the five hundred to buy a new one."

"Did you get a description of the man who paid him?"

"I was just coming to that, sir. I sat him down with our artist and here's what they came up with." Domjan unzipped his brown leather briefcase, which was bulging with law school casebooks for his evening class, and pulled out an Identikit sketch which he put in front of Loren on the mahogany. That was the man: lanky, thin-faced, cold-eyed, dark unkempt hair, stubble on his cheeks. Loren fought back a shout of joy. "So now do you believe me?" he demanded.

"Well," Domjan conceded, "this helps, sir. Yesterday I thought it was crazy enough that some street musician should conk you with his fiddle and bug off without trying to rob you or even to take the rest of the fiddle with him. Today I find out it's crazier than that. But—well, sir, it still doesn't confirm the part of your story about Ms. Hale and her phone call, does it?" He seemed desperate for Loren to agree with him.

"Okay," Loren sighed. "Get out your notebook." When Domjan had his Fordham pad and a gold-trimmed pen on the table, Loren told him about the second call from Kim in the depths of the night. The young cop's hand flew across the lined sheets of paper.

"I'm not surprised, sir," he said at the end of the recital. "I mean I did think, when I heard you running the seminar and just now while you were talking—well, I thought you looked remarkably calm and in control considering how uptight you were yesterday when you kept telling me she was maybe getting tortured or killed." He screwed the cap back on his pen and pocketed it. "I suppose I believe you. Tentatively anyway. I'll check with New York Telephone again but the answer's almost bound to be the same. She called you from somewhere within the 212 area code. By now of course she could be halfway across the country or the world."

"Or dead," Loren reminded him.

47

"Hold on a minute, sir. When she phoned you this morning, did she sound like someone was forcing her to make the call? Did you get the impression she was in danger?"

Loren squeezed his eyes shut, propelling himself back into the dreamlike haze which the call had shattered. "No," he admitted.

"Didn't think so," Domjan nodded sagely. "You wouldn't be taking things in your stride today if you thought there was a chance she was in trouble. Well, sir, I don't pretend to understand this situation, but so far the only crime we know of for sure is assault and battery on you by a slimeball with a violin. I'm not calling it quits, I still want you to come to the Island tomorrow and look at the mug books but—well, sir, I can't justify giving this a high priority."

"I understand," Loren said. That was the moment when he put firmly behind him the impulse to tell Domjan about Joyce Clarke and her father's murder. That lead he would pursue on his own, and leave the police out of it until and unless he learned something he couldn't handle without official support.

"You know, sir," Domjan told him earnestly as they shook hands and said good night in the seminar-room doorway, "I'd invest some of my own time on this case if I weren't in law school and didn't have finals coming up. I— well, you were a law student once, you know how it is."

"I was a law student once," Loren echoed, and watched the sergeant's trim figure merge into a cluster of students and law school staff waiting for a down elevator. *I was a law student once,* he said to himself. *That was when Kim was with me.*

Four

LOREN HAD NO TUESDAY CLASSES that semester. In the morning he retraced his Sunday route by foot and subway and ferry to the St. George terminal, where he caught a cab to the One-Twenty on Richmond Terrace. The two hours he spent leafing through photographs in the precinct station mug books were a waste of time. None of the vicious faces in those volumes belonged to the man with the violin.

Domjan was out but an obliging desk clerk to whom Loren introduced himself reached the youthful sergeant at the Borough Court House where he had gone to testify. "You guessed it, sir. New York Telephone has no record of your getting a call in the wee hours yesterday morning. Gotta go now, sir, my case comes up next, wish me luck." Loren wondered if Domjan was getting tired of him.

He stepped off the Manhattan-bound ferry at Battery Park a little before one in the afternoon and strolled through the financial district's lunchtime mobs to the World Trade Center, in one of whose lobby-level coffee shops he bolted down a chicken salad sandwich and an iced tea before boarding an Eighth Avenue express subway to West Fourth Street. A quick stop at Vanderbilt Hall to use the men's room and check his mailbox and he was out on West Fourth again. He turned in at the entrance to the Elmer Holmes Bobst Library, a redstone fortress twelve stories tall that guarded the southeast corner of Washington Square Park, and displayed his faculty card to the uniformed guard at the turnstile, then circumnavigated the vast atrium with its trompe l'oeil floor pattern until he found the reference room.

His first order of business was running down the name of U.S. District Judge Howard Clarke in *The New York Times Index*. He jotted down a list of all the dates on which stories about Clarke had appeared in the *Times*, took an elevator to the microform room on sub-basement Level A, hunted through file cabinets for the microfilm editions of the *Times* issues on his list, used the coin-operated reader-printer to make copies. There were five stories in all. The earliest dated back more than twenty years and covered his move from a partnership in the St. Louis firm of Anthony & Clarke to the federal bench. The article included a posed photograph of the new judge with his wife and their daughter Joyce, a slender grave-eyed child of eleven. The most recent of the five stories was three years old and dealt with the murder of Clarke by his housekeeper, a Ruth Schrader. Nothing about whether the woman had been put on trial or what had been done with her. For that Loren would have to consult the St. Louis papers. The account of Judge Clarke's death mentioned that he had been a widower and was survived by a daughter named Joyce who was an attorney in New York City.

Loren's eyes widened behind his glasses as he realized that he'd missed a bet. With the damp copies of the *Times* pages rolled into a cylinder in his breast pocket he went back to the reference room and the *Times Index* and looked up the name of Joyce Clarke.

Just what he'd hoped for: an article profiling her, in an issue published two and a half years before her father's murder. He retraced his steps to the microform room and left with one more glistening-wet copy of a page from the microfilmed *Times*, which he glanced at on a padded bench in the atrium, overlooked by half a dozen balconies high overhead on three sides. The focus of the article was on Women Crime Victims Legal Resource Center, a nonprofit corporation which Ms. Clarke had helped to form and which she served as associate director. There wasn't much biographical material about her beyond the facts that she had grown up in St. Louis and graduated from the

University of Michigan Law School in 1977 and that her father was a federal judge.

The photograph of her made Loren wince. Five or six years ago when the *Times* had taken her picture she couldn't have been more than thirty but the camera had made her look fat, dumpy, unkempt and at least twenty years older than her actual age. Maybe, he thought, she was just one of those people the camera didn't flatter. Newspaper pictures were always terrible and this was a photocopy, which would make it even worse. What the years since the picture might have done to her looks he didn't allow himself to dwell on.

He made one more visit to the reference room and found the shelves where telephone directories were kept. The Manhattan White Pages gave the address of Women Crime Victims Legal Resource Center as Ten Astor Place. At Loren's brisk pace he could walk there in five minutes. He scrawled down the phone number and replaced the directory on its shelf. His mind raced.

Outside the Bobst he headed east on Fourth Street, then swung north on Broadway to the corner of Astor Place. Number Ten was a gaunt red brick building with chipped gray trim, six stories high, faux columns in shades of gray flanking the entrance door. Loren slowed down as he passed but kept walking. At Fourth Avenue he did an about-face and came back on the other side of Astor, working out in his head a plan of approach from what he'd read in the *Times.*

When he was satisfied, he found a usable phone booth on Broadway around the corner from his target, dropped a quarter in the slot and tapped out the number he'd copied in the Bobst. On the third ring a woman answered in a nasal rasp that could have been born and nurtured only in New York. "Women Crime Victims Resawce Centa, please hold." A click exploded in his ear, followed by New Age music. He had to stuff another quarter down the coin slot before the voice remembered to come back. "Sorry to keep you waiting, Women Crime Victims Resawce Centa, may I help you?"

51

Loren tried to approximate the tone of a bored civil servant near quitting time. "This is Murphy over at Family Court. Got a lady here could use the Center's help, her old man's been beating up on her ever since she got pregnant again, he keeps hitting her in the stomach and she thinks he wants her to lose the baby. She moved out this morning, no money, no family in town, nowhere to stay. I want to send her over to Ms. Clarke but this lady's got paperwork to finish here first, she's filing charges against her old man. I don't think she can make it to the Center before, oh, say six o'clock. Will Ms. Clarke still be there at six, do you know?"

Loren heard the sound of papers rustling. "The appointment book shows Ms. Clarke is speaking to a women's self-help group in Brooklyn at six-thirty, Mr. Murphy, but someone else will be here to see the lady if she comes by at six. What name, please?"

Loren made up a Hispanic name, growled thanks for the receptionist's help and hung up.

His watch read 4:43. Even if Joyce planned to go straight from the Center to her speaking date, she'd have to leave soon. He crossed to the corner and watched the doorway of Ten Astor Place from behind an evergreen in a tub at the curbside.

The exodus began at five sharp. As the first wave of homeward-bound office workers poured out of the building, Loren began an aimless stroll along the opposite sidewalk of Astor Place. Waiting. Watching. For a woman who looked like the *Times* photo of Joyce Clarke. A few yards beyond Number Ten's entranceway he would swivel about and retrace his steps. In the cover provided by the scurrying pedestrians and the trucks and taxis on the street he was all but invisible. No one paid him the slightest attention.

There she was. Coming out now.

Suety body. Mannishly styled hair salted with gray streaks. Tan raincoat draped over her arm. Black Samsonite attaché case in one hand, tan purse in the other. She marched out of the building and swung left, and on his own side of Astor Place Loren kept parallel with her. When she paused at the southeast corner of Broadway to let a semi merge into the traffic stream, he knew she was headed north. He turned right on Broadway but reversed after a few steps and aimed himself on a collision course with her. Just as she had crossed the street and reached Broadway's northeast corner, he slammed into her soft loose body and flung out his arms to keep her from falling.

"Excuse me," he began, stepping away from her in embarrassment, "I wasn't looking. . . . Oh my God, Joyce? Joyce Clarke? Michigan Law, class of, let's see, class of '77?"

"I don't . . ." Her round doughy face hardened and she tightened her grip on the purse and attaché case as if she were afraid he'd try to grab one or both of them and run.

"Steve Harvey! Don't you remember me from school? I was a senior when you were a first year, in '74. God, I can't believe it's been that many years!" Loren kept it vague enough so that with a little luck she wouldn't be sure whether he'd been at Michigan with her or not, but he wasn't prepared for her reaction.

"Oh my God," she whispered, and the hostility that had flashed for a second in her bright grave eyes gave way to a look of stark terror that was replaced a moment later by a dead blank stare. "You're living . . ." She coughed and swallowed and had to start over as they stepped into a shop doorway. "You live in New York or what?"

"Just in town for a month or so," he said. "I'm with a firm in L.A. and we're getting ready for a trial in the southern district, copyright infringement case. How about you?"

"I work with a women crime victims' center around the corner on Astor Place. God, what a small world!"

"Microscopic," Loren agreed. "I thought it was up in Times Square where you meet everyone you ever knew."

"Only the scumbags," she said. "You staying in the Village?"

"No, over on Waterside Plaza." The instant the answer was out of his mouth he would have given a year of his life to take it back. For a split second he'd forgotten that he had to assume for now that she was an enemy. "Where are you off to? Got time for a drink and some catching up?"

She shook herself as if he had slapped her. "No, no," she said. "I have to . . . Look, uh, Steve, I wish I had an hour to spare but I'm late for a meeting and, here, here's my card, call me before you go back to the Coast and we'll do lunch." She twisted her mouth into an inane grin as she shook hands with Loren and broke away into the north-bound pedestrian tide. Whatever her skills as a lawyer and women's rights advocate, she was a dreadful actress. The terror on her face was palpable as acne. How could she know who he was?

When she was almost out of sight, he followed her.

Whatever had happened to Kim, Joyce knew about it or was involved somehow. Loren would have staked his life on it.

He pushed through the crowd on Broadway until he spotted her again, her walk so swift and graceless it was almost a waddle, the hem of her raincoat trailing on the filthy sidewalk, the black attaché case bobbing against her thigh as she scurried. Somehow she reminded Loren of the white rabbit from *Alice in Wonderland:* "I'm late, I'm late, For a very important date, No time to say hello, Good-bye, I'm late I'm late I'm late!" A traffic snarl at Union Square halted her. She stood undecided at the southeast corner of Fourteenth Street but as soon as the WALK signal bloomed she plunged into the pedestrian crossing and over to a subway kiosk. Loren darted into the stream of underground commuters in her wake. He almost lost her twice in the maze of tunnels. A legless man on a cushion against one of the passage walls held a violin to his chin and played a Brahms melody that echoed through the network of caverns. Loren remembered the man with the violin on the ferry and quickened his pace. He was a dozen feet behind Joyce when she came to the pair of passageways leading to the L train, the Fourteenth Street-Canarsie local line, and veered into the tunnel connecting with the trains going west. That surprised Loren. She wasn't headed for Brooklyn.

He followed her down the echoing staircase to the concrete platform. A train roared in while he was on the stairs.
He took the rest of them three at a time and caught a
glimpse of her in the midst of a mob fighting its way into a
center car. He joined the tail end of the horde, elbowed and
shoved like the others until he was in the car and the steel
doors behind him snicked shut and the train lurched into
motion. An indecipherable voice squawked the name of
each station over an intercom. There was no way Loren
could keep Joyce in sight through the crowd, but he
thought he knew where she was going.

By the Sixth Avenue stop there was breathing room and
even moving room in the car. Loren caught sight of her
again, standing near a door at the far end of the wheeled
cage, one hand wrapped around a support bar, the attaché
case planted between her thick ankles. Her back was half
turned to him and she seemed to be staring out the train
window in a fit of abstraction. Loren stayed where he was,
afraid that if he moved closer she might glimpse his reflec-
tion in the glass.

Early in his year at NYU he had made it his business to
learn how to use the subways. He didn't need to look at
the transit map framed on the car wall to know that after
the Sixth Avenue stop on the L train there is only one
more place to get off, Eighth Avenue and Fourteenth
Street, the end of the line. As the train thundered into the
station, he blended into the knot of passengers waiting to
exit by the door at the opposite end of the car from where
Joyce stood. The moment the twin doors banged open, he
stepped out to the platform. He was twenty feet behind her
as she went through an exit turnstile and up a stairway
past several panhandlers slouched on the landing and out
into the brightness of the West Village. He allowed her to
increase the distance between them as she went south on
Eighth.

She turned west on Jane Street.

Headed home as Loren had guessed. Trotting now, probably panting and sweating from the exercise.

He dropped further back and was a full block behind her

when she mounted the front stoop of the gray brick building numbered 79 and thrust a key into the lock.

Was it just that she needed time alone to recover from the shock of seeing him? Was there someone she needed to phone in privacy, to tell about the chance encounter on Broadway? Maybe the violinist from the ferry? Could Kim be in that house with her right now? Of her own free will? A prisoner?

Maybe she was dead. Maybe they had forced her to make that last call to Loren, and her body was somewhere in that house.

An insane urge swept through him. He wanted to kick in the door of the building and tear Joyce's rooms apart until he found some sign that Kim had been there. Only a quarter century of lawyerly inhibition restrained him. How likely was it that she was alive and in Joyce's place now, that by breaking in he could save her? Or even that she had been killed in there and her body hadn't been moved? The most he'd accomplish by forcing his way in would be to frighten Joyce worse than he had on the street. When he made himself think about the situation with a modicum of reason he realized that, assuming there was evidence that Kim had been in the apartment, he probably wouldn't know it if he saw it.

He backed away. Retraced his steps east on Jane Street without coming any nearer Number 79 and giving her a chance to spot him from a window. Better to keep her on edge, let her make the next move. Maybe it wasn't so bad after all that he had let slip to her where he was staying. It would give the other side, whoever they were, an opening to go after him. If he was prepared for it, he could make it backfire on them. His thoughts and feet had taken him that far when he reached West Twelfth Street and flagged a cab. "Waterside Plaza," he said, and slammed the passenger door as the taxi lurched into motion. By the time the driver set him down at the foot of the escalator, he had reached another conclusion. He couldn't handle this alone anymore. He needed someone to shadow Joyce and he needed someone to shadow himself.

He treated himself to a hot shower and a sherry on the rocks before he opened the desk drawer in the living-room alcove that faced the river and took out his permanent address book.

INSTINCTIVELY HE OPENED IT to the page headed H, to the neatly handwritten entry HOOFT, MARC followed by business and home phone numbers complete with area codes even though they were in his home city. Then he remembered that the genial and corpulent head of the private agency that had helped Loren on several past cases couldn't help him anymore. Marc had suffered a massive heart attack in the Jacuzzi of his condominium a week short of his fifty-fifth birthday. It had happened while Loren was in Europe. He heard of Hooft's death only months later and had never crossed Marc's name out of his address book. As Loren flipped forward through its pages he noticed at least a dozen other people listed who were dead and had not been crossed out. Maybe drawing lines through the names of the dead reminded him too vividly of his own mortality.

He held the book open to the page headed T and used the desk phone to tap out a number. After three rings a voice answered at the other end, a woman's voice but not the one he expected. "Good afternoon, Tremaine Investigations."

"May I speak to Ms. Tremaine, please? This is Professor Mensing calling long distance."

"Ms. Tremaine is out of town, sir, this is her answering service."

Loren restrained the impulse to say the four-letter words he was thinking. "Do you know when she'll be back?"

"She's expected in her office tomorrow, sir."

Loren thanked the answering service and hung up. If Val was due back tomorrow she'd probably be returning from her trip tonight. In a few hours he'd try her home number.

He wondered what had taken her out of town. A case? Another man in her life?

They had met almost ten years ago, when the state supreme court had asked Loren to act as a sort of detective without portfolio, looking into the provenance of $49,000 in cash which the widow of Justice Richmond had found in a shoebox in his bedroom closet. He had needed an assistant in the state capital to work with him, and Hooft had recommended Val Tremaine, who had carried on the small agency after her husband Chris had been murdered. Loren and Val had become lovers in the last shattering days of that mission, and afterward they had restored each other. They had been together off and on ever since. Their relationship had lasted longer than Val's marriage and longer than any other affair Loren had had with a woman but they each needed autonomy and private space as much as they needed each other. They had never spent more than a couple of weeks together. She was in her mid-thirties now but every time they saw each other something special still happened between them. He sat at the desk and gazed blankly through the window at the Brooklyn shoreline and the river traffic and wondered if he should simply ask her to recommend a New York agency without explaining why he needed one or whether he dared tell her about Kim.

He was worrying that question to shreds when the phone rang and lifted him an inch off his chair. *It's Kim again,* a tiny voice inside him whispered. His hand shook as he lifted the receiver to his ear and managed a hello.

"Loren? Hey, pardner, got a horned toad in your throat or something?" The prairie drawl of Tex Okamoto was unmistakable even over the phone. "Hope you haven't chowed down yet tonight."

The digital clock at the corner of the desk read a few minutes before seven. "I'm running late today, Tex," he said. "Figured I'd microwave something in a little while. What's up?"

"Got something better in mind. I'm at the Yale Club, Vanderbilt at Forty-fourth, couple blocks from Grand Central. Ever eaten here?"

"Not that I can recall."

"I'm about to put on the feed bag with a feisty old critter you need to confabulate with," Okamoto told him. "That is, you do if you still want to know what happened to our mutual friend Judge Clarke."

Loren said nothing, allowing Okamoto to savor the pleasure of keeping his colleague in suspense. "Tell me more, Tex," he said at last.

"Thought you'd never break down and ask! Well, you seemed so interested in Clarke yesterday, I made it my business to touch base with a few old federal judges I happen to know. Ever hear of Manfred Ostrander?"

"Just vaguely," Loren said. "Circuit Court of Appeals judge, right? My God, wasn't he on the bench before we were born?"

"Says he'll be eighty-six this winter, and he's still as rugged and feisty as a mountain goat. He's been on senior status since he turned seventy, takes cases as and when he feels like and draws most of a full-time judge's pay. He got bored a few years ago and offered to move out to St. Louis for a while and fill a temporary vacancy on the Eighth Circuit. Well, you know how overworked the federal bench is. He was serving out there three years ago when Clarke was killed. The FBI gave special private briefings on the case to all the federal judges in the district, and Ostrander's got the sharpest memory I've ever seen in anyone his age. Want to meet him over chow?"

Loren took less than a split second to decide that a leisurely meal with the old jurist might fill a gap in his knowledge of the situation and would certainly fill in time until his next attempt to get hold of Val. In any event the Yale Club cuisine was reputed to be excellent.

"Thanks, Tex, I'd love to. Can you dawdle over your bourbon and branch water till I grab a cab and join you?"

"I never dawdle over good liquor," Okamoto said. "But I do believe I can persuade His Honor to take another drink under advisement. Meet you in the roof dining room, twenty-second floor."

As he was changing into the pinstripe suit that he reserved for appellate court oral arguments and other special occasions, it occurred to him that these might be the clothes he would be buried in. Assume the worst-case scenario: that Joyce Clarke was involved in Kim's disappearance, that she had called her confederates from Jane Street and told them of her encounter with Loren, that they had had time since that conversation to cover Waterside Plaza, that whatever they were up to was so important to them that they were ready to do whatever it took to neutralize him. If all that were true, then when Loren stepped out of his highrise tower onto the quadrangle or the escalator to the street, or perhaps when he returned to Waterside a few hours from now, they might be waiting, to beat or maim him, maybe to kill him.

Paranoid, he mocked himself.

He was late already for his dinner date but made himself later by scrawling a hasty letter describing all he had done so far and sealing it in an envelope on which he wrote DETECTIVE SERGEANT DOMJAN, NYPD. In the lobby of the Waterside tower he deposited the envelope in his own mail slot before he left the building.

It was a cool spring evening, the eastern sky already dark purple like a bruise. Loren crossed the quadrangle at a brisk trot. Between the building entrance and the foot of the escalator to street level he passed perhaps a dozen people, all of them moving as purposefully as he. No one seemed out of place. No one seemed to be lurking in the shadows. He made it a point to exchange a few words with the security guard at the outer edge of the Waterside complex before he waved his hand for a cab.

Five

THE ROOFTOP DINING ROOM on the twenty-second floor of
the Yale Club was a cool mirror-walled cavern. At several
dozen linen-covered tables under the chandeliers, men and
women in casually elegant attire conversed and sipped and
partook of dinner amid the trappings of quiet dignity,
while servers glided across the diamond-patterned carpet
from table to table bearing cocktails, appetizers, soups,
stemware with dainty scoops of sherbet to cleanse the pal-
ate, entrees, wine, bounteous desserts, liqueurs, coffee in
gleaming pots. Glassware made soft tinkling sounds as
voices rose and fell in a restful hum and the majesty of the
evening skyline beckoned from the windows. Whenever
Loren entered such a place one part of him savored the
experience while another felt guilty.

"Professor Mensing, sir?" A smiling bald man in bow tie
and dinner jacket dipped his head as Loren stepped into the
entranceway. "Professor Okamoto described you, sir. This
way, please." Loren followed him across the room to a table set for three near the bar where Tex sat sipping a Jack
Daniel's and a compactly built man in a navy blazer with
wisps of snowy hair clinging to his skull was squirting the
contents of a lemon wedge on six succulent shrimp.

"Hope you don't mind us starting without you."
Okamoto set down his glass on the dazzling white tablecloth and hoisted himself to his feet, which Loren couldn't
see but assumed were shod as usual in cowboy boots.
"Loren, this is Judge Ostrander. Judge, my colleague Professor Mensing."

"Great pleasure," Ostrander said in a thin quavering

voice, offering a veined and liver-spotted hand which Loren shook gently. "Oh, come on, man, I'm no museum exhibit!" A waiter slid back the third chair at the table and Loren sank into its cushioned depths and unfolded his napkin.

"The pleasure's all mine, your honor," he replied mechanically, and retreated from his momentary confusion into a study of the menu, from which he selected the French onion soup and a filet mignon.

"Good choices," the ancient jurist cackled. "I eat here three, four nights a week and I know what comes out of that kitchen like I know my own name. Walk home most nights too, and I live way uptown, co-op on Park and Eighty-eighth. I've been offered seven figures for the place. Time comes when I can't take care of myself, the Club will give me a nice suite here for the rest of my life if I make a big enough donation."

"Looking at you," Loren said, "I don't guess that will happen anytime soon."

"Young fellow," Ostrander told him, lifting his glass as if in a toast, "you do know the way to my heart." He leaned forward until his mouth was an inch from Loren's ear and lowered his voice to a whisper. "I have a girlfriend sleeps over with me two, three nights a week. Young chick in her seventies." Suddenly Loren wanted to tell this spry and uninhibited old man that he would give almost anything to know that his own ninth decade would be as full of life as Ostrander's seemed to be. He wanted to know the judge better, penetrate his secret if he had one. *Later,* he decided. *Stay on track for now.* How to live as if old age and death held no terror was a subject for another time.

"Tex tells me," he ventured as the waiter set before him a steaming crock of soup topped with thick melted cheese, "that you still volunteer to sit on cases now and then."

"Haven't in the past few years," Ostrander said, "but I may do it again in the fall. Nice way to see the country at the taxpayer's expense." Okamoto lifted the half-empty bottle of Johannisburger Riesling from its coaster and filled Loren's glass and the judge's and finally his own.

"Didn't I hear," Loren went on, "that the last time you were on the bench one of your colleagues got himself murdered? Oh, hell, what was his name, Stark, Clark?"

"Boy," Ostrander cackled gleefully, "you can't pull anything on an old fox like me. You know damn well his name was Howard Clarke. You think I couldn't tell when Texas Tojo here pumped me about him this morning?" Okamoto spluttered and coughed down a mouthful of wine as he tried to suppress a giggle. "And let me make one correction in the record before we go any further. That son of a bitch was no colleague of mine."

Loren recognized the signal that the judge was about to open the conversational floodgates. As the waiter glided among them with the plates containing their entrees, Loren preserved a diplomatic silence which he broke the moment the three diners were alone again. "Sounds like you didn't think much of him," he said.

"I didn't and I don't." Ostrander sawed at his prime rib and lifted a heaping forkful to his mouth. Loren noticed that he seemed to have most of his own teeth. "When I think of the way he abused his power, the way he wrecked people's lives, I just wish the bastard would have been shot a lot sooner." He peered around him with narrowed eyes like a spy on the lookout for counterspies. "Don't you ever repeat any of what I'm telling you, boy," he warned.

Loren had known and worked with many judges but had never heard one speak so harshly of another before now. He sensed that age had put Ostrander beyond peer group pressure and the judicial code of *omerta*. "You saw Clarke as some kind of monster in a black robe?"

"Oh, hell, it wasn't just Clarke." The old man's Adam's apple bobbled as he washed down the meat with a long swallow of ice water. "You guys are lawyers, don't you feel it, too? That the whole system's been trashed by a pack of sorcerer's apprentices with good intentions? I mean, my God, these damn judges have decided they have the power to do anything they damn well please, to turn loose the most vicious scum in the country, to order employers to use hiring quotas by race and sex and whatever, to set local tax rates, by God! To take over whole institutions like an army of occupation! And these judges can't be fired, can't be disciplined, and most of the time they aren't even reversed on appeal. One of these days some federal judge is going to cancel a presidential election and declare the winner out of his own ideology. Burn any books or movies that have what they decide is a negative stereotype of some protected species of people. Condemn your house and give it to someone of the right shade of color or the right ethnic group. Maybe tell you who you can marry or have kids with. Mark my words, guys, we are sliding further down that slope every goddamn day."

Loren's traditional liberal instincts overcame him. He wanted Ostrander to return to the subject of Judge Clarke but couldn't resist the impulse to dispute the old man's philosophy. Okamoto meanwhile nodded his head mechanically in benevolent approval and applied himself to the duck à l'Orange. "But, Judge," Loren began earnestly, "surely you agree that if there's a violation of a Constitutional right or an entitlement under a civil rights statute, the courts have to—"

"Son," Ostrander cut in, "you're looking at the last active judge that was appointed by FDR. Back in 1939 that was. Goddamnit, I was a part of that judicial revolution and I still believe it was necessary. Up to a point! We went beyond that point a hell of a long time ago. We never intended to turn the judiciary into a goddamn dictatorship! But look what we've got now. A couple of generations of judges who've perverted the understanding this country was founded on, rewritten history to fit their own agenda, set themselves up as the ultimate branch of government, and then they piously declare they're just servants of the law, following the statutes and the Constitution, not inventing a dad-blessed thing. Guys, we've become what George Orwell dreamed about."

Loren was not convinced that the system had crumbled quite to that extent, but privately he had shared Ostrander's disillusionment for years and he suspected it had eaten into his enthusiasm for being a law professor, preparing young men and women for roles in a diseased order that might no longer have the resources to cure itself. He had suppressed his doubts as steadfastly as some of his colleagues had kept quiet about being gays or lesbians. Despite the guaranteed sympathetic audience around the Yale Club table he preserved his silence now and chose instead to divert the subject back to the man he was interested in. "Do you think Howard Clarke was somehow worse than the system?" he asked.

"Oh Christ, yes," Ostrander told him.

"Why?"

"He *enjoyed* using his power to hurt people. I got wind of this when I was out in the Eighth Circuit and asked around about Clarke. He was the same way off the bench. Drove his wife to suicide, which everybody hushed up; made such a mess of his daughter's life she hadn't spoken to him in years. As a judge he had—well, he seemed to have a genius for making rotten decisions that almost never got appealed and, when they were, almost never got reversed. Finally one of them came back to bite him." Ostrander chuckled fondly at the memory. "Ever hear of *Bloch* v. *Washington University?*"

Caught in the middle of a mouthful of baked potato, Loren shook his head no.

"Jonathan Bloch was a young fellow in his final year at the Washington University med school in St. Louis. How he got that far along in his education I'll never understand but one morning he just flipped out. Brought a surgical scalpel to class and cut up three students that sat near him and one of his profs. Scarred one gal for life. He was tried for aggravated assault and battery and found not guilty by reason of mental disease or defect and sent to the hospital for the criminally insane in Fulton, a couple hours drive from St. Louis. Meanwhile the medical school kicked him out. Eighteen months go by, the shrinks decide he's not dangerous to himself or others, court lets him loose. He reapplies to med school but he's turned down. Gets a lawyer and sues Washington University for discrimination against the handicapped in violation of the Rehabilitation

65

Act of 1973. As the luck of the draw would have it, the case was assigned to Clarke. He orders the school to let Bloch back in. The school doesn't appeal. So what happens? Five or six months later Bloch's doing a night shift in the university hospital's emergency room and all of a sudden he runs amok again, starts slashing everybody in sight with a scalpel. Kills an eight-year-old boy whose father had taken him in with a tummyache or something. Put a little girl's eye out. Naturally he pleads insanity again and gets sent to Fulton again. The father of the murdered boy kills himself. Clarke piously declaims that he was just following the law. Well, that time he was held accountable for his decision."

"I thought I'd heard," Loren said as one waiter removed their plates and another wheeled over a dessert cart laden with cakes and pastries, "that Clarke was shot by his housekeeper."

"Right." Ostrander ordered Courvoisier with his coffee and, when it came, poured the brandy into his cup and sniffed the fumes with a sensuous sigh. "She emptied a revolver in his face one evening as he was sitting in his study, then she picked up the phone and called the cops."

"I heard," Okamoto ventured between spoonfuls of parfait, "that she and Clarke were sleeping together. Or maybe I just assumed it."

"Old saddlemate," Ostrander cackled, "she was the last woman in the world would have gone to bed with Clarke. Bloch killed her son in that emergency room after Clarke ordered him readmitted to med school."

Loren blinked. The coffee spoon clattered from his fingers onto the bone china saucer.

"Yep," the judge went on, "she applied for that job as Clarke's housekeeper after all the flap about Bloch had died down. Used a phony name, of course. Bided her time for a few months, cooking, cleaning for him, then she made her move. Spunky gal, heh?"

"More like a vigilante," Loren replied mechanically.

"There's times vigilantes are needed," Ostrander said.

Loren said nothing. The dining room was three-quarters

deserted by then. The chandeliers seemed to shed a dimmer light. By Loren's watch it was a few minutes past eleven. The silence at the table deepened, became almost embarrassing until it was broken by Tex Okamoto.

"Killing a federal judge or almost any other employee," he pointed out sententiously, "is a federal crime as well as a crime under the law of the state where it happened. Do you know who put the woman on trial first?"

"I know all sorts of things about that case," Ostrander told him. "The FBI kept all the Eighth Circuit judges briefed. I can't recall how they decided who'd take first crack at her, but she was tried in the Missouri courts. Some downtown St. Louis hotshot represented her." He cradled his chin in his palm and shut his eyes for a few seconds. "Had a funny name . . . I've got it. Grimsby. Saul Grimsby. Naturally he put on the same defense Jonathan Bloch had gotten away with twice."

"What was the verdict?" Loren asked.

"The jury found her not guilty by reason of mental disease or defect. Guess there was a lot of local sympathy for anyone who'd been dumped on like that poor woman had. Far as I know she's still in the state hospital at Fulton."

"They put her in the same place with Jonathan Bloch?" Okamoto did nothing to keep the shock and disbelief out of his tone.

"Hell," Ostrander shrugged, "they'd let Bloch loose again before Mrs. Schrader was let in. Shrink said he was no longer a danger to himself or others, judge held a hearing, the creep walked."

"But Mrs. Schrader's still in the hospital?"

"Mrs. Schrader's an honest woman. She tells the shrinks the only thing she's got to live for anymore is to find Bloch and do him the way he did her kid. That makes her a danger to others. She stays in the loony bin. That's the law, son."

Loren ordered a brandy and downed it in a gulp, telling himself he needed it. "One thing I don't understand, Judge," he said then. "Why did the FBI give all those briefings to you and the rest of the Eighth Circuit bench?"

"Because lots of federal judges make lots of enemies,"
Ostrander said. "Now as far as I know, only a couple of us
have ever gotten ourselves murdered, but some of my
brethren wanted to be sure the Clarke case wasn't the start
of a pattern and others were worried about possible copy-
cats."

"And were there any?"

"I never heard of one," Ostrander told him.

So now, Loren thought as he swallowed the last of his
coffee, he knew how Joyce Clarke's father had died and it
was no help at all. Whatever connected that three-year-old
killing with Kim Hale's reappearance and return to the
shadows was murky as ever. By mutual consent the three
diners called it an evening minutes later. Ostrander invited
Loren to walk uptown with him to his co-op. Okamoto
wished the others good night outside the revolving door of
the Yale Club and trotted south on Vanderbilt to catch a
Village-bound cab from the stand at Grand Central.

It was just after eleven when they began their stroll,
north on Madison to Eighty-eighth Street and east one
block to Park. The night breeze kept them moving briskly,
hands in coat pockets. Ostrander's stride was as powerful
as Loren's. Twice, as if fearful the younger man might be
winded, he suggested hailing a cab. Loren laughed uproariously each time.

They shook hands in the ornately furnished lobby of the
co-op building. "I hope I've helped you with your problems, my boy," Ostrander said. "You keep them buried,
but I got a hunch you're wrestling with more than your
share."

"Judge," Loren replied, "I wish I'd had the chance to argue a case before you. Maybe I will someday."

"Oh, I don't plan to crap out anytime soon. But you
know, I sort of look forward to dying. As long as it's quick
and painless, that is. If there's an afterlife I want to look up
the ghosts of Brandeis and Cardozo and find out how the
hell we managed to screw up a perfectly good legal system
so badly."

The ancient judge marched straight-backed across the

lobby to the elevator at the far end. Loren visualized the assassin or booby trap that might be awaiting his return to Waterside Plaza and was tempted for an instant to crowd into the elevator behind Ostrander and beg to be allowed to stay the night. *No,* he commanded himself. *I will not let these animals mess with my mind.* With its security guards, Waterside Plaza was as safe as anywhere in New York.

He stepped out into Park Avenue and waved for a taxi. It was the first hour of the new day and traffic was thin but swift with cab after southbound cab streaking past him like tracer bullets in the night. After five minutes of standing at the curb and making futile signals he gave up, decided to cross Park and cut over to Lexington. If he couldn't hail a cab there, he'd take his life in his hands and risk the subway.

A dark-gray sedan swung onto Park from Ninetieth Street and jerked to a stop just south of where Loren was standing. Its dome light glowed as the right-side passenger door was flung open and revealed a woman's head and body. "Drop you somewhere, Professor Mensing?"

Joyce Clarke.

She was wrapped in a dark all-weather coat with imitation military fittings that glistened in the pale-yellow light. Loren flinched at the sight of her and his mind raced in multiple directions at once. What was she doing here? Could she have been following him all evening? He was convinced no one had shadowed him to the Yale Club, but someone could have seen him there or walking uptown with Judge Ostrander and gotten word to her. Her appearance on upper Park Avenue could hardly be by chance.

"I have things to tell you," she said softly.

Loren gazed at her in the doorway of the dark sedan and felt like a bird being hypnotized by a snake. She leaned forward in the backseat and seemed to beckon him, large and loose and unmenacing-looking with a bulky shoulder bag slung across her body. Was there a gun in the bag, or in one of her coat pockets? The imagination of disaster told him he was about to be taken for a ride like a character in a

69

thirties gangster movie, and every remnant of common sense told him that such things don't happen in the streets of New York in the eighties. He might be robbed or mugged or accosted by a violent panhandler or shot or stabbed or beaten to death but not taken for a ride. Besides, the dome light was shining on her and he could see the night man in the lobby of Ostrander's co-op building peering out at the two of them from behind the leaded glass of the vestibule door. If she was planning anything violent she wouldn't be going about it so stupidly. Would she?

He reached into his trousers pocket and fumbled around for a few seconds. "Damn." He said it just loud enough for her to hear. "I must have dropped my keys in there. Give me a second, will you?" He wheeled around and rapped on the co-op's outer door until the night man opened it a crack.

"I think my keys fell out of my pocket when I was saying good night to Judge Ostrander," he said. "Okay if I come in and look?" Without waiting for permission he stepped up and into the vestibule. The night man stood aside and relocked the door and trotted into the lobby where Loren on one knee was running his hands along the parquet beneath the chesterfield. "Got 'em!" he grunted, and thrust his hand into his pocket while lurching to his feet. "Thanks much." He reached into his other trousers pocket for his wallet and handed the night man a five. "My name is Loren Mensing," he said rapidly, and pulled a card from his wallet. "I'm a visiting professor at NYU Law School. Judge Ostrander knows me. The woman out there is Joyce Clarke. She lives at 79 Jane Street. This is her card." He held out the Resource Center card Joyce had given him on Astor Place. "Don't forget this if you read in the paper that anything's happened to me." The night man's sleepy eyes came open wide as Loren walked past him and waited for him to unlock the outer door, and then with his key container jingling in his hand stepped out onto Park and into the rear of the sedan as confidently as if he lived there. Joyce smiled and slid clumsily across the backseat to make room for him. In the split second of brightness before the dome light died with the slamming of the passenger door he caught a glimpse of a wedge of the driver's face: dark, dirty hair under an army-style fatigue cap, eyes buried behind sunglasses, strong brutal clean-shaven jawline. The car lurched into the traffic stream and hurtled south.

"Do I frighten you?" Joyce asked. The backseat was a cage rolling through patterns of light and shadow.

"I'm . . ." Loren edged to the middle of the seat but the rear vision mirror glass was tilted so that he saw nothing of the driver's face but only bursts of reflected light. "Right now I'm more puzzled than anything else."

"What by?"

"By you."

She maneuvered closer to him on the seat. The car turned west at Fifty-seventh and south again on Eighth Avenue. He guessed their destination was the West Village. "Ms. Clarke," he demanded, "what the hell are you mixed up in?"

"That's what it's time you know," she said. "That's why I came for you."

"How did you know who I am? How did you know where to find me?"

She ignored the questions. "We can talk best at my place. I have some things I want to show you. Books."

"What kind of books?"

"Sort of scrapbooks. A black one and a white one. You'll understand when you see them."

"Understand what you're involved in?"

"And what I want you to be involved in, too," she said with a quiet conviction that startled him.

"Was Kim Hale involved in it, too?" he ventured. Only after the question was out and beyond recall did he realize that he'd instinctively used the past tense, and the bile of despair came up in his throat.

The tip of Joyce's tongue peeped out as she moistened her lips. "Sort of," she answered after a stretch of silence. "Not really."

"Meaning she found out too much? Wanted out?"

The car turned off Eighth and wove through the surrealist twistings of the West Village. Loren lost track of where they were, kept focused on Joyce's eyes, her dark grave lovely eyes in that placid piglike face. "You're guessing," she said. Was there an undertone of fear there? A desperate effort to convince herself?

"I've always been a good guesser," he told her. "When I was in law school I could usually tell what answers the professors wanted even when I was just as lost as everyone else."

"Maybe you could psych out your professors," she said. "But we're not playing school games now. This is not about the intellectual bullshit they feed us in law school, it's the real world, the horrors, the—the stinking jungle they've made of everything, lawyers, bureaucrats, judges, God damn them all to hell!" Her voice filled the car with an anguish that made Loren drop his eyes in embarrassment. He made himself pay attention to where they were and recognized some of the stores the sedan was passing. He had seen them Sunday evening on his taxi excursion into the neighborhood. The driver made another turn and Loren recognized Jane Street. The car slowed to a crawl but every parking place along the street was taken. The night was velvet dark, quiet, empty. Like Loren himself. The driver turned again.

"If you've hurt Kim," Loren said, "you tell me now."

"She wasn't hurt," Joyce told him.

"Where is she?"

"Far away from here. If you—if you come in with me I'll tell you where. You can . . . you can see her." She caught her lower lip between her teeth and bit down hard. "You still love her, don't you?"

"I don't know," he said. "I have to know she's all right."

"You want to find out if she still loves you." She flung the words at him like an indictment.

"My God, it's been close to twenty-five years since I've seen her! The way she left then without saying a word, I've, well, I've always felt maybe I said or did something that drove her away."

"She told me you had an overdeveloped sense of guilt back then," Joyce said. "You still do." For a moment as the car's interior was bathed in ochre light from a street fixture something in her eyes seemed to soften. "Look, I'll tell you this much. You didn't drive her away. She's still very fond of you but she knows it can never work between you."

"Why not?"

"Come in with me," she said again. "With us. Then I'll tell you where she is and you can ask her yourself."

"Who is us?"

"Give me some time," she said. "A few more years and there'll be thousands of us. Almost, well, a counterculture but not out in the open like in the sixties. A resistance movement. A secret army."

That was when some of the fragments in Loren's mind began to cohere into a picture. The murder of Judge Clarke by his housekeeper. Joyce's long-standing hatred for her father, her center for women crime victims, the radical disillusionment of so many veterans of the legal system like Ostrander and Okamoto and himself, the endless countless stories of gross injustice cloaked in legality. The shape of the pattern he saw blotted out every other thought.

"You were part of the movement in the sixties." Joyce made her voice soft and breathy as if she were seducing him. "Why not now?"

Loren kept silent. The car writhed in the labyrinth of night-cloaked streets, searching for a place to rest.

"You can't hide behind your professor title. Others don't. No one's above this battle. I want you. We want you. We need you. You— Kim said you used to care about injustice so much."

"I like to think I still do," he lied.

"Then you will join us!" A sort of holy joy seemed to possess her as she slid against him and took his hand in hers. "Oh, I knew you would!" And suddenly Loren knew. She wanted him not only in this movement of hers but sexually. Repulsion and fright struggled inside him like interwined snakes while he let her caress his fingers and flailed about for escape.

The driver nudged the sedan into a space just barely large enough and shut down the engine. "Best I can do," he muttered without even slightly turning his head. Loren had no idea where they were parked but he saw the fronts of a health food store and a gay and lesbian bookshop and made out the hum of traffic a few blocks off and knew they weren't far from the West Side Highway.

"Thanks, Morgan." Joyce unclasped Loren's hand and reached into her shoulder bag for a ten which she passed to the driver over the seatback. "Here, take a cab home. Call me at nine and I'll give you the schedule for the day. My friend and I can walk from here." She opened the left rear door and lumbered out into the silent empty street, and as Loren slid out after her she took his arm between hers and hugged it. The driver strode away in the direction the car was facing. Joyce turned Loren the other way and they lurched together along the dark sidewalk, her bag on its long strap bobbing against her left side while the right side of her body rubbed against him. There was certainly no gun in her coat pocket. He felt clammy. He was afraid he might be sick. He forced himself to encircle her waist. His hand brushed against her shoulder bag and tested its weight. No gun there either. She pressed herself against him, her lips nuzzling his neck. He shut his eyes and tried to think of lying next to Kim on Sunday evenings and the touch of her thighs against him as she offered herself. If not for Kim, if not for his need to find her, he would have flung Joyce away from him and run headlong out of this dark glistening labyrinth. He made himself stay and stagger with her along whatever street this was. Dead storefronts flowed by them.

"I want you," she whispered into his ear. "She made me want you. She said the time she was with you was the last happiness she'd ever known. I've never had even that much happiness. My father started raping me when I was seven. I was a pretty child. I gorged myself on food so I'd get fat and repulsive and he wouldn't rape me anymore and

74

then I had to stay fat, and by the time I left St. Louis I was addicted to food and couldn't lose weight but I'm losing it now, oh I swear I'll lose it all, I've lost ten pounds this year already, oh trust me, give me six months and I'll be so beautiful for you and you'll kiss me all over my body and we'll give each other pleasures we never dreamed of before."

The torrent of whispered revelation poured out of her and assaulted Loren until something in him crumbled. He wrenched free of her frantic embrace and stood apart in a patch of shadow, facing her. "Ms. Clarke," he faltered, "Joyce . . . I can't . . . I just can't . . ."

"Fuck it!" she shrieked and broke away from him. "Fuck you!" He saw unshed tears shine in her eyes, watched her sniff and fumble blindly in her shoulder bag for a handkerchief. "Go find the bitch yourself if you think you can! You ever come near me again and I swear to God I'll call a cop and say you tried to rape me. Fucking bastard!" She jammed the handkerchief into a coat pocket, groped again through her bag, pulled out a key ring and stalked off in a sort of waddling trot and disappeared around the next corner. Loren stood in the womb of shadow and shuddered.

The roar of a car motor filled the night like a bomb exploding. A dark shape without lights cut across the intersection where Joyce had turned and there was a sick thump-plop of impact and a tiny scream cut off and another impact sound and the dying away of the motor. Loren stood rooted to the sidewalk. Then he ran. Around the corner, into Jane Street. Joyce Clarke's body lay crumpled across the hood of a parked Buick, her head hanging over the hood's edge upside down against the front bumper and something oily oozing down the metal grillwork into the curbing. Loren fell to his knees and threw up.

No windows cracked open, no lights flooded out over the street, no one came down to see what had happened. New York, New York.

Phone. He had to find a phone on this dead street and get help. He lurched to his feet and began to run east, toward

75

Sheridan Square and maybe a pay phone that hadn't been vandalized.

He took three steps and stopped. Saw something gleaming on the black pavement under a lamppost and stooped to pick it up.

The key ring. Flung out of her hand on impact.

He darted across Jane Street, and halfway down the block he jammed one key after another into the front door lock of Number 79, and it wasn't until the last one on the ring that he found the key that worked. He stumbled into a narrow stifling vestibule like an upended coffin with another door at the far end. He used the key ring again and this time got it right on the third try and stumbled up a flight of carpeted stairs to a door at the top. This time he made it with the first key he thrust into the upper lock but it took several tries before all three locks gave way and he was in a large open square of darkness. From somewhere in the empty space he heard the whisper of stringed instruments. An old show tune. She was one of those who kept the radio on while she was out so that friendly sounds would greet her when she came in. Lonely people tended to do that. Loren did it himself, only he preferred classical stations over those that offered easy listening. He pushed through the yielding dark and bumped against a low table and felt a lampshade and groped for the switch button. Warm light bloomed golden-brown. His eyes probed the room for a phone and found it, on the long table-desk against the far wall, peeping out from a jumble of books and papers.

Halfway across the room he heard the siren, ululating through the street like the howl of the tortured. He swung around, raced to the bay window that looked out on Jane Street. A boxy EMS vehicle was blocking the only usable traffic lane, blue roof globe lazily whirling. Two men in white uniforms huddled over the hood of the Buick across the street. Loren saw an NYPD cruiser screech to a halt behind the ambulance and two cops pour out on the double. So someone had called in for help after all. He ducked below the windowsill and sat on the floor and tried to sort out his options.

He had Joyce's keys but her shoulder bag must still be out there unless in the few minutes since the hit-and-run a neighborhood derelict had snatched it. Once the police found it, and in it her wallet and ID, they'd come up here and catch him. Even if they didn't find him tonight, surely when the news hit the morning papers the doorman at Ostrander's co-op would remember how Loren had given him her name and his own less than an hour before her murder, and would tell the police.

He had no choice. He had to go out there and tell them what had happened. He crossed the room to the untidy table-desk, followed by soft lush stringed sounds from the radio. "I thought that you want what I want. Sorry, my dear . . ."

The desk was a door lying on its side and mounted on two low file cabinets, its surface cluttered with books, papers, letters, manila folders, a box of pink facial tissues, a pen set, a memo pad, a digital clock, a stapler, a paper clip tray, and a telephone half buried in the rubble. A personal computer and printer stood on a hutch at right angles to the door desk. Loren dropped into the posture chair before the hutch and reached for the handset again. And stopped again.

This was where Kim had been. Where she'd told Joyce about her love for Loren. This was the phone from which she'd called him. He felt it. He felt her recent presence in this room almost like a scent and he knew he could never prove it.

Unless she'd left fingerprints or other traces the police could find.

He poked under the chaos of papers on the door surface, found two razorpoint pens and used them, clumsily as a person manipulating chopsticks for the first time, to lift the phone handset from its nest. With the eraser end of a pencil he tapped out 411.

"Manhattan Directory Assistance." Bored voice with a hint of Cuban accent. "May I help you?"

"Do you have a listing for a Domjan?" He spelled the name, pausing for a second between letters. "I think his first name is Theodore or Ted. Begins with a T anyway."

The line went silent and Loren imagined the invisible operator scanning a computerized directory. "We have no listing for a Theodore or Tee Domjan, sir. There is a . . . I'm sorry I can't pronounce it. T-A-D-E-U-S-Z."

Tadeusz. Sounded Hungarian enough, and any American born with the name would likely go by Ted. "Let me have his number," Loren said. "Please."

He jotted it on a scrap of paper with the lead end of the pencil and used the eraser end to tap out the number. After three rings came the familiar voice, still exuberant at 1:30 A.M. "Domjan."

"Loren Mensing, Sergeant. Sorry I had to wake you but . . ."

"I wasn't asleep, sir. Reviewing for my Labor Law exam at Fordham tomorrow. What can I do for you?"

"I hate to pull you away from the books but I just missed being a witness to a murder and I think I just missed being a victim." He gave the Jane Street address and a quick summary of the evening.

"Stay where you are," Domjan ordered. "Don't move, don't touch anything. If local cops drop by, tell them I'm coming." He hung up.

Loren used the pens to replace the handset and sat in the posture chair with his chin propped in his fist. He tried to think, gave up, crossed to the bay window and peered out. They were putting Joyce's body on a gurney, wheeling it into the ambulance's maw. Blue globe light streaked the pavement and the parked cars and the people who had ventured out from their caves to gawk. There were three NYPD cruisers now, parked at grotesque angles. Two uniformed cops were setting up a portable floodlight. Others with notebooks in their hands were questioning bystanders in nightclothes. Someone must have identified the body by now, told the police her address. Loren's hands and feet felt frozen. He wanted to be gone from here, out of it all. He wanted Domjan to arrive before any other cops.

He wanted a drink desperately and sleep even more. Most of all he wanted to toss this apartment, find the black book and the white book that Joyce was going to show him.

Domjan had ordered him to sit still. He went back to the door desk, sat in Joyce's chair and tried to wait in patience.

The opened box of facial tissues sat atop a heap of file folders at one corner of the desk, the front edge of one soft pink tissue peeping out of the container, waiting to be plucked and held to a runny nose or tearful eye. Loren could taste the residue of vomit when he ran his tongue over his lips. He pulled a handful of tissues from the box.

And found a paper of another sort sandwiched between two of them. Of a similar softness and pink shade but longer and narrower and with neat symmetrical perforations. A strip of toilet paper.

With writing on it.

He took it to the table lamp he had lit when he entered the apartment and, holding the paper six inches from his glasses, read the cramped hand-printed message.

J

    I am still locked in this horrible cage I did everything you wanted & said nothing about you or why but three yr is too long when I think the butcher who murdered my child was out of this hell hole in 18 mth Your people MUST have me out by the end of June or I will have to tell who came to me & gave me the plan & the gun If I spend much longer with these screaming lunatics & their filthy keepers I will truly go insane I want to see Kim again she was good to me I am sorry to bother you

R

J had to be Joyce. R must be Ruth Schrader. The horrible cage would have to mean the Missouri State Hospital for the Criminally Insane. If the note was to be believed, it was Joyce who had inspired Mrs. Schrader first to apply for the job as Judge Clarke's housekeeper and then to murder him. Was this why Joyce had been so eager to enlist Loren in her movement, so that he'd represent Mrs. Schrader, sue to have her released?

Whatever else he did, he would have to go to Fulton and see the Schrader woman. She had known Kim. Kim had been good to her. Maybe she knew where Kim was. Maybe.

With infinite care Loren folded the toilet paper along its perforations and slipped it into his hip pocket. Then he sat in the posture chair again and let his eyes wander across the wild assortment of items on the table-desk and from there to the bookshelves at right angles to the work surface.

Cheap pine shelving, painted white. Lower shelves packed with lawbooks, upper with legal periodicals, feminist tracts, handbooks on crime victims' rights. Two middle shelves held paperback romances. Some diet and exercise books were lying on their sides with a brass owl figure roosting on them.

Flanking those volumes like bookends, one on each side, was a pair of loose-leaf albums or scrapbooks. One bound in black, the other in white. Hidden in plain sight like Poe's purloined letter.

Loren had them in his lap when the door buzzer exploded.

Six

DOMJAN STOOD ON THE THRESHOLD alone and yawning, his blond hair tousled. He wore beach slippers, a velour bathrobe over gray silk pajamas, and a shoulder harness. Loren gaped at him, and at the .38 police pistol he was pointing at Loren's middle. "Back away, sir," he ordered politely. Loren lurched backward across the front room with his hands in the air. "Sit." Loren dropped into the nearest armchair as Domjan eased the door shut behind him.

From where he sat Loren had a clear view of the digital clock on Joyce Clarke's door desk. The ruby numerals confirmed his internal time sense. Less than ten minutes had passed since he'd phoned the young sergeant. "You live in this building," he said.

"Have for the past three years. I was here before the Clarke woman moved in. If you don't mind my saying so, sir, any fool could tell I live here if he saw me come in like this."

Loren felt his head whirling. "And you just happen to have been the cop who investigated the business on the ferry, right?"

"Something like that." Domjan smiled but only with his mouth. "One of my profs at Fordham likes to say God put so many coincidences in the world so we wouldn't think it made sense. You know, sir, if you'd mentioned Ms. Clarke back on Sunday we maybe could have saved her life. It's not nice to hold things back from cops." He holstered the .38 and perched on the arm of a couch at right angles to Loren.

"It's not nice for a cop to be hand in glove with a vigi-

81

lante group," Loren said. "Domjan, you're in this up to your eyeballs. I think I understand now why Joyce was so frantic to come back here yesterday evening. She wanted to see you here and have a nice private chat with you about how I'd bumped into her on the street and pretended to have known her from law school."

"Maybe." Loren saw the sergeant's eyes brighten and had the unsettling sense that Domjan was proud of being found out by someone he admired. "But, sir, if I'm in some kind of vigilante conspiracy and you know about it, don't I have to take you out?" He smiled again and caressed his shoulder harness lightly. "In my jammies, yes? With my own weapon, which whenever it's fired for any reason there's an internal investigation, right?"

"No," Loren said. "If you were going to kill me, that's not how you'd do it. I figured that out the minute you walked in here. Why do you think I'm sitting here talking to you like this instead of either quaking in my boots or trying to take the gun away from you? You came down to tell me something and I want to hear it."

"You *are* sharp tonight!" Domjan pursed his lips in a parody of awestruck amazement. "Listen," he said then. "Listen hard." Loren heard nothing.

"Get up," Domjan ordered. "Go over to the window and peek out. Tell me what you see."

Loren pushed up from the depths of the upholstered armchair and backed to the bay window. With one wary eye on Domjan he parted the flowered drapes and glanced out into the dead quiet of Jane Street. Except for the row of parked cars gleaming under night lamps there was nothing to see.

"Where did all the cops go?" he demanded.

"*Very* sharp tonight!" Domjan said. "They were told to resume their other duties, sir. I made a few calls before I came down here. Come on now, we're going up the fire stairs to my place." The sergeant rose from the arm of the couch and moved away from Loren, toward the pine shelves near the door desk, and pulled down the black-and-white scrapbooks. "Never could find these before," he re-

82

marked idly. "She must have kept them squirreled away except when she brought 'em out to study or show to somebody special like you." With the bulky volumes tucked under his arm he sidled over to the entrance door and nodded for Loren to join him. When they were in the outer corridor Domjan stood on one foot, lifted his other foot, tugged off his beach slipper, hooked its leather strap around the doorknob and pulled the door shut. Then he shod himself again and led Loren down the hallway to a cream-painted steel door with EXIT in glowing letters above the frame. They climbed three flights to the top floor. Domjan twisted the knob of the apartment door across from the fire exit and motioned for Loren to go in.

It was the messiest place he'd ever seen in New York. Mismatched chairs sagging with age. High-backed lumpy-cushioned couch upholstered in maroon velvet. Dust bunnies along the floorboards. Coffee cups, plastic glasses and cans of diet soda sprouting on every flat surface. On the particle board coffee table an open container in which a half-eaten slice of cold pepperoni pizza lay forgotten. How could the same person keep himself so neat and his home such a pigsty?

Two men sat motionless on the couch as if they were waiting for something. The black man wore a gray chalk-stripe suit of quiet elegance and perfect fit, the white man a tweed jacket and jeans. They rose in unison as if joined by invisible wires and squeezed past Loren in the narrow entrance hallway and went out through the door Domjan held open for them. The sergeant locked and deadbolted the door, set down the scrapbooks on the coffee table, unstrapped his shoulder harness and deposited it meticulously atop a heap of law school casebooks. Then he dropped onto the couch. "Come on over," he invited.

Loren crossed the room on hesitant feet and gingerly settled himself on the other end of the couch. He thought he felt a burning sensation where the toilet-paper letter lay in his hip pocket.

"Those two guys are FBI," Domjan said. "They'll spend

the rest of the night tossing her pad. No one'll ever know they were there unless one of us talks."

Loren said nothing.

"Time to tell me what went down out there." The sergeant kept his eyes fixed on Loren while he groped under the couch and pulled out a midget cassette recorder. "Not the *Reader's Digest* version you gave me over the phone. Full details. Okay, sir?" He pressed the Record button and recited his name and the time and place of the interrogation in a low monotone, then signaled to Loren to begin.

Fidgeting on the seat to find a halfway comfortable position, Loren recited the events of the afternoon and evening. His confrontation with Joyce Clarke at Broadway and Astor Place. Her frantic retreat to Jane Street. Dinner at the Yale Club and the walk uptown with Judge Ostrander. The way Joyce had accosted him outside the old jurist's co-op. The drive down to the West Village and everything Joyce had told him. Even her clumsy move to seduce him. Everything but the note that seemed to be eating through his hip like acid. Three times during his recital the phone rang and Domjan shut off the recorder, scooped up the handset, listened, made noises into the mouthpiece that could have meant anything, hung up, pressed the Record button again and gestured to Loren to go on. The whole story with interruptions took him more than half an hour. Domjan touched the Stop and Eject buttons and stowed the microcassette in his bathrobe pocket. "We're off the record now, sir," he said, as if Loren were an idiot. "Any thoughts on what happened tonight?"

Loren kept still.

"Well, I have a few, sir, and I'd like your reactions to them if you don't mind. First, you say you stopped her outside her office and scared the wits out of her, but you also tell me she'd never seen you before yet you're convinced she knew who you were. Now, sir, how is that possible?"

For a manic moment Loren imagined he was a law student again, being slyly cross-questioned by old Hirschberg.

"She could have learned about me from you," he suggested.

"Didn't happen that way, sir. Don't forget when I first talked to you Sunday morning at the ferry terminal you saw fit not to tell me that your lady friend had mentioned Clarke and her father's murder. Why would I have told Clarke what happened to you on the Island? No, sir, if she knew so much about you, and from your story she knew a hell of a lot, she must have learned it from your Ms. Hale."

Loren's intuition while prowling downstairs came back to him full force: Kim had been there recently. God, if only her prints were on file somewhere so they could be matched with whatever prints the FBI men might find in Joyce's apartment! "Okay," he said, fighting to keep his tone neutral. "I'm with you so far. The two of them were together sometime before—before all the trouble started."

"So what started the trouble?"

Loren said nothing.

"Something," Domjan went on. "Something that sent Ms. Hale off by herself. Maybe something she found out here. Maybe something that made Clarke have a tail put on her. Right, sir?"

"It doesn't have to be a piece of information Kim came across," Loren pointed out. "It might have been something tangible. She stumbled on it, saw it meant something important, took it and went on the run. Joyce misses it and sends her people, whoever they are, to get it back and shut her up." He said it as if the women were characters in a movie or figures in a video game. It was the only way he could think about it without going over the edge.

"Anything's possible," Domjan said. "Now, sir, let's flash forward to the hit-and-run. You say this fellow she called Morgan drove the two of you downtown and parked a few blocks from here between a health food store and a gay bookshop."

"Right."

"And he didn't hand her the car keys."

"I didn't see him give her anything."

Domjan nodded toward the phone. "FBI found the place.

Car's not there now. Are you thinking what I'm thinking, sir?"

Loren was silent.

"I think this Morgan waited till you and Clarke turned the corner. Then he went back to the car, started it up, drove around till he was back on Jane Street and waited to hit the two of you when you crossed over to this building. I think if you'd held your nose and played along with her proposition and crossed the street arm in arm with her you'd both be in the morgue now."

A shudder rocked Loren's body.

"FBI's been on the phone to the head honcho at the Women Crime Victims Resource Center." Domjan jerked his head toward the phone again. "This Morgan wasn't employed there. That means he worked for Clarke personally. Does that suggest to you what it does to me?"

"He was in this vigilante movement with her," Loren said dully.

"Exactly, sir. Now Clarke sort of wanted you in her organization, or maybe she just wanted you and was using the way you feel about Ms. Hale for bait. But I flat out need you, sir." He seemed to rethink what he'd just said and then let out a giggle. "On my team, that is, sir, not sexually. You've been checked out and I think I'm ready to trust you."

I know something you don't know, Loren sang to himself, and felt the piece of toilet paper in his pocket burning him. "How far?" he asked.

Domjan took the black scrapbook from the coffee table with his right hand and the white with his left and held both of them toward him. "Which one you want to start with?"

LOREN CHOSE THE BLACK. Took it from Domjan's hand, opened it on his lap and began turning pages. It was a standard ring-and-binder scrapbook with a capacity of three or four hundred pages. The sheets that filled it were a mixed bag. Photocopied newspaper stories. Police and medical examiner reports from dozens of jurisdictions. Copies of judicial decisions on every subject, from criminal law to divorce and child custody law to the law of decedents' estates. Summaries of all sorts of legal developments from the past several years. Blank sheets of paper headed LAWYERS FOUNDATION FOR JUSTICE with no address but varying logos, clearly devised with the help of a word processor program, as if Joyce Clarke had been experimenting to find the most striking signage for an organization. Loren read the first dozen items through, then began skipping around the scrapbook. After about twenty minutes he understood its dominant theme.

If asked to give the compilation a title he would have called it a catalogue of outrage. The earliest entry was dated five years ago, the most recent last fall. Each item dealt with a particular injustice perpetrated by the American legal system. Innocent persons convicted of crimes and sent to prison for years. Sociopaths let loose. Victims vilified in court by lawyers defending the indefensible. Judges ordering violent criminals released from prison in droves, the criminals maiming and murdering fresh victims, the cycle starting over. A law professor was quoted: "Our Constitution explicitly protects the rights of criminal defendants both before and after conviction. It doesn't say a word about rights for victims." Every time the name of a functionary of the legal system was mentioned in a story it was highlighted in yellow.

Loren leafed forward to the pages covering events of three years ago and skimmed from one miscarriage of justice and decency to another until he found the single story he knew would be there, the account of how Joyce Clarke's father had ordered Jonathan Bloch readmitted to medical school. He read with care and struggled to keep a poker face so that if Domjan should glance up from the white book he wouldn't wonder what Loren was so engrossed in.

All the photocopied news stories on the case came from the St. Louis *Post-Dispatch*. The first included a capsule biography of Jonathan Bloch, who was portrayed as a brilliant, moody loner with a gap of several years between college and the start of medical studies. The story said he'd spent part of that time on the West Coast with his brother Clifford, a bit-part movie actor and auto stunt coordinator, and the rest of the interval in various institutions. Clifford Bloch had refused all requests for an interview.

The second *Post-Dispatch* report summarized the arguments made before Judge Clarke by Washington University's general counsel and by Bloch's lawyer, a St. Louis practitioner named Garrett Anthony. The third covered Clarke's decision and included a photo of Jonathan Bloch.

Triangular face. Strong cheekbones, savage jawline, eyes behind granny glasses glittering with hate for the world. *Swell doctor he'd have made,* Loren thought. He was clean shaven in the picture but there was no doubt in Loren's mind. This was the man with the violin who had assaulted him in the St. George ferry terminal.

Replace the John Lennons with mirror-lensed sunglasses and he also looked frighteningly like the driver of the dark-gray sedan in which Joyce Clarke had accosted Loren on upper Park Avenue in the last hour of her wretched life.

His mind fought that conclusion as absurd. How could the man whose case had led to Judge Clarke's murder be driving his daughter around Manhattan three years later? Then an even wilder thought occurred to Loren. *What if the driver wasn't Jonathan Bloch but his brother?* Hollywood stunt coordinator. Experience staging auto smashups for the screen. If the dark sedan Loren and Joyce had ridden in was the car that had run her down, it made a crazy sense. The driver with the sunglasses had kept the keys, and if he was Clifford Bloch, using an auto as a murder weapon would be natural for him.

Trying to keep his movements controlled, Loren set the black book on the middle couch cushion, sauntered to the window, looked out at the empty street. He felt light-headed and dizzy. He put a hand on the sill to support himself and waited out the weak spell.

Open up to Domjan or tell him nothing? Loren's instinct sensed something out of kilter with the fawning sergeant.

If he made the wrong decision and if Kim were still alive, it might kill her.

There was no way he could sort it all out with Domjan sitting across from him and no way he could get rid of the man anytime soon. He had to forget what he'd just seen. Buy time with his silence. Without the benefit of Loren's glimpse of the face of Joyce's driver, it might take Domjan a few days to make the connection. As soon as he came upon that third *Post-Dispatch* story in the black book with the picture of Jonathan Bloch, he'd see the resemblance to the Identikit sketch of the violinist on the ferry and know that this was the man. The account of Clifford Bloch the auto stunt specialist would suggest to Domjan exactly what it had suggested to Loren. But even an obsessive like Domjan had to sleep. He couldn't possibly master the hundreds of pages of material in the white book on his lap and then tackle the black book without calling it a night and arranging to meet with Loren later. Or maybe he could. Something about him wasn't quite human.

"You okay?" Domjan called from across the room. "Want some coffee? Soda? Need to use the john?"

"Right," Loren said gratefully. "The john."

HE BLINKED HIMSELF out of a half-doze and squinted through his glasses at the quartz clock on the unpainted pine credenza. 2:47. A fresh Silex pot of coffee steamed on the dime-store table in front of the couch. Beside it were two cups, a half-empty quart of Jack Daniel's and a can of mixed nuts. Domjan with red-streaked eyes sat erect in his robe and pajamas, chewing a mouthful of nuts that made his face resemble a squirrel's. The white book lay shut on his knees. Soft light from a table lamp formed a bright cone against the surrounding dark. "You awake?" the sergeant whispered.

"Sort of." Loren shook himself and felt exhaustion covering him like a blanket.

"I'm through with the white book. Want to trade?"

That was the last thing in the world Loren wanted at the moment. "I want to go home and sleep," he answered irritably. "My God, I have a class to teach in a few hours!"

"What time's your class?"

"Not till two in the afternoon," Loren yawned. "Thank heaven."

"I have to clock in at eight ayem. Give me the black book." He reached to Loren's side and put his hand on the dark binder.

"You can't guess what's in it sight unseen?" Loren challenged.

"I assume it's a pile of horror stories about lawyers and judges shitting on people. Now you guess what's in Mr. White here."

"Doesn't take any brains," Loren said. "It's a death book. News stories, reports, all sorts of stuff about lawyers and judges who've died in the past several years."

"Not quite on the nose but close enough," Domjan told him. "It's a death book all right but it goes beyond lawyers and judges. State and federal legislators, a few government bureaucrats, fifteen or twenty corporate muckymucks, couple dozen I'd just classify as people with lots of money. The earliest entry's four years and nine months ago, the latest is dated last October."

"Roughly the same time frame as mine," Loren said. "She must have started a new pair of books seven or eight months ago. And there may be earlier pairs for cases more than five years old, if you think these vigilantes go back that far."

"If any more books like these are in her pad, those FBI guys'll find them."

Loren braced himself and took a long gamble. "Anything about her father's murder in there?"

"Probably everything ever published," Domjan told him. "Plus a transcript of the trial where the housekeeper was found not guilty by reason of insanity. Just a Xerox but I wonder where whoever put this book together got hold of it." He yawned and took a swallow of coffee. "Someone'll have to sit down with these books and the PD computer

90

and cross-index all this stuff, see how much correlation there is between the bad guys in the black book and the dead guys in Mr. White. Then the real fun begins."

"Tell me about it."

"You'll see for yourself when you look at old White here. A few of the deaths that get coverage there's no doubt were murders, like Judge Clarke. Most of them look on the surface like natural deaths. Heart attacks, cancer, a few cases of AIDS. Twenty or thirty could be almost anything. Bunch of auto accidents, some suicides that maybe weren't. Every single one of these has to be checked out. Exhumation orders, autopsies, the works. And it'll have to be done without the media picking it up. Jesus," he sighed.

"Do you believe it?" Loren asked. "Do you believe there's some kind of national organization that kills people who've used the legal system to kick around other people?"

"Does sound crazy when you put it into words," Domjan conceded. "But, you know, it could just be true. Look at all the serial killers who've murdered dozens of people and the cops didn't know anything till years later!"

"Serial killers usually target drifters," Loren said. "Prostitutes, homeless people, runaway kids. We're talking about lawyers, judges, prominent people. I don't think this vast underground of conspirators can exist."

"Sir," Domjan reminded him, "just a few hours ago you were invited to join it. I was asked in last fall."

"And that's when you went to the FBI and they asked you to sort of be a mole?"

"Well, the feds had the same doubts you do but they did ask me to pretend to play along. And I've been doing that, sir. On top of my regular caseload, plus law school three nights a week. If I get one good night's sleep in three it's a miracle."

"How do you keep it up?"

"Being young," Domjan said. "Benzedrine helps too. Want to hear how I first got involved?"

Loren abandoned all hope of being allowed to leave the building in time to snatch a few hours rest. He filled his cup with coffee and a healthy splash of Jack Daniel's and settled back in his corner of the torture couch and forced himself to listen.

"EVER WATCH any of these law professors on TV?" Domjan began.

"Almost never," Loren said. "I'm too busy being one in the real world."

"It was one of those clowns opened my eyes. A couple years ago I was hanging around my place on a day off and turned on the tube and this great legal scholar on the talk show said if you catch a burglar or a rapist in your home you better be damn careful not to use unreasonable force to defend yourself and your family or the perp will sue you and likely wind up owning your house himself. And he laughed! He thought it was a neat joke. Said he'd represented a couple of scumbags in cases like that and won big. Told about that teenage hood in California who climbed to the roof of a school building one night, trying to break in and rip off something, and he fell through a skylight and broke both his legs and sued the school district for a couple of million, saying there should have been a sign on the roof warning perps the skylight was dangerous. He got a settlement in seven figures and the lawyer kept a third. Oh, this prof had a pile of stories like that. I was in my first semester at Fordham Law and this wasn't the system they were teaching me about."

"Couldn't have surprised you," Loren said. "How long have you been on the force? How many times have you seen bad guys and their lawyers get a friendly judge to rule that they can walk away?"

"Oh, none of that stuff on TV was exactly *news* to me, sir. But—well, until that day I'd been keeping all those experiences in a corner of my mind. I was sort of idealistic about becoming a lawyer till then and—well, I don't know if you're religious, sir, but watching that jerk on the tube

92

was like St. Paul on the road to Damascus when the scales
fell from his eyes."

"Changed your life, did it?"

"Oh, not at all, sir! I studied harder. Made up my mind
I'd never be that kind of lawyer. Then I took the course on
professional responsibility and it dawned on me that lawyers aren't given a choice. My duty is to my client and no
one else in the world. If he raped a woman and cut her
eyeballs with a razor so she couldn't pick him out of a
lineup—this is a case I handled last year—well, my job, my
solemn obligation is to mix up that woman on the stand,
and dig into her sex life, and try to get the jury to think she
was either asking for it or is a racist or whatever, just so
long as I get a not guilty verdict. Even if I know the black
son of a bitch is guilty as hell! And if the jury finds him
guilty, then I have to appeal, and make any argument I can
to get a reversal. Like there weren't enough blacks on the
jury panel, or the guy's confession shouldn't have been let
in because his chosen language is Swahili and he was given
his Miranda warning in English. And there are enough ass-
hole federal court decisions going the defendant's way on
issues just like those that I just may win! Remember when
Sirhan Sirhan tried to get the California parole board to let
him walk? He said he'd already served more years than
most murderers and it had to be because he was a poor
oppressed Lebanese, and if Bobby Kennedy were alive he'd
be the first to agree that holding Sirhan any longer was
discrimination. That was a lawyer talking, sir. Carrying
out his sacred ethical duty to represent unpopular causes.
And, by God, half the time those fuckheads win and their
clients get to commit more rapes and more murders!" He
cut off his tirade and half filled his cup with straight Jack
Daniel's. "I dropped out of law school," he went on, more
softly now, in control again, "till I could sort it all out."

"But you went back."

"Yeah, a year later I went back. I wanted that J.D. degree
so bad I could taste it like I taste this bourbon."

"What for?"

His eyes glistened with memory and desire. "I want to

become the chief legal counsel to the Department," he said. "Before I'm fifty I want to be police commissioner of the City of New York. And then one day I met Joyce Clarke and I saw how I could do it."

"You just happened to meet her? Just happened to live in the same building with her?"

"I was here before she moved in. We met at the laundromat around the corner and found out we'd both been living in the same building for months. We got to shooting the bull over the spin-dry cycle. She was a lawyer but she hated the system too. She identified it with her father and hated him worse than anything. You wouldn't believe the crap he got away with because he was a federal judge."

Loren saw no point in suggesting that perhaps her emotions had led Joyce to exaggerate her father's defects. Whatever his vices, his housekeeper had paid him back for them.

"After a while we made it a point to do our laundry on the same night when we could. We had a lot of long talks about the law. Of course I didn't tell her I was a cop, I said I worked on Staten Island for the Port Authority. She kept harping on how thousands of ordinary decent people had gotten tromped on by lawyers and judges and the system and wanted to take their freedom back and wouldn't it be great if there was a way of getting even for all those folks. Then she began hinting that maybe there *was* a way and maybe she was a part of it and maybe I'd like to be."

"She hinted she was part of a murder organization?"

"Nothing that blatant, no, sir. She mentioned a black book and a white book and said she'd show them to me someday. And every few weeks I'd see her on the street or in the elevator and we'd be alone and she'd put a big grin on and say 'A bug was squashed in Chicago last night' or whatever. Or she'd recite the Carl Sandburg line about the hearse horse snickering when he takes lawyers to the grave."

"And you took these remarks to mean the organization had scored another hit?"

"Well, lots of people hate lawyers and judges but, well, I did get the sense these guys weren't dying natural deaths."

"And that," Loren said, "was when you went to the FBI."

"Yes, sir. I do plan to run the PD by the time I'm fifty. A world-class undercover bust in my personnel file, that's a neat credential, sir. I've been a sort of mole since last fall but she still wouldn't let me see these scrapbooks or meet anyone else in what she called the New York cell. She did say they were organized into tiny cells like the Commies used to be so if things went wrong no one could give away more than a couple of other people."

"There must be a top echelon somewhere," Loren said. "At the rate you were going it might have been years before you found it."

"I was making good progress, sir. There was to be a meeting of the local cell in a few weeks. The last time we talked before yesterday, she said she thought I'd be invited. That's all out the window now because she's dead and I don't know anyone else in the group. But we have these babies." He petted the scrapbooks on the couch as if they were a pair of puppies or kittens. "These may be worth more to me. A short cut into the heart of the vigilantes if I get real lucky."

"You really don't give a damn that she was murdered, do you?"

"Not much," Domjan said. "She was basically a good person, I guess, but sort of pathetic. Overweight, lonely, frustrated, full of hate, but a good person deep down. I bought her an exercise video last Christmas. She'd dropped some weight and promised to take off a lot more."

So she could gain it back on starchy prison food after you busted her, Loren thought.

"In fact, sir," Domjan added, "the FBI's going to see to it the PD doesn't work overtime trying to catch this Morgan guy who ran her down. Too much publicity on her might drive the organization underground."

"Smart move," Loren said. He was convinced by now that he'd been right to say nothing about the toilet-paper note in his hip pocket or his certainty that Joyce had been murdered by Jonathan Bloch's brother. He needed time to think, someone to talk to that he could trust. Domjan wasn't that person.

"Which brings us," the sergeant said, "to your part in the play. Professor, what are your plans for the summer? Staying in town? Got some travel in mind?"

"Nothing definite," Loren told him. "I certainly hadn't planned to stay here."

"What I mean is, you're free as a bird for the summer, right? Not teaching anywhere else? No commitment to a particular place?"

"None." Loren wondered where this strange conversation was headed now.

"Good." Domjan rubbed his palms together as if he were coming down with a chill. "You're working for me as of now."

There was something in his eyes as he said it, the look of a hawk that has a rabbit in its talons. Loren glared at him, made a move to get up and out of the apartment.

"Sorry, sir." The deferential mask was back on Domjan's face as he stood and thrust out his hands in a sort of pleading gesture. "I mean I'd like very much for you to work *with* me on this case. There's one aspect of it that you can investigate a lot more effectively than I can or even the feds can."

"What?" Loren growled.

"What you'd probably be doing anyway," Domjan said. "Trying to find your Kim Hale. Trying to see how deeply she's mixed up in this mess. Saving her neck if you can."

In fact that was all Loren had thought of doing over the next few months, and he was already counting the hours until he could finish his work at NYU and get started. That Domjan knew him and his desire so well sent a rush of fear through him.

"We won't stop you," the sergeant smiled. "We *want* you to find her."

Loren had had close to twenty years experience with police thinking. If Domjan could read his mind, he could read

96

the other's too, and knew he was to be cast as the staked goat. To move around, ask questions, follow leads, draw attention to himself, make enough noise so that the organization might decide he was a nuisance and take steps to put him out. Maybe send Clifford Bloch on his trail. And that in turn meant that wherever he went and whatever he did, Loren would be kept under tight surveillance by Domjan or the FBI. That he would not tolerate. He decided he had no choice but to force the issue.

"Suppose I agree to be the bait," he said. "How do you stay on top of me? Make me wear a wire? Put a video monitor on me?"

Domjan beamed on him the bright-faced beatific smile of an infant warm with milk. "Ehyeh asher ehyeh," he recited solemnly.

Loren tried not to let his eyes pop.

"I guess I never got around to mentioning it, sir," Domjan hastened to explain, "but I spent a couple years in a seminary before I left and joined the PD." He paused as if confident all was now clear but must have seen the continued bewilderment on Loren's face. "You know who Martin Buber was, sir?"

Loren was not one of those lawyers who read nothing but law. "Probably the greatest Jewish religious writer of this century," he said.

"No probably about it. Anyway, when Moses in Exodus asks God what his name is so he can tell the children of Israel, God says: 'Ehyeh asher ehyeh.' That's Hebrew, sir. It means 'I am that I am.' Buber says it means: 'I shall be present as whoever I shall be present.' In other words, sir, you won't know when or where or how, but believe me, I will be with you." His smile was so incandescent it might have lit the world, and in that moment Loren understood. He was locked in a room with a man who had a badge on his chest and a mind out of joint.

"So," that man asked him, "are you with me?"

The need to answer made Loren feel ripped down the middle. He could tell Domjan to go to hell and walk out, but what would the other do in return? Forgive like a loving god? Frame him for Joyce Clarke's murder? Have his fed buddies kill him and make it look like a random street crime? But if he said yes he could buy himself some freedom of movement, some chance to find Kim and, with great skill and greater luck, save her. Years later, when the affair is a blur of memory, what do you owe your love?

He stood there unmoving for what to him were days and to the clock was no more than a minute before he took three steps over to Domjan on feet that seemed encased in concrete and looked into his moist God-intoxicated eyes and said: "Yes." Neither man offered his hand to the other.

"Good," Domjan sighed. "I knew you would, sir."

All the adrenaline that had sustained Loren through the long night was gone now, leaving him stale, used up, swaying on his feet, seeing strange shapes in front of his eyes. Fit for the trash heap. He wanted to fall onto Domjan's shag rug and die there. He shook himself and looked at where the sergeant had been standing and the space was empty. For a wrenching moment he thought Domjan had made himself vanish. Then he heard a sound behind him and saw the other standing at a wall phone just inside the doorway to the kitchen, speaking low. Domjan cradled the handset and swung around to face Loren, his body dappled by the half-light from the living-room lamp.

"Just called you a cab," he said. "You need some rest, sir, that's for sure. Taxi'll be at the door in five minutes and drivers don't wait for people this time of night. Can you make it on your own?"

"I'll make it." *Better lose an arm,* he thought, *than spend another minute with this lunatic.* He shambled to the entranceway, pawed at the deadbolt and released himself into the gray corridor.

The instant he stepped outside he felt the chill and moisture in the air and knew a storm was coming. He saw the cracked roof light of the owl cab bumping down Jane Street and hailed it with a wave. "Waterside Plaza," he croaked as he tugged open the passenger door. "Number Forty." He slumped in a backseat corner and was in a half-doze before the cab turned north on the West Side Highway. The first gentle drops brushed his shoulders as he was mounting the staircase to the Waterside quadrangle. He trotted to his building and crossed the tiny lobby under the night guard's baleful eye and punched the elevator button for his floor.

Five minutes and three Valiums later he was curled in a nest of pillows and blankets in a fetal position. Thunder pounded in his ears like a drum tattoo. The soft pink toilet paper note lay folded in his wallet among the credit cards. He was exhausted but the storm and dread of what he might dream kept him lying awake till just before dawn. He slept fitfully for six hours. At noon he made himself get up and shower and shave and dress for class. That day he was more poorly prepared than his worst students.

Seven

HALF A WEEK LATER and almost half a continent away, he sat belted in an aisle seat on a TWA jet gliding southwest over parched Illinois farmland. He didn't see the planeful of travelers around him or the flight attendant who served him roasted peanuts and orange juice or even Val Tremaine in the center seat beside him. He was looking inside himself, into his own recent and distant past. Trying to make sense of what had happened in New York.

He had called Val from NYU late in the afternoon on the day following Joyce Clarke's murder. He would have phoned her from Waterside Plaza the first thing after waking up but a voice kept whispering to him that Domjan or the FBI might have had his line tapped during the wee hours. *Wait till you get to the office*, the voice told him. *Safer.* Then he began worrying about his phone at the office. The NYU law faculty included some of the best known civil liberties activists in the country but that didn't mean his office phone couldn't be bugged too.

Just before his two o'clock class he had leafed frantically through a copy of the *Times* in the faculty lounge. Not a word about Joyce's death. Either a federal coverup was under way or the hit-and-run story had broken too late for the paper's deadline. Small wonder his students that day did not see him at his best.

Back in his office after class he had checked the master schedule for the semester and confirmed what he vaguely remembered: Okamoto's seminar on The Jurisprudence of Judging met from four to six on Wednesday afternoons. He loped one flight up the fire stairs and tapped on Tex's office door. "Come!" the prairie drawl boomed out.

"Hi, Tex." Loren let himself in and took the only spot on the faded davenport that wasn't piled with books and papers. "Could I ask you for a favor? I need to borrow your office while you're in your seminar."

Okamoto kept his face blank as a desert landscape.

"I can't tell you why," Loren went on. "Not for a while anyway. I have to make a call I can't place from my own shop."

Okamoto reached into the teakwood box on his desk which held an inexhaustible supply of his business cards, took one out and tapped its edge against his teeth. "Is this by any chance tied in with what happened to you Sunday on the ferry?"

"Your carpet," Loren replied, "is getting frayed looking."

"Like that, huh?" Tex dug into his pocket for a cowhide key holder, snapped one apart from its mates and tossed it across the room. "No sweat, hoss. Just lock up when you're done and leave the key in an envelope in my box downstairs, okay?"

"Thanks," Loren said. "I owe you a big one."

HE TOOK THE SEAT behind Okamoto's desk two minutes after Tex left the office. Reaching for the phone on the credenza at right angles to the desk, he saw a plastic cube for photo display nested in the shelter of two high stacks of advance sheets. The photos showed an Asian girl four or five years old: lustrous black hair, shining eyes, ecstatic smile. If Tex had ever mentioned having a family, Loren couldn't remember it.

By luck he caught Val in and free. It took him most of an hour to tell her the story and when it was told she had just one question. "How soon can we get together?"

"How long will it take you to get what you need?"

"Two or three days probably. How does Saturday night sound?"

"Fine by me."

"Will you meet me at the airport or do I cab to your place?"

Loren thought a minute before he answered. "Neither. There's a good hotel on Lexington and Fiftieth, the Beverly. Make a reservation for Saturday and Sunday nights. Might as well get a suite. Use your own name and credit card. Leave a message at the desk so I'll know when to expect you or if you have to change plans. The message should be for—let's make it Mr. Witney. I'll write you a check for your expenses and a lot more as soon as I see you."

"As soon as you see me?" He sensed the naughty chuckle in her question. "My dear, have you forgotten how long it's been since we've seen each other?"

He thought it was at least a year, maybe a year and a half. Each week time flew more swiftly with him in its claws. "Much too long," he said. "My fault, I fear."

"Still want me?" Under the bantering tone of that question he heard a note of uncertainty.

"Always have," he told her softly. "Always will."

THE FRIDAY MORNING *Times* devoted two perfunctory paragraphs to Joyce Clarke's death, a simple hit-and-run with police seeking information that would help identify the driver. Domjan's name was never mentioned.

That was the last class day of the semester. Loren could have packed and left New York that night for his home or any other destination. In the morning he brought a small softside suitcase to school with him and at day's end, with good-byes said to Okamoto and other friends and all the personal items from his NYU office stowed in the bag, he cabbed back to Waterside Plaza. As far as he could tell, no one followed him.

Saturday morning he filled his big suitcase with enough clothes for a week and his attaché case with what he needed for the next two nights. The passion and anguish of the Schoenberg *Transfigured Night* drifted through the apartment from the CD player as he straightened the place and packed. She was coming to him. Only a few hours more.

Early in the afternoon he realized that she might not be coming at all and a wave of panic lapped at him. With the Beverly's number from the directory in the apartment jotted down and in his wallet he left the building and made his way through the sea of weekend shoppers on Twenty-third until he found a deli. He sat facing the street at a table for two and ordered a tuna on wheat and iced tea. Others came in after him, took tables or counter stools and buried their noses in the menu. None of them looked like a shadow but what does a shadow look like? He couldn't believe he wasn't being followed.

With half the sandwich still on his plate he sauntered to the rear of the deli where there were restrooms and phone booths, slipped into a vacant booth, shut the door behind him and punched the number. "This is Mr. Witney. Any message for me from Ms. Tremaine? She's staying with you tonight and tomorrow."

There was indeed a message. Ms. Tremaine would be arriving between four and five that afternoon. Did Mr. Witney care to leave a message for her? "Just tell her I called," Loren said. He went back to his table and finished his sandwich and strolled back to Waterside Plaza. No one seemed to follow him.

A few minutes after four he took the suitcase and attaché case down to the street-level bus shelter where a few cabs usually waited. "Grand Central," he called out to the first driver in the line. The first thing he did at the station was to stow the big suitcase in a locker. Then in case someone was still behind him, he took more steps to lose himself. Browsed in a bookstore, wandered through a florist's, stepped into a liquor store where he bought a bottle of Pouilly Fuissé. As far as he could see, no one cared who he was or where he went. At five to five he took the pedestrian tunnel that connected Grand Central with the Roosevelt Hotel. In a booth on the Roosevelt's mezzanine he put in another call to the Beverly a few blocks north and, willing himself to keep his voice calm, asked for Ms. Tremaine's suite.

He heard three rings and then her voice and felt a current run through him. Just that one word did it to him. "Hello?"

"Hi," he said. "Had a good flight?"

"Little bumpy. I'm in 909, love. Are you coming soon?"

"Very soon," he said, and hung up. He took Madison to Fiftieth, swung east past the Waldorf to the corner of Lexington and entered the mirrored lobby of the Beverly, moving with the assurance of one who was not only a registered guest of the hotel but owned a piece of the building. At the ninth floor he left the elevator and turned right and followed the hushed and elegant corridor to 909 and tapped.

The door opened and she stood there and the next moment she was reaching for him and deadbolting the door behind him while they clung together in breathless silence and he tasted the tears sliding from her eyes and felt her body purring like a cat's as he stroked her. They curled together on the couch in the silky twilight between pools of gold from two floor lamps and after a time of quiet cuddling they undressed each other, first slowly as in a ritual and then with a sort of frenzy. He gasped with desire at sight of her breasts and touched his mouth to her nipples and felt them come alive on his tongue. Awkwardly they danced to the bathroom where they showered in each other's arms and dried themselves on a huge white cotton towel and massaged one another with cream lotions before they scuttled into bed. There were no words that night, only the sounds of a man and a woman together.

Over a very late Sunday brunch of mimosa cocktails and chicken crepes in mushroom wine sauce and fresh strawberries and Viennese coffee he told her what had been happening inside him, the growing depression, the disgust with himself and his life and the law, how he had stayed away from her because he didn't want her to see what he'd become. Hating himself for sharing the wretchedness with her. Then he felt her reaching for his hand under the table-cloth and looked into her grave blue eyes and could have sworn she was not so much concerned for him as relieved.

"And that's all it was? That's what was keeping us apart?"

"My God," he said, "don't you think it was enough?"

"Loren, you'll never know what you put me through. I was terrified you'd gotten cancer or AIDS or something and had crawled into a shell to die. I—well, this is Let It All Hang Out time so I'll tell you. I investigated a bit. There's this computer hacker who works for me now and then and I had him break into your health insurance file at school. That's how I learned that there didn't seem to be anything wrong with you physically. So, well, you understand I couldn't help wondering if maybe there wasn't another woman in your life."

"There's no other woman," he told her. "I'm not even sure there's a me in my life anymore."

"There's Kim Hale," she reminded him.

Afterward in the living room of Suite 909 in the Beverly, over the Pouilly Fuissé which somehow one or the other of them had managed to remember to put in the refrigerator the evening before, they began to talk about Kim and the rest of what had happened to him over the past week. It took them the balance of the day.

"This is insane!" Val said, not for the first time in their conversation. "It's like a roller coaster out of control. You're crazy to let yourself ride in it and I'm crazier for riding with you." She reached into the tan leather portfolio beside the living room couch and handed Loren a sheaf of computer paper. "I paid another visit to my friendly neighborhood hacker after you called Wednesday. Here, read this."

Loren began to skim the first page but had covered only a few paragraphs when Val cut into his concentration. "What those documents mean is you can stop tearing yourself into confetti wondering about your friend Domjan. Yes he is a religious nut of sorts, yes he is hand in glove with the feds and yes, they're taking this idea of a vigilante network very seriously."

"Mind telling me where you got all this?"

She leaned over and whispered into his ear as if she thought the suite might be bugged. "I can read most of the FBI's computer files whenever I need to." Behind his glasses Loren blinked. "Which isn't often, thank heaven. By the way," she went on, her voice back to normal, "there was a break-in at Joyce Clarke's apartment yesterday morning."

The scrapbooks, Loren thought. *The vigilantes want her scrapbooks.* "The feds catch the guy?" he asked.

"They weren't trying to. They let him search for an hour and come up empty and then they let him go. Obviously he was sent to take her scrapbooks and anything else that could connect her with vigilantes. Domjan and the feds want to find out who the burglar reports to. I think he's just a small-timer, and when the people he goes to find out the scrapbooks are gone they're not going to just assume Joyce stuck them in a safe-deposit box, they're going to take it for granted the police have the stuff and probably dispose of the burglar the same way they got rid of Joyce."

Loren looked up from the computer paper. "You picked up all this information from your friend the hacker?"

"Some of it I got from phoning Chicago," Val told him. "My best girlfriend from college is a wheel in the FBI office there. A few years before she joined the Bureau I—oh, the hell with false modesty, I saved her life and her child's life and she owes me big. I'll tell you the story sometime when we're not distracted. Anyway, I called her and routed myself through Chicago on the way here and got together with her in a bar and pumped her. I had to tell her some of what you told me Wednesday. She didn't ask how I knew so much but I could see she was terrified that the media and maybe even the vigilantes might find out about the operation too. I had to make her a lot of promises before she'd come through."

"And?"

"The gist of it is there's a high-level investigation under

way. Agents all over the country are very quietly checking out the deaths of every lawyer and government bureaucrat and judge and bigwig who died in the last three years if there was anything even the least bit sleazy in the person's history or doubtful about the way he died."

"Domjan said that would happen," Loren remembered. "Something on that scale will probably take months."

"I can get us a progress report anytime I want to take a quick trip back to Chicago," Val said.

"Ah. Good. That fits in. We'll fly to Chicago tomorrow and then go on to St. Louis."

"What's in St. Louis?"

"The center of the web," Loren said. "That's where Jonathan Bloch went to medical school. It's where he brought the discrimination suit that Joyce Clarke's father decided in his favor. It's where Judge Clarke was killed and where the woman who did it was found not guilty by reason of insanity. Do you know where the institution is where they're still keeping her?"

Val shook her head no.

"Fulton, Missouri," he told her. "I looked at a state map yesterday and it's about two hours drive from St. Louis. If you believe that toilet-paper note I showed you, Kim Hale saw Mrs. Schrader there. That means she was in Missouri sometime during the past two or three years."

"I know you, darling," Val said. "You have a plan up your sleeve, don't you?"

"Worked it out yesterday morning while I was packing," he confessed. "We're going to St. Louis and stir the pot all we can. I don't think it will take much effort because it's boiling over already. Once we're set up in St. Louis we're going to Fulton and visit Mrs. Schrader. Again if you believe that note, she's desperate to get out of the mental hospital. From her point of view, she did what the vigilantes wanted and they're letting her rot in the nuthouse. Suppose I offer to get her sprung?"

"Loren, how can you possibly do that?"

"The point isn't to do it, it's to convince her I can. If I can win her over, maybe I can get her to open up to me.

107

Including what she knows about Kim. Anyway, that's the deal I'll try to make with her after we're organized in St. Louis."

"This is going to take time," Val reminded him. "Don't you have to come back here to give exams or something?"

"Proctors will handle that and the exams can be sent to me later. I wish I could get back here next Saturday, there's an honors convocation and Justice Blackmun of the Supreme Court's going to be the guest speaker, but this is more important and I'll give it all the time it takes." He hesitated, looked into her eyes again. "You'll need to get back to your own business in a few days, I guess."

"Tremaine Investigations is a high-tech outfit now," she said. "Give me a fax machine and a modem and a cellular phone and a laptop and I'm as close to my work back home as I need to be. For a week or two anyway." She reached for his hand and took it between hers as if she were reading his palm. "Are you subtly hinting that you only want me on a short-term lease?"

He had always loved the way she could seem to laugh at him without hurting or mocking him. Once, a few days after they'd met, before they'd become lovers, she had knocked on the door of the hotel room in the state capital where he was staying and roused him from a sorely needed nap, and when he shuffled blindly to the door and opened it for her she had glanced at his feet and told him with a gleeful light in her eyes that his shoes were unlaced. That was when he had first thought they might have a future: ten years ago; no, closer to a dozen. He saw the same light dancing in her eyes now.

"Most women wouldn't dream of putting their own lives on hold even for a few days on something like this," he said.

"You mean to help you find another woman you may still be in love with?"

"Something like that," he mumbled.

"What would most women do?" she asked.

"Be jealous?"

"I refuse to be jealous of any gal who's got half a dozen

years on me," she said with the joyous gleam still in her eyes.

"She's still damned attractive," Loren ventured.

"You could tell from a few seconds glimpse of her all the way across that big old ferry barn, right?"

"Wasn't that big a barn," he said. His voice changed then. "Anyway I think she may still love me."

"I'll take my chances, darling." Loren thought he detected a new tautness in her tone, something different in the way she looked at him and held his hand in hers. He wished he could read her mind. "I know she needs your help," she went on. "Our help. We'll sort out the rest of it later if we have to."

"Let's start now," he said, and gently pulled her against him.

It was only by a fluke that he jerked awake two hours later and remembered that he'd left his big suitcase in a twenty-four-hour locker. He eased himself out of her sleeping embrace and kissed her hair lightly and threw on his clothes and dashed out of the Beverly in a frantic search for a cab that would take him to Grand Central. When he let himself back into Suite 909 he found her in a robe and on the phone, making plane and car and hotel reservations for both of them, reciting her credit card number without having to go into her purse and look it up. *How am I going to pay her for all this?* he wondered. *If I write her a check and Domjan or the feds are tapping into my account, there goes what little edge I have.* Just before they went to sleep that night, he raised the question. "Write me a check and postdate it the thirty-first of next February or something," she yawned.

————————

IN THE MORNING they flew to O'Hare where Val left Loren to his own devices for almost three hours and kept another clandestine rendezvous with her old college chum the FBI woman. She returned just in time to jog with him through corridors choked with once and future air travelers to the gate where their connecting flight to St. Louis awaited them.

"Look here, darling." Val in the window seat handed Loren the AAA map of Illinois and Missouri that she'd been studying as the jet gained altitude. "Our flight path will take us right over the city of Normal."

"First thing normal I've seen in ages," he grunted.

Fifty-five minutes after takeoff they collected their checked baggage at the Lambert International Airport carousel and found their way to the car rental booth where they claimed the 1987 Toyota Cressida Val had reserved. With her behind the wheel and Loren navigating they took Interstate 70 east into downtown St. Louis. All the rush hour traffic was clogging the highway in the other direction. Wrapped in privacy for the first time since they'd checked out of the Beverly, Val told him about her lunch meeting between flights.

"The feds are getting excited about a couple of the deaths they're checking out," she said. "Ever hear of a judge in Chicago known as Understanding Blanding?"

Loren searched through his memories of the late-night session on Domjan's couch with Joyce Clarke's scrapbook. "Blanding . . . Oh of course, Blanding! He was the one who sort of made a habit out of excluding evidence against murderers, rapists, child abusers. There were some clippings in the book about a Marielito knife killer. He grabbed a black teenage girl from off the street, kept her chained for four days, raped her a dozen times, gave her a choice between him burning her breasts with a cigar or cutting them with a straight razor. Blanding threw out the bastard's confession because the cop who read him his Miranda rights did it in correct Castilian Spanish and not Cuban Spanish. In some quarters that decision was called a blow for civil rights. There were rumors His Honor might have been motivated by something besides ideology. Meaning he may have been on the take. One of the dirty judges Operation Greylord missed. The scrapbook said he died, oh, two years ago I think. Late-night auto smash on the Eisenhower Expressway."

"It was closer to three years," Val corrected. "He piled his Cadillac Coupe de Ville into a bridge overpass at eighty miles per hour. I won't try to describe what was left of the car or him. Blood alcohol test read more than double what it takes to be legally drunk in Illinois. But I am told in strictest confidence that it now begins to look as if someone may have forced His Honor to down a quart of bourbon before they plowed his car into that overpass. Nothing conclusive yet."

"Sounds too tricky to work," Loren said. "How does the killer get out of the Cad before it hits? Do the vigilantes have stunt drivers on call? And you know, there are less conspicuous places to kill a man than an urban expressway even in the small hours of . . ." He was jerked back in his seat as Val stamped on the brake and swerved into the far left lane. In the side window he caught a flash of a twisted golden shape sprawled in the center lane before it vanished behind them. "I think it was a collie," Val shuddered.

"Want to pull over and let me drive the rest of the way?"

"No, I'll be okay in a minute. I didn't see the poor dog lying there till I was a split second from hitting him myself. God, if that had happened in the westbound lanes . . . Funnily enough, that's a bit like the other death the feds are getting excited about."

"A dog getting killed crossing a highway?" Loren blinked.

"No, no, a man who was killed in a multi-car pile-up on the Dan Ryan during the morning rush hour on a foggy day. Actually there were three people killed and five or six others permanently injured, but one of the three dead guys was the CEO of a family corporation his father had founded back in the twenties. A couple million dollars plus control of this huge corporation passed to other members of the family when the son died."

"He wasn't a lawyer or a judge or anything like that?"

"Just a prosperous businessman as far as I know," Val said. "But didn't you tell me there were people like that in those scrapbooks too?"

Loren said nothing. He stared into the center of the

111

windshield as if the Gateway Arch looming up ahead had transfixed him.

"I know it's hard to imagine someone staging a terrible accident like that just to kill one person but . . . Loren, what's the matter with you, are you ill?"

"The brother," Loren mumbled.

"What?"

"Jonathan Bloch has a brother. Cliff Bloch, remember? The guy who used to be an auto stunt coordinator in Hollywood."

"Oh, God, Loren!"

"And this is the third death we know of that was connected with an auto. Blanding, your CEO, and Joyce Clarke. These vigilantes do have a stunt driver on call!"

"Loren, that's impossible," Val said.

"Why?"

"Those Bloch brothers just don't make sense in the picture. First Jonathan gets a break from sleazoid Judge Clarke and is let back into medical school and carves up some kids in the emergency room. Then another lawyer saves him on an insanity defense and he's sent to Fulton. Then the shrinks let him out of Fulton because the judges say it's unconstitutional to keep him there if he isn't dangerous to himself or others. So what happens next? Both he and his stunt driver brother sign up as hit men for a vigilante group that wants to kill off precisely the kinds of lawyers and judges that gave Jonathan his freedom! And then, if you're right, little Clifford coldbloodedly murders one of the key people in the group and the daughter of the judge that let his brother go! Loren, that simply doesn't rhyme and you know it."

"They're both crazy," Loren said. "Not responsible for their actions. Can't be punished even if they're caught. They'll just be sent to another institution till another lawyer and another judge say they're un-dangerous again and have a constitutional right to be free."

"Darling." She took her right hand from the wheel and offered it to him without taking her eyes from the highway. "You're a lawyer and I'm not but aren't you exaggerating the rottenness of the legal system just a little? It's not that easy to get off on insanity anymore and a lot of the criminal psychos stay institutionalized for years and years. Look at the creep who shot Reagan back in '81, no one's let him out yet."

"I know," Loren said. "Okamoto and Ostrander and those scrapbooks and, oh, hell, it's all fed into this sense that's built up in me about how the system's gone haywire and being a law professor's like teaching irresponsible people how to use guns. My job is to help them master the tools they'll use to hurt others."

"No wonder you've been so depressed," she said. "Feel like maybe joining these vigilantes?"

"Part of me does," he said. He glanced casually into the rear-vision mirror and his eyes narrowed. "Shit," he muttered.

Val half turned and frowned at him. "Problem?"

"Look what's behind us."

She adjusted the mirror and narrowed her eyes at what it showed her. A blue-and-white sedan with roofbar lights pulsing silently less than a hundred yards behind them and gaining. She said nothing but slowed to fifty and signaled and turned into the center lane. The police car swept past them and vanished around the next curve.

"Dear paranoid," she teased him. "Loren, you can't let that loony Domjan yank your chain. He spouts a couple of words in Hebrew and all of a sudden you're convinced he and his people are all around us like the pods in *Invasion of the Body Snatchers!*"

"The pods were all around the guy in that picture," Loren said. "And no one believed him either . . . I'm sorry, Val. The last week's just been too much for me to handle, I guess."

"You're forgiven." She reached with her free hand for his. "So let's go over the game plan, okay? Once we're settled I'll be my usual self and dig around for leads in newspapers and official documents. Meanwhile you do whatever you can to be conspicuous, maybe get yourself on local TV, and hope that Kim sees you and knows you're

113

in St. Louis and makes a move. If she's here and if she can."

"And if she can't, maybe the people who have her will. If anyone does. Sounds like a waste of time when we put it that way. Can you suggest any improvements?"

"Maybe just one," she said. "How's about we make a U turn and take this car back to the airport and catch a plane to someplace where we can spend the summer making love?" With a mock seductive gleam in her eyes she released her right hand and undid the top buttons of her blouse. For a dazzling moment Loren was thrust back into the room in the big isolated house she had built on a mountainside and the smells of sweet plants and freshly planed wood. Their first time together, more than ten years ago. She was in her late twenties then and he had not yet begun to dread the approach of forty. The next moment he was in the Cressida again with a block of ice in his belly chilling him and the taste of clammy sweat on his lips.

"Oh, Christ, Val, you don't know how much I want to do just that," he said. "But Kim . . . She meant everything to me once and then she just vanished out of my life and I still don't know why and a week ago she calls and begs for my help and then she vanishes again. I . . . can't leave things this way." His voice rose. It was as if he were arguing in court before a jury of one.

"I know," she said quietly, and offered her hand again. "Don't you think I understand it's not really her you're looking for? Loren, darling, you're the brightest man I've ever known, but you're not terribly well acquainted with yourself." She half turned in the driver's seat so Loren could look into her eyes. "There's a you that got lost somewhere between your affair with Kim and now. That's who you're really hunting for, love."

It was a clear cloudless afternoon with the sun an unseen burning ball falling slowly to the western horizon behind them. Loren felt torn and exposed and impotent. He wanted to melt into a lump. He wanted to rip open the car door and leap out to the ground under the wheels of eastbound traffic. She kept stroking his hand gently, and after a few minutes the spasm of fright disappeared. The Cressida rounded another curve and the downtown St. Louis skyline reared up in front of them, the highrise towers of steel and mirror glass, the Gateway Arch struck with fire from the sun.

"Nothing's . . . keeping you here," Loren made himself tell her.

"Oh my dear," she said, "you're so wrong." The low intensity of her voice made him shiver.

Eight

"WELCOME TO ST. LOUIS." Loren turned from the hotel window and lifted the tumbler of single malt Scotch in a toast. "Home of the Cardinals, the Anheuser-Busch brewery, the courthouse where the Dred Scott case was tried, a great symphony orchestra, a bowling museum and a dog museum."

"You forgot the mighty Mississippi out there." Wrapped in a peach cotton bath towel, Val joined him at the window and touched her glass to his. "We saw it from the plane just an hour ago. Didn't that Greek philosopher say you can't look at the same river twice?"

"I don't think that's quite what Heraclitus meant." Outside and below a tug was dragging a string of barges under the Eads Bridge and down the brown river.

They had made advance reservations at the Laclede Suites, a seven-story hotel of red brick that might once have been a warehouse, facing First Street and the river in a neighborhood of cobblestoned roads and trendy restaurants and art galleries and jazz clubs. Unpacked, showered and at ease in the living room of their suite, Loren went over to the couch, snapped open his attaché case and pulled out two photocopied pages at which he squinted through his glasses as if the small print hurt his eyes.

"What's that?" Val wondered, and came across the room to curl up on the other end of the couch.

"A few pages from the stud book," Loren said.

First she looked blank, then she flashed him a lascivious grin and wriggled until the bath towel exposed most of her breasts. "Are you listed in it?" she inquired innocently.

116

"We all are," he replied in a moment of absentminded-
ness, and then saw how she was posing for him and realized what she was thinking and collapsed in an orgasm of
laughter such as he hadn't enjoyed in months. Restored to
what passed with him for normal, he moved the attaché
case to the coffee table, tugged the towel lower on her and,
when it was bunched around her waist, offered a fuller
explanation. "By the stud book," he declared solemnly, "I
refer to the directory of the AALS."

"All American Lovers Society?"

"Association of American Law Schools, you adorable
uninformed, ahhh, layperson." Somehow the last word
sent both of them into the giggles. "Which is to law professors more or less what the ABA is to practitioners. My
God, you mean we've been together most of ten years and
I've never mentioned AALS before?"

"All you lawyers talk alphabet soup and none of the rest
of us can keep it straight. Okay, so what are those pages
for?"

"They're the lists of faculty on the two law schools
here," he said. "St. Louis University and Washington University. I copied this stuff just before I left NYU the other
day. I want to see if I know any of these people well
enough to ask a favor."

"What's the favor?"

"Sitting down with me for a few hours. Telling me about
any recent legal outrages around here which might tempt a
vigilante group to take out the lawyer or judge who committed it. Not asking questions about why I'm interested
. . . Nope . . . Nope . . . Damn it, I don't know anyone
here well enough. Time to check out the practitioners."
He crossed the carpet to a deep-drawered end table and
pulled out a thick yellow-covered phone book. "Lawyers,
lawyers," he mumbled, leafing through the volume's middle pages. "Wait a minute, they call them attorneys out
here. Backtrack." He let his eyes and fingers roam through
the running heads until he found the place. "Here we go.
Column after column of attorneys." He settled back on the
couch and began reciting names to the room at large. "Ab-

ington, Abrams, Adams, Ahrens, Allan, Anderson, Anthony. . . . Garrett Anthony, see Garrett Anthony Associates. Remember that name, Val?"

"Wasn't that Jonathan Bloch's lawyer? The one who sued Washington University for discriminating against a handicap?"

"Yes, and he's still in practice here. Definitely someone I need to see this trip." He went on running down the columns of lawyers' names, his droning voice acting on Val like white noise after a rough day. She was half dozing on the couch when a sudden bull roar from Loren shook her awake. "Grimsby!" he cried out. "Does the name Saul Grimsby ring any bells?"

She squinted at him blankly.

"The lawyer who defended Mrs. Schrader when she killed Judge Clarke," he reminded her, "and got her off on insanity."

"Somebody else you need to see, I suppose."

"You bet. I wonder how many more . . . Irwin! Irwin!" He began yammering suddenly. "I don't believe it, I don't believe it! Gael T. Irwin!" He threw down the phone book and turned to Val in a whirlwind of excitement. "Do you remember Gael?"

"Gael I remember distinctly." Val gave a practiced semblance of a yawn. "The little nut who was a student of yours when we met."

"She's practicing in St. Louis! My God, I haven't thought of her in I don't know how many years and she's precisely who I need."

"I thought I was precisely who you need," she reminded him pointedly. "Darling, I hate to be a stick-in-the-mud, but just how many old girl friends of yours are we going to be having passionate reunions with this season?"

"This is the last one," he promised, then backed up and did a comic double take. "Wait a minute, what am I saying? Gael is not an old girlfriend. We were . . ." Having no idea how to finish the sentence, he abandoned it in midflight and reached for his drink.

"You were . . . ?" Her voice reminded him of a third-

118

grade teacher quizzing a backward student. He gulped for the right word but it continued to elude him and he knew that the longer he sat there tonguetied the guiltier he looked. "Buddies," he ventured at last. "Comrades in the great crusades of the Vietnam years."

"Comrades in arms, you mean?" She winked at him lewdly. "And you expect me to believe you just discovered this minute that she's hung out her shingle in St. Louis?"

"Val, I swear, we dropped out of touch, oh, seven, eight years back. My God, she could be married by now, have three or four kids! Besides," he added after a moment of Machiavellian contemplation, "you have to keep in mind what she and Kim Hale have in common."

"Besides having had you?"

"Very funny. Very amusing. What I was driving at, my dear, is that they're both older than you."

Val sidled across the couch, leaving the peach bath towel at the far end, and looked thoughtfully into his eyes. "You're determined to call her today, aren't you?"

"It's not even four-thirty yet and the phone book says her office is at 500 North Broadway. That's walking distance."

A strange disturbing smile came into her eyes, a smile that was knowing and wily and shameless and lustful. She slid naked to the floor at his feet and took an ice cube from his empty glass and rubbed it first against one nipple and then the other until they were dark and hard as rubies. "I'm cold," she whispered, and drew him down to her.

He didn't manage to make the call to Gael's office until half past five and by then there was no desire left in him at all.

THE FIRM OF Bryan Cave McPheeters & McRoberts filled several floors of the steel-and-glass hive at 500 North Broadway, ten minutes brisk and sorely needed walk from Loren's hotel. One look at the building and the endless list of names on the lobby directory board and he knew this was the St. Louis version of a Wall Street law factory. The Gael he remembered wouldn't have been caught dead in such a place. He stepped out of the elevator onto the deep-piled carpeting on the eleventh floor and received precise directions to Ms. Irwin's office from a receptionist with the poise of a fashion model who sat behind a sectional information desk in the center of the atrium. Being Loren, he forgot the directions ten seconds later and got lost in the maze of corridors before he found her name on a dignified plate on the grasscloth-papered wall beside a closed door. He knocked and a muffled voice called: "Come in." It sounded too low for Gael, too well modulated and lawyerlike. Half afraid that a different woman with the same name would be inside, he edged the door open.

"LOREN!!" she screeched as she flew out of a black leather executive swivel chair and bounded around the corner of her double-sized mahogany desk and threw herself into his arms with a leap and a yip of ecstasy and smothered him in a hug so hard he had to repress a gasp. Fifteen years fell away in a split second and they were young again, he the firebrand new professor and she the firebrand new law student, their torches blazing together as they struggled for a decent world. Then the veil of illusion lifted and a dignified man of forty-five and a dignified woman of forty were sitting like business acquaintances in matching wingback chairs at the far end of the office. She had let her dark frizzy hair grow out and was wearing a prim navy skirt and jacket with white silk blouse and polka-dot bow tie. Power ensemble. Behind her glasses, which he'd never seen her wear in her student days, he noticed a network of fine lines around her eyes that weren't in his memory image either. But her eyes were shining with the old delight and in his presence her voice had reverted to the old uninhibited high-pitched squeal. "I can't believe it's you!" she kept saying.

"But I called your office an hour ago and spoke to your secretary. She said you'd be back from your settlement conference around six."

Gael's eyes widened in instant comprehension. "So *that*

120

was what that phone message meant! Shalonda told me somebody named Professor Benson was in town and wanted to know if he could come by and see me and I couldn't remember any Professor Benson but my *God*, Loren, I never dreamed she meant *you*! What are you doing here? What's been happening with you?"

"Still teaching," he said. "Just finished being a visiting professor at NYU. Still getting messed up in people's problems now and then. And that's really why I'm here, Gael. I need your help and I can't say much about why, not yet anyway. Are you, well, free for dinner tonight? Got anyone to go home to?" He held his breath waiting for her answer.

The question seemed to pluck the old wild delight from her voice and restore the cool professional tone in which she'd invited her unseen visitor to enter. Suddenly she was forty and successful again. "I've got someone," she said with a shy smile, "but not tonight. He's out of town on business all week."

Loren focused on her ring finger and noticed a marquis-cut diamond in a platinum setting which he hadn't observed there before. Maybe, he told himself, because it was the last thing he wanted to see. "You going to marry him?"

"Looks like it." Her voice was softer than he had ever heard from her. "The date's set for next month. Big church wedding, Episcopal bishop, truckloads of bridesmaids and flowers . . ."

"Who's the lucky guy?"

"His name's Don, Donald Eastman, and his family is old money and he owns three shopping malls and a condo complex out in West County. We met when I drew up the condo charter for him. He's divorced and has a son and daughter by his ex and he sort of looks like Cary Grant in *North by Northwest* and I know we're going to be very good for each other."

Loren felt a strange amalgam of emotions. Pleasure at Gael's success and happiness, sorrow at the loss of the younger and more mischievous Gael, the one who was vivid and bright as a peacock. He wondered if he would ever make Val as happy as this Eastman seemed to have made Gael. He stood and held out his hands to lift her to her feet and hugged her like a father hugging his daughter and was astonished to feel a weight slipping from him, a thankfulness that at least one complication had been avoided.

On the street, walking hand in hand with Gael through the last wave of the homeward bound, along Broadway to Washington and then east into Laclede's Landing, he was overwhelmed by a sudden fantasy. Kim was somewhere in the crowd, maybe only a few steps behind them, or ahead of them, or across the street, or having a drink in one of the bars whose windows they passed, and she would see him and recognize him and cry out his name and run into his arms, and the three of them would make their way to the hotel where Val was waiting and he would introduce them to her, Gael tucked under one arm and Kim in the other. It was insane, he shouted soundlessly at himself. Never happen in a million years.

He kept telling himself to be reasonable, that Kim was not on the street, but a voice louder than reason kept shrieking at him that she was, she was. Somewhere in this city, somewhere near him, maybe a dozen stories up, maybe a block or a mile away, but somewhere in St. Louis.

They made their way toward the river without exchanging a word. If Gael wondered what was wrong with Loren, she left him undisturbed in his fit of distraction and walked at his pace while he darted glances in all directions like a fugitive.

EIGHT O'CLOCK CAME and went, and Gael and Val were still on the couch laughing and waving their arms in the air and finishing the bottle of Missouri burgundy that Loren had bought under Gael's prodding at a trendy little wine and cheese shop on the way to the Laclede Suites. Within five minutes of their introduction the two women were relaxed amid the couch cushions with their shoes kicked off and chattering with the uninhibited sprightliness of a pair of former schoolmates who hadn't seen each other in years. Loren might as well have been a thousand miles away. When they began swapping anecdotes about him he wished he was. He sat isolated in an armchair and watched and listened to them probing and forging bonds and getting to like each other, and beneath his momentary discomfort he glowed with a warmth that had nothing to do with the wine. His stomach growled for supper but he hesitated to intrude on the mysterious process that was happening between these two women who in different ways meant so much to him.

It was almost nine when by mutual consent they cabbed to the Clarion Hotel on South Fourth and took the express elevator to the Top of the Riverfront, the revolving restaurant on the roof. In the dim hush, with riverscape and cityscape gliding along the panoramic windows in a dance of darkness and light, Loren waited for the server to refill the coffee cups and set down a bowl of chocolate bonbons filled with ice cream and step nimbly off the moving track below the window line to the solid floor that supported the rest of the room. When he was sure no one else was within listening range he brought up the business of the evening. Casually as anyone making shoptalk with no ulterior motive, he began asking Gael what he hoped were leading questions; questions that would lead him to the vigilantes. Did any recent litigation in the St. Louis area strike her as outrageous? Had there been any unusual deaths among the lawyers and judges and movers and shakers? She nibbled at her lower lip and tried to fight the wine and concentrate but came up with nothing Loren found useful. Time to see what she knew about the other lawyers in the mess, he decided. Might as well take them in alphabetical order.

"Garrett Anthony," he said softly, popping a bonbon into his mouth. "Know him, Gael?"

He watched her eyes dart from him to Val and back to him and saw her expression shift from puzzled studiousness to wild excitement. "So *that's* what brought you

123

here!" she shrieked like the Gael of old. He grimaced and ground his teeth at her in a shushing signal and thanked dumb luck that the tables around them were vacant. "You're in one of those detective things again!" she accused him in a stage whisper.

Val began laughing so uproariously she dropped her coffee cup and spilled half its contents into her saucer. "Darling," she spluttered from behind her napkin, "you've trained this one too well. She can read you like the Sunday comics."

"I checked him out in the Martindale & Hubbell directory before we flew in," Loren said, "and found out his specialty is planning and managing trusts and estates. Your reaction tells me you know more about him than I do."

Gael nibbled at a bonbon and kept her eyes on the tablecloth. "He's about sixty or a little older. Very well fixed. His firm has most of a floor to itself in the Mercantile Tower and branch offices in Chicago and Kansas City. I happened to see him in the corridor a few hours ago when I was in court for that settlement conference but I don't think he saw me, thank heaven. He's creepy."

"Why do you say that?"

"I met him at a Missouri Bar reception last year and five minutes after we were introduced he was asking me if I was prepared to die. Loren, there's something insidious about his voice, it's very soft and low so you have to get really close to him to hear. For a minute there I couldn't tell if he wanted to get me to hire him to plan my estate or if he wanted to slit my throat."

"You don't think he was making a pass at you?"

"Not him," she said.

"That mean he's gay?"

"He's never been married or involved with a woman as far as I know so naturally there are rumors. He lives with his mother and sister and his mother's nurse in a gorgeous place on prime real estate out in Ladue, which is a *very* ritzy suburb. He has a country house outside Hannibal, a few hours drive from here—you know, where Mark Twain lived—and I've heard his property is crawling with old unexplored caves that run underground for miles. I think it fits him, Loren, because caves have bats and they don't come any battier than Garrett Anthony."

"What does he look like?"

"Petite," Gael said. "He's an inch shorter than me. Very trim and neat, sort of vain about his appearance. Has suits handmade by the priciest tailor around."

"Does he litigate any cases himself?"

"Loren, can you imagine what a jury would make of that spooky whisper of his? Maybe he's tried a will contest once in a blue moon but I'd never call him a courtroom lawyer. Of course I've only been in St. Louis . . ." She let the sentence fall apart. In the flame of the candle in its glass shield on the tablecloth Loren saw her lips tighten. "Something's coming back to me!"

He sat still, hardly daring to breathe.

"Right around the time I moved here, the papers were full of this case where a student maniac cut up a professor at Wash U Medical School and got expelled and he was suing them for discrimination against the handicapped. Anthony was the crazy's lawyer and the federal judge who heard the case used to be Anthony's partner. He made the school take this monster back and then the crazy snapped again and killed some people. I can't remember all the details but . . ."

"Hold it. Stop." Loren bobbed his head groggily as if he'd just been rabbit-punched and raised a palm. "Judge Clarke and Anthony had been law partners? Are you sure?"

Gael looked blankly at him. "They were in practice before my time here but I'm sure that's what I heard from the older lawyers at Bryan Cave. They'd been partners. Anthony & Clarke."

That was when Loren remembered. Old Judge Ostrander had mentioned the firm name during their dinner at the Yale Club, and there was something about the partnership in one of the *Times* articles he'd copied in the Bobst Library. He knew from the material in Joyce Clarke's scrapbook that the lawyer representing Jonathan Bloch before her father had been named Garrett Anthony, but if those clippings said anything about the attorney and the judge having once been law partners, Loren had blinked and missed it.

"Loren, are you all right?" Gael asked. "You know, it's not unethical to argue a case in front of a former partner who's been made a judge."

Yes, but why had he taken the case? What was the link between the mouselike estate planner and the madman who had taken Kim Hale from the Staten Island ferry and the madman's brother who had crushed Judge Clarke's daughter under the wheels of a car in the West Village? Loren thought he heard a voice welcoming him to the heart of the labyrinth. Now if only he knew where in the world he was.

The only other name he needed to try out on Gael was Saul Grimsby, the lawyer who according to Judge Ostrander had defended Ruth Schrader in her trial for Judge Clarke's murder and whose insanity plea had led to her confinement in the same place where Bloch had been sent. "I don't know anyone named Grimsby," Gael insisted. The dinner party broke up ten minutes later.

Gael chauffeured Loren and Val back to the Laclede Suites in her car, which was parked in the multi-level garage across from the Clarion. Loren wasn't surprised to see that she drove a BMW. When he kissed her good night in front of the moon-shadowed hotel, his thoughts were still a thousand miles away and stampeding everywhere at once.

"I like her." Val snuggled against him as the elevator door hissed shut. "If the vigilantes get me, she'll be good for you."

Loren wasn't sure if there was a layer of seriousness beneath the banter. "She's marrying a millionaire next month," he reminded her absently.

"If you suddenly came on the market I bet she'd change her plans."

Loren fumbled in his wallet for the coded card to their

suite. "You'd never know," he said as he dropped the rectangle into the slot. "You'd have to be dead for me to be free. Anyway," he added, "she's too old for me." He deadbolted and chained the door and reached for her.

Nine

A FEW MINUTES BEFORE SEVEN he was driven from bed by thunder. He stumbled to the east window, took a look at the sheets of rain slanting on wind gusts into the turbid river and knew his deal with Val had been a mistake. Just before turning out the light they had agreed that in the morning he would take the Cressida and drive the hundred miles to Fulton and try to interview Ruth Schrader. Val would spend the day combing library and court records for whatever she could learn about Jonathan Bloch's and Mrs. Schrader's various encounters with the legal system and Garrett Anthony. Loren was especially curious to find out who had represented Bloch on the two occasions he'd been tried on criminal charges and, like Mrs. Schrader after him, been found not guilty by reason of insanity.

When he turned from the window looking out on the river he saw Val sitting up naked in bed and flashing an I-won-the-wishbone-pull grin at him. "You heard a weather forecast last night," he accused her solemnly.

"Not last night," she said. "While you were up in that law office rubbing thighs with your Portia. Still going to make the drive?"

"How long's the storm supposed to last?"

"Clearing by early afternoon." The look in her eyes and the set of her lips didn't change but were somehow different: sensuous and reminiscent. "You do know how to make a woman wake up happy, darling," she said softly. "Were you fantasizing I was Gael or Kim, or both of them?"

"Three's better than two," he teased her, "at least when

128

you're one of them. Still jealous?" He climbed back into bed and kissed her eyes and mouth and shoulders and breasts. "What are you thinking about? You look like you're in another galaxy all of a sudden."

"I'm flying back into the past like you," she said. "I swear, Loren, I had this exact same conversation with Chris, oh God, fourteen, fifteen years ago." Chris was her husband and he'd been murdered a few years before Val and Loren had met. If she hadn't left their parked car to make a routine phone call, she'd have been dead too. "There was this beautiful woman he was working with on a case and I was making jealous-bride noises and you know what he did? He read me a poem. A German poem, I think it was by Goethe. It was about how this woman felt whose husband saw a lot of other women, and it ended up something like: Go ahead, gals, excite him all you want to. What you sow by day, I reap by night. And then we made love." She lay in bed like a sculpture, indifferent to his touches, and that was the moment when Loren knew the terror and pain she felt at the way he was fighting to step back into the river of his own past.

But he knew also that he couldn't stop.

IT CAME TO HIM suddenly, over sausage and scrambled eggs and hot biscuits in the Laclede Suites coffee shop with Val in the upholstered booth across from him. He would wait till afternoon to drive to Fulton, and the morning's target would be Garrett Anthony. He couldn't approach the man as Loren Mensing and had neither the time nor the contacts to prepare a false identity properly, but with a little boldness and luck he wouldn't need one. There was risk: if Anthony recognized him, the other side would know Loren was in St. Louis. But if Loren saw that Anthony recognized him, wouldn't that prove his connection with what had happened in New York?

"You're not eating, dear," Val said, "but something

seems to be eating you." She set down her cup and gazed at him curiously.

"Just an inspiration," he said. "Back in a minute." He slid out of the booth, asked a passing busboy the way to a pay phone, and two minutes later after a call to Directory Assistance he was listening to an artificially perfect female voice reciting: "Garrett Anthony Associates, good morning."

"This is Federal Judge Tremaine," Loren said. "I'm in town for a day or two to look St. Louis over before I decide whether to transfer here and accept a position I've been offered on the U.S. District Court. A colleague told me that Mr. Anthony is the man to see about any changes in my will that might be necessary if I move my domicile to Missouri and I'm calling to make an appointment. I know this is short notice but I won't be in town long and, well, could Mr. Anthony squeeze me in sometime before noon today?"

"Please hold, sir." Loren spent a good minute listening to silence blessedly unbroken by canned music, then the perfect voice came back. "Sir, Mr. Anthony won't be in till around eleven-thirty, he's driving in from his country place in Hannibal. Would this afternoon be acceptable?"

No it wouldn't, Loren decided. He was determined to see Ruth Schrader in Fulton this afternoon. "I have other commitments then," he said, and was on the brink of suggesting tomorrow when he had another inspiration. "Ah— by any chance would Mr. Anthony be free for lunch today?" He fought to keep from nervously licking his lips through the dead time while the receptionist checked her employer's schedule.

"He does seem to be free, sir . . ." she began.

Loren cut in with the curtness of one whose word literally is law. "Then it's settled," he said. "I'll take Mr. Anthony to lunch and we'll discuss my estate situation then. I'll come by at, say, eleven-fifty. Thanks very much for your help." He hung up, threaded his way past tray-laden waitresses and thronged tables and rejoined Val in their booth.

"You know what I'd do if I wanted real power in this world?" he said. "I'd become a federal judge. You wouldn't believe what doors those words can open."

Over coffee refills he told her of his hopes for the morning, and after she left for a day among the court records he sprawled on the davenport in their suite, working out his moves, honing his impersonation. Just short of eleven-fifty, on Seventh between Locust and Washington, he paid the cabdriver, ducked into the shelter of One Mercantile Center and scanned the lobby directory board. An express elevator whisked him to the twenty-third floor. On instinct he turned right, marched down the gray-carpeted corridor and realized after a few seconds that he'd gone the wrong way. Garrett Anthony Associates might occupy most of this floor as Gael had said, but other firms were renting part of it too. Moxley Harrison & Summers. The DuBoff Partnership. Saul Grimsby, P.C. *That name.* Was it possible? The lawyer who had represented Ruth Schrader had his office on the same floor of the same building as the lawyer who, at least once, had represented Jonathan Bloch.

If that fact meant nothing, Loren decided, then the world meant less. He swung around to the other end of the corridor and opened the fumed oak entrance door to Garrett Anthony Associates.

The receptionist stationed at an L-shaped cherrywood desk leapt to her feet like a Marine private whose brigade commander has just entered the barracks. Loren came very close to blushing.

"Judge Tremaine, sir?" She was a tall anorexic white-blonde and the tension of a visit from a federal judge turned her perfect voice into a squeak.

"I'm Judge Tremaine." Loren tried to keep his tone low and unthreatening.

"Mr. Anthony's expecting you, sir, I'm buzzing him now." Her finger stabbed at a button on her desk and missed. Loren took off his trenchcoat, crossed the paneled foyer to a black leather couch and pretended to immerse himself in a copy of the ABA *Real Property, Probate and Trust Journal* he found on a gleaming lamp table. He had hardly turned a page when the door at the end of the foyer clicked open and a man came through and trotted over to him. Short, trim, iron-gray hair, hazel eyes alight, hand outstretched. For a moment Loren had the impression he had met the man before. Had there been a photo of him in Joyce's scrapbook?

"Garrett Anthony, Your Honor." Loren caught beneath the intimate whisper a trace of real or assumed British accent. "It's a pleasure to meet you, sir." He carried a Burberry and a bumbershoot over his left arm. If he'd worn a hat, Loren guessed it would be a bowler.

"The pleasure's all mine," he replied as he rose from the couch. "I really appreciate your seeing me on such short notice. The court isn't giving me much time to decide on this move."

Anthony kept the deferential expression fixed on his prim face as they walked to the elevator. *If he knows who I am, he deserves an Oscar.* The lawyer pressed the button and the cage doors sighed open.

Outside, under the building canopy waiting for a cab, Anthony turned to Loren with a quizzical look. "Forgive me, Judge," he said, "but you mentioned that a colleague of yours had recommended you to me. Would you be free to tell me who?"

Loren had no idea which of the local federal jurists Anthony might be acquainted with but he had anticipated the question and had an answer ready. "Judge Ostrander," he said. A cab splashed to a stop at the curb and Anthony opened the rear door for him. "Merton Ostrander. He's on senior status, served with the Eighth Circuit a few years ago."

"Clarion," Anthony told the driver, then settled into the cushions and twisted around to face Loren. "Funny. I don't recall ever meeting the man."

"He's a delightful old gentleman, well into his eighties," Loren said. "Claims to be the last active judge appointed by FDR. He can be, well, outspoken at times. Insisted I had to see you on this estate question."

If Anthony had stiffened in his seat, he seemed to relax

again as the cab crawled south on Eighth to Spruce, then east to the corner of Fourth, within sight of the entrance ramp that led to the silolike Clarion. It wasn't until they were struggling out into the rain that the lawyer spoke again. "Well," he said, "I'll take any free endorsements I can get." Loren wondered whom he was addressing.

They took the elevator to the Top of the Riverfront. Loren focused on keeping hidden the unease he felt at coming back to the place where he had eaten with Val and Gael just fifteen hours before. Talk about stepping into the same river twice! *It has to be coincidence,* he insisted to himself. *There's no way he could know.* But a single stroke of bad luck, like a server who'd been on duty last night too and remembered him and made the wrong remark in Anthony's hearing, could wreck the impersonation beyond salvage.

He was suddenly grateful for the storm. If he broke out in a sweat he could pass it off as rain.

THEY TOOK A TABLE along the moving belt by the panoramic windows. Loren sipped Chardonnay and frowned at the bleak sodden cityscape below and occupied Anthony with a barrage of questions about the law of wills and estates in Missouri. As the level of wine in the bottle dropped, his queries grew broader. About current issues in the St. Louis legal community, about relations between bar and bench, between the state and federal judges. Every reply out of Anthony's mouth was a model of legalistic propriety, with never a hint of outraged idealism or insider cynicism or any other sentiment that might suggest a connection with vigilantes. No matter what subject Loren raised—abortion, reverse discrimination, judicial release of murderous psychopaths—Anthony's comments were sober, balanced, detached, as if he were a robot without values or commitments. Or could his commitments be so radical he had schooled himself to hide them? Loren couldn't maneuver him into mentioning having been Jonathan Bloch's lawyer and didn't dare introduce the name himself. Halfway through his shrimp salad entree he decided he was wasting money and time and taking a senseless risk. The storm clouds had parted to let shreds of clear sky through and even now and then a touch of sunlight. Better cut this lunch short and hit the road for Fulton.

It wasn't until they were toying with coffee and declining the server's suggestion of a brandy or liqueur that Loren caught something peculiar about their talk. At least four times Anthony had used the phrase "when you die." Natural enough when the subject was estate planning, but Loren would have sworn that every time Anthony pronounced the words his eyes seemed to glow. Hadn't Gael mentioned his habit of speaking about death on the least appropriate occasions?

Nothing else over the meal had worked. Maybe this would.

"The way you keep saying when I die," he began. "Do I look as if I've got one foot in the grave or is this something all estate lawyers do?"

Anthony's face went pale. Coffee spilled over the rim of his bone china cup as he set it in the saucer with a clatter. "I'm terribly sorry, Judge," he said. "I . . . suppose I may have a bit of a fascination with death and dying."

Encourage him, encourage him! "Me too," Loren admitted, "a little. Comes of trying murder cases maybe." An instant later he was groping for the wine bottle he knew was empty, desperate to cover his confusion. A federal judge trying murder cases? "I was a state trial judge before I was appointed to the federal bench," he said, and begged that Anthony wouldn't question the impromptu addition to the curriculum vitae. "Christ, those capital murder cases!"

"The power." Anthony's whisper seemed to come from another world. "The knowledge of the last moment. The bond between murderer and victim is stronger than the strongest sexual relationship two people can have. Haven't you felt that too, trying murder cases? Don't you *know* it?" His gaze ate into Loren's eyes like acid. "Judge, have you ever killed anyone?" He paused for a fraction of a second. "In combat? Vietnam perhaps?"

There was something obscene in this conversation. The memory of how chance had spared him from choosing between submission to the military and exile in Canada tore through him like a chain saw. Keeping in character as a judge and answering calmly from within his persona was almost beyond him. "My wife and I had a baby just in time to keep me out of the draft," he said. "I was never in the service."

"I commanded an artillery battery," Anthony said. "Korea, 1952." The moving beltway had made a full circuit. Outside the windows and below lay the gray-brown river. "I killed a lot of people but it was all at long range, I never once came close to death myself. I sought it out, I courted the experience but it was denied me. And in all the years since Korea I've never once had a close call, no auto accidents or bouts with cancer or anything." He lowered his voice even more so that Loren less than a foot away could barely make out the words. "At times I think I'm not meant to die. I want so much to know what it's like." His whisper was a fever of sound. Loren had the insane notion that Anthony was trying to seduce him.

"You will someday," he promised.

"I have a country home in Hannibal," Anthony said. "I would like to invite . . ." He froze in mid-sentence, reached for his water goblet and took a long sip and patted his mouth with a napkin as the waiter materialized from behind Loren and deposited at his place the tooled leather folder within which rested the check. Loren found his Master Card amid a heap of others in his wallet and, positioning the plastic so that his embossed name faced him and not Anthony, handed it to the waiter, who picked up the folder on its tray and glided out of sight. *Now if only Anthony isn't one of those people who can read writing upside down,* Loren thought.

"If you accept the judgeship here," the lawyer resumed as if nothing had happened, "I do hope you'll come spend a weekend in Hannibal with me and some . . . friends. No one else will be an attorney and my practice isn't federal so you wouldn't need to worry about the appearance of impropriety."

It couldn't be, Loren told himself. This simply could not be an invitation to join the St. Louis cell of the vigilantes. He was a total stranger to Anthony, and nothing in their conversation until now could possibly be construed as a build-up or a recruiting pitch. *Maybe he is trying to seduce me,* Loren thought. *Or maybe he knows who I am and is out to get me in a trap.* It was all he could do to wrench himself back to the reality of the dandified lunatic across the linen-shrouded table.

"What do you do on these country weekends?"

"Explore caves," Anthony said. "I have a network of wild caves on my property, they run for miles. In summer they're cooler than the finest air-conditioning on the market. We read and discuss books. Have you ever read Chesterton?"

Loren almost winced. In his first year of law school when he was living with Kim Hale he had had to read Chesterton just to make sense out of old Hirschberg's paradoxes. His thoughts raced wildly. *Kim had remembered that and told Anthony. Somehow the two knew or had known each other. Anthony knew who he was. This lunch was a trap.* Then his critical reason rebelled against his paranoid side. Millions of people have read Chesterton. Why not Anthony as well as Loren himself? "He wrote those old Father Brown detective stories, didn't he?" he asked as if the author's name were only vaguely familiar.

"Oh yes, and so much more." Anthony's voice glowed as his eyes had glowed before. *"The Man Who Was Thursday, The Club of Queer Trades,* oh so many fine pieces of work. He first wanted to be a painter, you know, and he wound up painting with words. Someday we must read him together in my cave, under the earth."

Loren had another paranoid vision. He was surrounded by Anthony and his nameless friends and they read Chesterton over him like priests reciting prayers over a coffin and then they left him in one of those endlessly twisting caves to starve to death in the darkness, his body decomposing, never found.

With raincoats draped over their forearms the two men stepped off the moving belt and across the restaurant floor to the elevator alcove. In the mirrored cage that dropped them to the lobby they were alone. Loren tried to hold back a shudder but failed. Under the building marquee Anthony waved for a cab.

"Thanks again for your time and advice." Loren offered the lawyer a hand clammy with the sweat of fear. "I'll write in a week or so and let you know if I'm making the move. And, well, I'll think over your invitation. Sounds intriguing. Sorry I can't go back with you but I have an appointment in the other direction and I'm running a bit late."

It was the first thing he'd said since meeting Anthony that was even slightly true. He watched the other's cab slip down the ramp into the traffic stream, hailed a taxi of his own and rode back to the Laclede Suites. He used the bathroom, rummaged in a bureau drawer for the Gideon Bible, retrieved Mrs. Schrader's toilet-paper note to Joyce Clarke, shielded it in a sheet of hotel stationery and slid the papers into his breast pocket. By two o'clock he was in the Cressida and blundering through the maze of one-way streets around the hotel, eyes straining to pick out the I-70 signs while his right-hand fingers toyed with the radio buttons. He found a classical station and the Interstate in the same minute. KFUO's afternoon program of Ravel, Chausson and d'Indy kept his thoughts company as he maneuvered into the slow lane and pushed at just above the speed limit past the airport and the bridge across the Missouri River and through St. Charles County. The nearer he came to Fulton, the more his own thinking disturbed him.

Just after three-thirty he exited at Highway 54 and peered through the caked mist and filth on his windshield. He found no road signs and swerved into a service station for fuel and directions. While the freckled young attendant used a squeegee on the windshield, Loren stepped into the station office and mini-mart, paid cash for the gas, asked the way to the state hospital and, passing along an aisle of the convenience store area, saw a pyramid of facial tissue boxes, each one priced at about twice what it would cost in a regular store. He snatched the topmost box, went back to the clerk behind the counter and reached for his wallet again.

Out of sight of the service station he turned into a Burger King and slid the Cressida into a vacant slot behind the building. It was too late for lunch and too early for dinner and the lot was almost empty. He opened the box, pulled out a handful of pale-blue tissues and tossed them and the box top into a waste can. Then he took the sheet of Laclede Suites stationery from his jacket pocket, removed five more tissues from the box, inserted Mrs. Schrader's note and covered it with the five tissues, tossed the box to the backseat floor and drove out of the lot. He might need the note to persuade the woman that he knew more than in fact he did but saw no need to carry it openly into the hospital with him.

The dashboard clock read two minutes to four when he swung onto two-lane Highway O and saw the Missouri State Hospital complex a few hundred yards ahead on his left. At the BIGGS DRIVE sign he turned into the grounds. Then he hit the brake, hard. The Cressida shuddered to a halt. A lean young black man in the tan uniform of the state police had come from nowhere and was standing in the center of the drive with his hand raised. When the car was still he approached the driver's side window and motioned Loren to open it. "May I help you, sir?" He kept his right hand on the polished butt of his revolver and his eyes were bright and blank.

"I'm Professor Mensing." Loren took a law school card from his wallet and handed it to the trooper. "I'd like to see whoever's in charge of the criminally insane section. It's in connection with some research I'm doing for a law review article."

The guard unstrapped a walkie-talkie from his belt and spoke softly into the mouthpiece. Loren shut the car window and his eyes and rehearsed once more the reasons he would give for requesting an interview with Mrs. Schrader. He had to get the message through to her that he'd come from Joyce Clarke and to hint that if she refused to see him he could make trouble for her by telling the hospital administrator about the toilet-paper note to Joyce that she had smuggled out. A tapping on glass aroused him from introspection and he rolled down the window again. The guard's eyes had changed, the blankness replaced by a veiled look, wary, expectant.

"That's the Biggs Building straight ahead." He enunciated each word as if he were talking to a child. "Park anywhere in the lot. The man you want to speak to is Dr. Cameron."

"Right." Loren thanked the trooper and eased the Cressida into motion. The Biggs Building was four stories tall, of orange-red brick with cream trim, surrounded by concertina wire on spring arms set in concrete. Scattered among the civilian cars in the parking lot Loren counted five state police cruisers and an evidence van. He locked the Cressida, followed the sidewalk to the entranceway and strode through glass doors into the lobby.

It looked like the lobby of every other hospital he'd ever seen except that a short broken-nosed thirtyish man in state trooper tans was standing at attention beside the information window. "Yes, sir?" the officer challenged him.

"I'm Professor Mensing," Loren said. "I believe the trooper outside called about me a few minutes ago?"

"Yes, sir. You want to see Dr. Cameron but you don't have an appointment."

"It won't take long." Loren made a stab at a rueful smile. "I thought my secretary had made the appointment for me weeks ago. I'm a law professor, I've just finished a visitorship at New York University. It really won't take much time."

"Let's see what we can do. Follow me, sir." The trooper about-faced and led the way to a metal detector of the sort Loren had walked through in dozens of airports. "Keys out of your pockets." He handed the trooper his key ring and passed through the barrier. The trooper unlocked a door

139

into a square boothlike area. Loren saw neat round little outlets on the walls. "We can flood this place with gas if we have to," the trooper said. "Stay close behind me, sir." He unlocked a second door and escorted Loren along first one sterile corridor and then another. There was a hospital smell but no people, anywhere. Except for the bright lights it was as if the trooper was leading him into the center of one of those immemorial caves to die of starvation.

They came to an unmarked door whose knob the trooper twisted without knocking. The office they entered was empty too. Bare desk, functional chairs, file cabinets. Painted wooden ducks on the cabinet tops. Loren felt a surge of the same panic he had felt with Anthony at lunch. *They know me. They're watching me.* If he had thought he could find his way out alone he would have bolted. He stood paralyzed six feet inside the doorway, waiting for the unimaginable to happen.

The trooper rapped on an oak door at the room's far end and stood away, facing Loren, hands at his hips. Loren heard muffled footsteps. The inner door opened and a man stood framed in the dimness of the doorway, smiling at him.

"Ehyeh asher ehyeh," Sergeant Domjan pronounced. "How you doing today, sir?"

Ten

LOREN FELT HIS EYES LOOSENING in their sockets, heard a high whistling sound in his head. The sergeant looked like a Wall Street arbitrageur in a dark-blue cashmere suit and gray silk shirt and regimental striped tie and glistening Guccis but there was a stubble of white gold on his cheeks and he stood unsteadily as if reeling from sleeplessness. Behind him in the inner office lights blinked on. Loren glimpsed four other men around a conference table haloed by tobacco smoke. One was a heavyset black man who struck Loren as vaguely familiar. Then he remembered: the black FBI agent from Domjan's apartment.

"You came to see Mrs. Schrader, sir." The sergeant seemed to sense that Loren was stunned by his presence and knowledge, and managed a modest smile that did not conceal his delight. "No magic involved in figuring that out. No one else in the hospital has any connection with our case, right?"

"Okay. Right." Loren tasted the bile of fear and almost gagged. "You're here for . . . for the same reason?"

"Not quite," Domjan replied softly. "I'm here because the lady got her throat slit from ear to ear last night."

Loren felt himself falling into nothingness. He thrust out his hands for support, stumbled to the nearest chair, sank into it, bent forward and breathed deep. "Here?" he mumbled between gulps. "In the state hospital?"

"Upstairs. Night nurse found her in a storage closet a little after midnight. Preliminary medical report says she was grabbed from behind in a corridor, her mouth taped with gauze, dragged to the closet and butchered."

141

"Here in a state institution. Insane," Loren said without thinking, and went red with embarrassment when the black FBI man chuckled.

"We're pretty sure who did it," Domjan went on. "Guy on the housekeeping staff by the name of Elmo Trane who was working the three-to-eleven shift. Sort of a janitor. He came on duty yesterday as usual but no one's seen him since nine or ten last night. He didn't clock out at end of shift and his apartment at the other end of town's empty. His car's still in the lot outside but that doesn't mean much, it's a fifteen-year-old clunker he bought when he came to work here three months ago. There's, ah, some evidence of sexual assault. He seems to have pulled down Mrs. Schrader's panties and played around in her vagina with his knife while she was gagged and bleeding to death."

Loren heard old Professor Hirschberg's philosophic singsong: God, chance, absurdity. An underpaid menial, seething with who knew what rages, goes haywire and slaughters precisely this woman less than twenty-four hours before Loren might have prevailed on her to tell what she knew about Kim. He boiled with his own rage at the way the world was made. He wanted to kill someone.

Then reason took hold again and he began to think.

"Sergeant." He looked up into Domjan's burning eyes. "If this murder isn't connected with what you call our case, what the hell are you and these FBI men doing here?"

"Quick recovery, sir." Domjan nodded like a benevolent father watching his child make a wise move at chess. "I'd called Dr. Cameron a few days ago about Mrs. Schrader because the Judge Clarke murder was in those scrapbooks but she told the doc she wouldn't talk to anyone without her lawyer and that's what he told me. By the way, sir, I'm not working Staten Island anymore, I've been transferred to liaison with the FBI special unit that's been set up to work these vigilante cases. Anyway, before we could figure our next move, this happened. Cameron was sent for in the middle of the night and decided to call me right away. I'd left him my home number. You know, sir, my last exam at

Fordham was yesterday, seven to ten P.M. I was sacked out like a corpse when he phoned from here with the news. Could have killed him at first." He yawned and patted his mouth with fingertips. "Christ, I haven't had a real night's sleep in two weeks."

"So you and the FBI team flew a thousand miles to investigate a murder that's not relevant to your case? That makes no sense. Where's your jurisdiction? What's your interest?"

Domjan beamed at him again. "Well, you see, sir, as soon as Cameron hung up, I called the Bureau and reported, and they told me to get dressed and meet with them, and then they phoned here and had this Elmo Trane's picture and prints faxed to them just to make certain the murder wasn't connected with our case. And you know what, sir? When I saw what came off the fax machine I nearly keeled over just like you did a minute ago. Can you guess why?"

Loren sat there in slack-mouthed silence.

"This Trane character," Domjan said, "looks enough like Jonathan Bloch to be his brother."

Loren wanted to scream. He wanted to cry out that this was too insane even for a world gone mad. Clifford Bloch working as a janitor in the hospital where his brother Jonathan had twice been confined, murdering the woman who had killed Judge Clarke less than a week after murdering Clarke's daughter. He didn't hear the sergeant close the inner office door, pull up a second hard chair and drop into it beside him.

"I'll bet you thought we didn't know he had a brother," Domjan clucked disapprovingly. "I did take the time to read every page of those scrapbooks, sir. We've learned a bit about Clifford since last time I saw you. We're fairly sure he's the one that called himself Morgan and did Joyce Clarke last week."

"Wait. Wait a minute," Loren muttered. "You just finished telling me Clifford Bloch was calling himself Elmo Trane and working the three-to-eleven shift in this hospi-

143

tal till last night. So how could he have been here and in New York at the same time?"

"He couldn't of course," Domjan readily admitted. "I didn't say Clifford was working here as Elmo Trane, sir. What I said was that Trane looked enough like Jonathan Bloch to be his brother. The one who worked here was Jonathan himself. He came back to the hospital three months ago as Trane and got himself a job. Guess he must have liked the place."

Loren raised his head and shook it from side to side until Domjan reached out and made him stop. "I know it sounds crazy," he said. "But they don't pay much here and in a booming economy like we have now, it's hard to find people who'll do scutwork for loonies. The hospital's got a huge amount of personnel turnover. No one did a security check on Trane and none of the staff remembered him as Jonathan Bloch."

Voices thundered in Loren's whirling head that it still wasn't possible. If Jonathan had been working here as Trane, how could he have been in New York, snatching Kim Hale from the ferry terminal?

He felt something in his lap but couldn't focus on it. His eyes were going. For a moment he thought he'd gone blind. Then he groped in his pocket for a silicon-treated tissue, wiped his glasses with it and looked down again. What lay in his lap was a photograph. A harsh black-and-white of a dark-haired fox-faced man in his thirties, eyes bright with what might have been pleasure or hate, lips thin, jaw underslung.

"Is that the man who hit you with the violin on the ferry, sir?" Domjan asked.

Loren hesitated, blinked, lifted the picture closer to his eyes. There was an institutional quality about it, like a driver's license or passport photo but not like a police mug shot. Loren guessed it had been taken when Trane started working at the hospital, probably for use on an ID badge.

"It's the same man," he said slowly. "Elmo Trane?"

"Right, sir. Also known as Jonathan Bloch."

Now it began to fit. Ruth Schrader had written that note

to Joyce, demanding to be sprung from Fulton, threatening to tell whatever she knew if her release wasn't arranged. Either Joyce had passed on that message or Mrs. Schrader herself had smuggled out similar letters to others. Either way, a decision had been made: to send in Jonathan Bloch, have him get a job in the hospital and await his chance to dispose of her as long as it was done well before her June 30 deadline. The sexual assault was for Bloch's private enjoyment or else a blind designed to hide the real reason she had to die; maybe both. The ideal candidate to commit a murder in a hospital for the criminally insane would be a former inmate, someone with intimate knowledge of the layout, security arrangements, work schedules. And who had dispatched Jonathan to commit this murder? Well, if Mrs. Schrader had sent word to someone besides Joyce that unless she was released she would talk, who would that someone be? Most likely the lawyer who had handled her defense. Saul Grimsby. Who just happened to have his office on the same floor of the same building as Garrett Anthony!

"You're wondering." Domjan's voice pierced his thoughts. "I said, sir, you're wondering how little Elmo managed to take time off and go after Ms. Hale and you in New York. Right?" Loren nodded dumbly. "I knew you were. So were we. The answer's in his personnel file, sir. He was out with a bad case of flu for nine days. Got a note from a doctor. Just came back to work last Friday."

"A genuine doctor's note?"

"Cameron tells me the man's a local internist, been in practice here for twenty years."

"You've had someone check with this doctor?"

"Not yet, sir," Domjan said. "Think a minute and you'll see why we haven't."

Loren sat motionless on the hard chair, staring at the wall. There was a glass-framed diploma or citation above the bank of file cabinets, flanked by two wooden mallards with their beaks touching. Loren didn't see them or anything else except what was passing through his mind. He had no idea how much time had gone by before he straightened and looked into Domjan's eyes.

"First possibility," he said. "Bloch forged the doctor's name to the note. That's not likely because first of all as far as I know he has no track record as a forger and secondly it's so damn risky. If a supervisor happens to call the doctor's office and ask if the note is genuine, there goes the whole three months' masquerade. Second possibility, which I think is much more probable. Remember Bloch used to be a medical student. He faked the symptoms and fooled this doctor into diagnosing flu." He paused, showing puzzlement. "But why should that keep you from checking with the doctor?"

"You're missing the third and likeliest theory, sir," Domjan told him. "That the doc's part of the vigilantes." The sergeant beamed at Loren as if he expected applause for a particularly clever move. "Which is why there's a watch on his office even as we speak. Bloch might be holed up in there. More likely he's hundreds of miles away by now but you never know. Meanwhile we're looking at the doc's contacts with lawyers over the past several years. Maybe we'll find some reason why he might hate them, like an ex-wife cleaned him out or he got screwed by a big malpractice judgment."

"You may find something like that," Loren told him. "But it won't matter a damn."

Domjan gave him a fish-eyed scowl and rubbed the sandpaper stubble on his cheeks and chin. "You have to be kidding, sir. Look, I spent months back in New York trying to worm my way into the outfit and couldn't get beyond the Clarke woman. Now I'm handed a lead into the vigilantes on a silver platter and you sit there and tell me it doesn't matter?"

"There are no vigilantes," Loren said.

Domjan sat with a stunned look on his face as if he were watching a dear friend come apart.

"Give me a couple of hours alone with you and I think I can convince you."

"Jesus," the sergeant muttered. Loren sensed that the

ambitious young cop had never been so shaken by a thought in his life, not even when for whatever reason he'd made up his mind to leave the seminary. He saw Domjan's lips quivering and wondered if he was saying a prayer and sat patiently waiting. When the sergeant spoke again, he seemed to have forgotten what Loren had said. Denial stage?

"You know how I got here, sir?" he asked, but didn't wait for an answer. "FBI plane. We landed at Columbia and picked up a government car for the run to Fulton. I think I can explain to my fed buddies in there that it's time I explored some leads in St. Louis. How would you like to drive me in, say your piece on the road?"

"Makes sense," Loren agreed. "It wasn't till I was on the road out here a few hours ago that I began to see what this mess is really about. Sure you don't want to grab a nap first? I'm going to throw some mind-bending stuff at you."

"My bennies will keep me going a little longer." Domjan stood and stretched lazily. "I left my overnight bag inside there, sir. Just let me go get it and tell the feds where I'm off to and we can bug out of here." He smiled but it was the ghastliest smile Loren had ever seen, like the grin on the face of a long-dead corpse. "I trust you to keep me awake."

IT WAS NOT quite six when Loren turned the Cressida onto I-70 East. Domjan sprawled in the front passenger seat, which was tilted back as far as it would go. Every so often a gentle snore came from his half-open mouth. St. Louis-bound traffic was light, a few cars and vans and the occasional tractor-trailer or semi. The eastern sky was teal blue with not a cloud in sight. Loren relaxed and let the car all but drive itself while he rehearsed what he'd say if and when Domjan came awake.

Fifty minutes out of Fulton the sergeant's body twitched. He sat erect, raised his seat to the upright position, shot a glance at his Rolex and did deep-breathing exercises until with a grateful smile he twisted to face Loren as best he could. "So much for the bennies," he said. "Where are we?"

"Next exit's Wright City. Another hour or so to St. Louis unless we hit traffic."

"Damn," the sergeant grunted. "I was hoping to see a little of Fulton. You know, sir, that was the town Henry Bellamann wrote about in *King's Row*. The book they made into a movie with President Reagan back in 1942. *'Wheeerrre's the rest of me?!!'* " He rendered the line in such a nerve-shattering screech that Loren instinctively jammed his foot on the brake and the Cressida slewed over the still-damp highway into the next lane, which happened at the moment to be empty. "Sorry, sir," he said when Loren had regained control of the wheel. "If I wasn't wide awake before, we both sure are now. Ready to tell me what's on your mind?"

"If you're ready to listen."

"I don't even need coffee. So." Domjan gave Loren a grotesque look like a prisoner just sentenced to death facing his judge. "You say there are no vigilantes. Then I guess I'm just imagining I'm liaison to an FBI task force that's after this group. The year I spent sucking up to the Clarke woman, that was just a dream, right? That story you gave me last week about her inviting you to join up was a lie. Jesus Christ, where the fuck is your head? You just about witnessed one murder these clowns pulled and we just left the scene of another!"

"You don't understand," Loren told him quietly. "I didn't either until I started thinking very carefully on the drive to Fulton today. Look, how would you define the objective of these vigilantes?"

Domjan took the hint. The Cressida was transformed into a moving classroom and Loren into one of his professors. "Sir, those scrapbooks tell us loud and clear. They're out to get even with the scumshit lawyers and judges who like to piss on decent folks' lives."

He had used more profanity in the last two minutes than in all their conversations before. *Good*, Loren thought. *I'm rattling him.* "They're trying to reform the legal system by force, then? Kill off the bad lawyers and judges so they can be replaced by good ones?"

The sergeant rubbed his chin stubble and squeezed his eyes shut. "What good ones? . . . Well, sir, if that was their aim they'd have to make themselves known, I guess. Take credit for their hits like the Islamic terrorists do. Make demands. And they haven't done any of that."

"So?" Loren pressed him.

"So I'd say their motivation is pure *Network.*" Loren looked blank. " 'I'm mad as hell and I'm not going to take it anymore!' " This time Loren was ready for the outburst and didn't lose control of the wheel. Domjan smiled at Loren again, this time shyly like a child. "I sympathize with that a little, sir."

"Who doesn't? But you're still nowhere near the truth. Do you really believe a national vigilante organization could set itself up and bring in the Bloch brothers and who knows how many others to be their pet hitmen and have them kill dozens of lawyers and judges and keep the whole operation so secret that not one of their hits was even suspected of being a murder till recently?"

Domjan squirmed in his seat belt, eyes half shut as if he were afraid of the setting sun even though they were driving east.

"Ready for an alternate theory?" Loren asked. "One that accounts for everything more credibly?"

The sergeant said nothing but out of the corner of his eye Loren thought he saw him nod.

"First I want you to think back to those scrapbooks. Remember you said someone would have to compare the outrage stories in the black book with the death stories in the white book and see how much correlation there was between them?"

"I remember."

"I'll make you a bet there was nowhere near as much as you expected," Loren said.

Domjan still said nothing.

"Back in your apartment," Loren went on, "you also told

me that a fair amount of the material in the white book dealt with the deaths of people who weren't part of the legal system but were either corporate bigwigs or just rich. Remember that?"

"Yes, sir, I remember, but I have no idea where you're going with it," the sergeant said. "Except to St. Louis," he giggled.

"Now," Loren said, "since you brought up St. Louis, what do you know about a law firm there that used to call itself Anthony & Clarke?" *Unfair question,* he chided himself. The old firm name had been mentioned in the *Times* articles he'd copied at the Bobst, and Gael had discussed it with him last night, but as far as he knew it hadn't figured in any item in the scrapbooks. As a seasoned law professor he wasn't bothered at all by the unfairness. He asked questions like that in class whenever they served a purpose.

This one worked superbly. Domjan hunched in his seat with perplexity written all over his face. "Doesn't ring a bell, sir," he admitted at last. "A guy named Anthony was Jonathan Bloch's lawyer in that handicap discrimination suit, and the judge of course was Clarke, but . . ." He sprang erect like a jack-in-the-box as comprehension dazed him. "Are you trying to tell me the two of them used to be law partners?"

"Until Clarke went on the bench," Loren said. "That's when the firm name became Garrett Anthony Associates. Now, how about a lawyer by the name of Saul Grimsby? Tell me what the scrapbooks gave you on him."

"Bing bong," the sergeant responded without hesitation. "He was Mrs. Schrader's lawyer. Got her off on insanity when she blew His Honor away."

"Suppose I told you Grimsby's office is on the same floor of the same building as Anthony's?" Loren asked.

Domjan said nothing.

"Now I'm going to offer a theory," Loren continued. "I can't prove it, not yet anyway, but I think it accounts for what's happened so far, and I don't see any other theory that does. We start with the firm of Anthony & Clarke. On the surface they have an ordinary respectable practice but over time they develop a secret sideline. Now we both know that all sorts of things are done in the legal system that—well, the only way to describe them would be if you could say insane, obscene and absurd all at the same time."

"Amen!" Domjan cut in. "Couldn't agree with you more, sir."

"Some of those things come about because judges or bureaucrats or legislators are lazy or incompetent or don't care a damn about the human consequences of what they decide. But every so often we find a dirtier explanation." For a few seconds Loren's thoughts parted from his words and his mind flew back to when the highest court of his home state had asked him to serve as its own private detective, investigating the shoebox full of cash that had been found in the closet of the dead justice who had been Loren's mentor. That was when he and Val had met. God, could it have been a dozen years ago?

"I think that was Anthony & Clarke's sideline. They became the conduit, with a bunch of judges and legal functionaries on the take at one end and a bunch of lawyers at the other end with bribes in their hands. Then in time something like Gresham's Law operated, and the rotten side of their practice drove out the rest and grew. They became the conduit between people who wanted murders committed and the hit men."

"The Bloch brothers," Domjan said in a near whisper.

"Someone wants to take over as CEO of a corporation, or get rid of a competitor, or come into an inheritance, whatever."

"Who ya gonna call?" Domjan sang to the tune of the *Ghostbusters* lyric. "Anthony & Clarke!"

"You get the idea," Loren said. "The lawyers call one or both of the Blochs or maybe some other killers. An accident happens. When Clifford Bloch makes the plans, more often than not a particular type of accident happens. An auto smashup."

"Rubenstein," the sergeant said under his breath.

"Fuller. Judge Blanding." Loren knew nothing of the first two but remembered what Val had told him about the Chicago jurist who had died in a one-car wreck on the Eisenhower Expressway and guessed that the others had also been killed on the road and memorialized in Joyce Clarke's scrapbooks.

"And that type of accident then gets refined into something even more obscene," Loren went on. "Ever read Chesterton?"

In the rear-vision mirror he saw Domjan blink like a mole forced into sunlight. "Gilbert Keith Chesterton?" he asked. "The guy who wrote all the paradoxes?"

"Not to mention tons of journalism, religious writing, poetry, a few novels and dozens of short stories. His best-known character was the priest detective, Father Brown."

"Oh, yeah," Domjan muttered. "There was a movie . . . I think Alec Guinness was Father Brown. Pretty awful picture, sir."

"You ought to try the original stories someday," Loren suggested. "I had to when I was in law school because one of my professors kept throwing these paradoxical one-liners at us and I decided to find out what they meant. One of the Father Brown stories I read is called 'The Sign of the Broken Sword.' Where does the wise man hide a leaf? In the forest. Suppose there is no forest? Then he makes one. Where does the wise murderer hide a body? In a forest of bodies. Suppose there is no forest of bodies? Then he makes one. That's the idea behind Chesterton's story. A general kills one of his young officers and then orders out all his troops on a suicidal charge so the body of the man he killed will pass as just another casualty of war."

"Oh, Jesus." Domjan kept repeating the words softly like a prayer. Loren remembered Val's report on the Chicago executive who along with several others had been killed in a multi-car pile-up on a foggy morning and sensed that the sergeant knew of more accidents of the same type that had made their way into Joyce's scrapbooks.

"Garrett Anthony," Loren said, "is a Chesterton nut."

Domjan didn't speak or move. He seemed to accept the

statement without wondering how Loren knew that. *Don't give him a chance to think. Keep hitting him hard.* Loren darted into the fast lane to pass an eighteen-wheeler.

"On top of his sideline or maybe because of it," he continued, "Clarke has made political friends. He's offered a federal judgeship and accepts. The firm name changes to Garrett Anthony Associates but the dirty business goes on. Maybe Clarke makes a clean break from it or maybe he demands a piece of Anthony's take like an actor getting residuals. Time goes on. Jonathan Bloch decides to give up murder and go to medical school. He runs amok with a knife, is put on trial and gets off on an insanity defense. He's sent to Fulton. A doctor says he's no longer dangerous and they have to let him out. He wants to get back into med school and goes to his pal Anthony for legal advice. Anthony sues for handicap discrimination. Who manipulates the system so he gets to sit on the case? Clarke. No wonder Bloch wins! Then he goes haywire again and kills a small boy."

". . . And justice for all," Domjan said. Loren couldn't tell if he meant the pledge of allegiance or the movie.

"By this time Anthony sees the whole stinking operation in danger of coming apart. Time to start eliminating whoever might drag him down. Beginning with Judge Clarke. So he makes contact with the dead boy's mother, Ruth Schrader."

"Hold it, sir," Domjan broke in. "Objection. Anthony represented Jonathan Bloch in the case that gave Bloch the chance to kill the kid, right?" He didn't wait for a reply. "So wouldn't Mrs. Schrader just spit in his face if he approaches her?"

"Of course she would. Good point. He can't get in touch with her directly but he can through another lawyer. Maybe it was through Grimsby but my hunch is it was Joyce Clarke who did the honors. We both know how much she hated her father. The night she was killed she told me he'd started having sex with her when she was seven. I'm not saying she knew about the dark side of the Anthony & Clarke practice, but if Anthony could play the

Iago part, manipulate Joyce into a friendship of some kind with Mrs. Schrader, get her to work on the woman, turn her into a vigilante . . . Remember, her family's been wiped out, she's sick with rage and grief. If another woman, another victim of Judge Clarke, should tell her there was a vigilante underground group that was willing to train her, give her a gun and forged references, help her get a job as Clarke's housekeeper under an alias so when the right chance came she could blow him away . . . Well, if you were Mrs. Schrader, wouldn't you buy the story?" Loren fought to keep his eyes on the highway. If Domjan ever guessed that some of this reconstruction came from the toilet-paper note concealed in the tissue box on the backseat floor almost within reach of his hand, Loren might easily wind up in jail for withholding evidence.

"Professor," Domjan said, "you sure know how to paint a picture. Okay, so what happened then?"

"This is mostly guesswork but I think Anthony counted on Mrs. Schrader to go on the run after she killed Clarke. He would have hid her for a while and then quietly got rid of her." He thought of the cave network behind the country house near Hannibal. "But of course she didn't run. She emptied her gun into Clarke and then sat down and called the police. Suddenly Anthony faces a new crisis. If she tells the cops too much, there goes his whole rotten operation! So what happens? An attorney comes forward who vigorously defends her rights, pleads insanity and gets her sent to Fulton, the same place where Bloch had been sent a year or two before. He was out by then, of course. And who was Mrs. Schrader's lawyer? Grimsby." He remembered a line from the toilet-paper note and fit it into place. "Likely Joyce or Grimsby or someone promised her a quick and quiet release with help from vigilante sympathizers in high places."

"So," Domjan said. They crossed the Missouri River on the new bridge and passed into west St. Louis County. "But, sir," the sergeant added after a few minutes' thought, "she actually served three years there . . . Oh, now I see

154

your point! You think she got antsy and threatened to spill the big secret, so Anthony sent Bloch down to get a janitor's job there and . . ."

"And wait for his chance to kill her just as she'd waited hers to kill Clarke," Loren finished. "But before that chance came, Anthony was hit with another crisis. We don't know what it was but we know it involved Kim Hale and couldn't be put on hold. So he had Bloch fake flu symptoms and get off work for a while—"

"And track down and get rid of her before *she* blew the show!" Domjan interrupted in turn.

"Exactly. We'll never know the details unless we find Kim alive or make Anthony talk but the general pattern's clear. Somehow or other she found out some or all of the truth and for some reason or other she couldn't take it to the police. So she ran."

"She ran to New York and tried to reach you?"

"Sergeant, when we first met in Staten Island you already knew about the cases I've been messed up in over the years. It's reasonable to assume she did too. She was desperate for help, we'd been close once . . ." His voice trailed off into nothingness. Suddenly he noticed how dark the early-evening sky had turned and switched on the headlights.

"How would she have known you were in New York this year?" Domjan wondered aloud.

"Anybody at my own school could have told her. It was hardly a secret. So she came east to see me." Loren accelerated to 70 mph and set the cruise control knob. He sensed that somewhere around this spot there was a hole in his hypotheses but he couldn't put his finger on it and chose for the moment to ignore it. "We know from her first phone call to me that she knew Joyce Clarke was involved somehow. Maybe she found out how Anthony had manipulated Joyce over the killing of Judge Clarke and went to tell her. Maybe Joyce betrayed her to Anthony and Bloch or maybe they found her another way, but they certainly did find her. Bloch and his goons grabbed her in the ferry building."

155

"And what did they do with her?" Domjan demanded.

"We know they didn't kill her right away because at two o'clock Monday morning she made the second call to me, begging me to stay out of the mess. Maybe somehow she got away from Bloch before she made that call or maybe he forced her to do it. If she did get away, maybe he found her again and killed her or maybe she's still out there alone on the run." *Please let her be alive,* he kept saying to himself.

"Either way," the sergeant pointed out, "we know for sure Bloch was back at his Elmo Trane job in Fulton on Friday which was, let's see, about four and a half days after the second phone call you had from Ms. Hale. Doesn't help us much though. The timing might mean he'd found her and killed her during the week or it might mean he never did find her but Anthony called him off and told him to go back to Fulton and finish off Mrs. Schrader because that job couldn't wait any longer."

She must be alive she must be alive. Loren repeated the words silently as if they had power to keep her safe.

"Sir," Domjan broke into his mantra, "one point I still can't make head nor tail of. Just what was Joyce Clarke up to back in New York? I mean, she really did believe in these vigilantes. She tried to recruit me, and the last thing she did before Clifford Bloch ran her down is she tried to recruit you."

"I'll risk some more guesswork," Loren said. "When Anthony used her to help get rid of her father, when he had her come on to Mrs. Schrader as part of a vigilante group, he created a Frankenstein monster. Joyce hated her father and hated the legal system she identified him with. A lot of the material in those scrapbooks must have been given to her by Anthony as part of the scam to get Mrs. Schrader to pull the trigger. I think reading about those outrages gave her an idea. *Why not make this mythical organization a reality?* That's what she was up to, I think. But she was such a klutz at conspiracy she wound up trying to recruit a man who happened to live upstairs from her and also happened, although she didn't know it of course, to be a cop! God knows what other stupid mistakes she made but—either/or, here we go again—either Anthony got wind of what she was trying to do or on general principles he decided she was too dangerous to live, so he sent in Clifford Bloch to get rid of her."

"Which would put both the brothers in New York at the same time but to kill different women," Domjan said. "I wonder if Clifford could have been one of the goons at the ferry terminal. In any event, sir, we did find the hit-and-run car abandoned over in Jersey with a clear print of Clifford's forefinger behind the rearview mirror. If we find him, we've got him for Murder One."

"You know, Sergeant," Loren said, "there have been a remarkable number of violent acts within this group in less than two weeks. Do you sense what I do? That Anthony's operation is coming unstuck?"

Domjan stifled a yawn and pawed wearily at his eyes. "Seems to me that's the understatement of the week. If we don't make some arrests soon there won't be anyone left to arrest, they'll all have killed each other. By the way, sir, better slow down. Speed limit's fifty-five here." He gave Loren one of those death's-head grins and cushioned the back of his neck against his London Fog.

"Don't drop off on me," Loren warned. "I'm not through yet. There's a map of Missouri in the door pocket on your side. Pull it out and open it up."

With his eyes still shut, the sergeant groped for the map. "Is this really necessary, sir?"

"Look at what's in front of you and see for yourself. Now find Hannibal. Up in the northeast part of the state. Mark Twain's boyhood home, remember?"

"I've read *Huck Finn*, sir." Domjan folded the map into a compact rectangle and bent over to study it under the dashboard lights. "Found it."

"How long do you think it would take to drive to Hannibal from Fulton?"

The sergeant squinted at the folded map and measured distances with a finger. "I don't see any world-class roads between them but the distance looks like something over a hundred miles. Say two, three hours drive time?"

157

"Now comes the interesting part," Loren said. "Anthony's home is in a fancy suburb of St. Louis County but he has a country place near Hannibal with a network of unexplored caves on the property. I had dinner last night with a former student of mine who's in practice downtown and she happened to mention that she'd seen Anthony in the courthouse corridor very late in the day. Now if you were stuck in downtown St. Louis till five-thirty or so on a weekday, and had the choice of going home to Ladue or trekking out to Hannibal for the evening, which would you take?"

Domjan made the map crackle as he neatly refolded it and set it on his lap. "Unless I was just crazy for driving, I'd spend the night in Ladue. Wherever that is."

"Yet I know for a fact," Loren told him, "that when he drove into work this morning he didn't come from Ladue. *He came from Hannibal.* Now why do you suppose he made a quickie visit to Hannibal last night and stayed there till this morning?"

Domjan tapped his fingers against the map on his knees as if it were a musical instrument. His eyes were bright with the blue fire Loren had seen in them in New York. "He went to take a meeting with one or both of the Bloch brothers and open up one of those caves for him!"

"Or *them*," Loren said. "That's my hunch too." A descending jet roared over the highway. "We're half an hour from downtown," he added.

"No time for a decent nap, damn it." Domjan dug in his pockets for a squat plastic cylinder from which he rolled two pills into his palm. *More bennies,* Loren guessed. He drove mindlessly, past the airport and the maze of exits and interchanges, and caught glimpses of the Gateway Arch and the light-studded city skyline. His thoughts kept returning to that note. To the squares of toilet paper that Ruth Schrader had smuggled past her keepers and mailed to Joyce Clarke and that Loren himself had smuggled past Domjan and out of New York only to have the fierce-eyed young zealot be sitting so close to the tissue box where it was hidden that he could have reached back with his hand

and touched it. Loren fought to stop thinking about it because a tiny irrational part of him was still afraid Domjan could read his mind, but the words scrawled on the thin paper kept drawing him as the candle flame draws the moth. He saw them as clearly as if it were broad daylight and the note in his hand. How could Mrs. Schrader have known Joyce's New York address? Where could she have met Kim Hale? Why did her note to Joyce speak of Kim as someone known to both of them?

That was when he knew.

"Sergeant," he said.

Domjan rolled his head around lazily. "Sir?"

"You and the FBI men were working on the Schrader murder for several hours before I showed up, weren't you?"

"From the minute we rolled in this morning. What about it?"

"I was just wondering." *Keep it slow, keep it calm!* "Did you happen to make a list of whatever visitors she had while she was a patient in Fulton?" *Please, please let the answer be yes.*

"Normal routine," the sergeant told him. "One of the first things the state cops did."

"Long list?" *It couldn't be, it couldn't be.*

"Three names," Domjan said. "No help at all."

"Try them on me." Loren stopped breathing. Reason told him nothing now but the voice of instinct was deafening him with its rocket-fire shriek *This is it This is it!* "If you remember them," he added.

"There was one visit from Joyce Clarke. Long time back, maybe eight months after Mrs. Schrader was locked up there. That was sort of a surprise, sir, but I knew how much she hated her dad and I figured she wanted to have a look at the lady who'd done him. Mrs. Schrader didn't object. Of course if your reconstruction's on target the visit makes a lot more sense."

So now I know how she'd known where to send the note. Roll the dice again. "One of the other two visitors must have been Saul Grimsby," Loren offered. "After all he was her lawyer."

"Easy guess, sir. He visited her, oh, ten or twelve times over the three years she was confined. Of course the staff couldn't ask what the visits were for or eavesdrop on privileged communications." He let loose a soft chuckle. "I doubt they could have overheard anything even if they'd tried. Security guys said he had the softest voice they'd ever heard from a lawyer in their lives."

Soft voice Soft voice! Something imploded in Loren's head. "Soft hypnotic voice?" he asked very quietly. "Little guy, early sixties, dressed very expensively and neatly like a wealthy Englishman?"

"Yeah, that's about the way the security people described him. Saul Grimsby."

Wrong. Garrett Anthony. Loren screamed at himself to pay at least minimal attention to the road and the traffic.

"If your theory's right, sir," Domjan went on, "at least some of those visits must have been to . . . well, hold her hand. Keep her pacified. Tell her he was pulling strings to get her released even while Jonathan Bloch was waiting his chance to kill her. But they sure looked like genuine lawyer-client conferences. I mean, he brought his secretary with him four or five times."

"Secretary?"

"You know, to take notes or whatever."

"Anthony brought a secretary to Fulton to see Mrs. Schrader."

Domjan stared as if he thought Loren belonged in the state hospital with the other crazies. "Not Anthony. Grimsby," he said. "Her lawyer, Saul Grimsby. His secretary was the third visitor. She had to sign in too of course. Regulations."

"What was her name?" Loren had never tried so hard to keep every hint of emotion from his voice.

"Rhodes," the sergeant replied. "Kay Rhodes I think it was."

And there it was. So neat and simple it dazzled the eyes. In the three years of her confinement Mrs. Schrader's only visitors were Joyce Clarke, Garrett Anthony and Kay Rhodes. If it was during those years that she had come to

160

know Kim Hale, it followed as night followed day that Kay Rhodes and Kim Hale were the same person.

Kim worked for Anthony. That was how she'd come to know too much. She had worked for him in the same suite of offices Loren had visited this morning as Judge Tremaine. That was how near he had been to her. That was how far.

Please, God, somebody, he begged, *please let her still be alive.*

Eleven

DOWNTOWN ST. LOUIS was dark and near deserted when Loren exited I-70 and retraced his tortuous groping toward the riverfront. The Cressida bumped along the steep cobblestoned streets of Laclede's Landing, jolting Domjan wide awake. Loren swung into the lot next to the Laclede Suites and parked. "Home," he announced, and pulled on the floor lever that popped the trunk open. "Might as well take your bag in with you. You won't have any trouble getting a room."

"Gotta touch base with the local FBI office first." The sergeant lifted his overnight case from the trunk and they trudged toward the side entrance of the hotel. "See if any instructions came through for me. Uhhh . . . this is one of those hotels where every room's a suite, right?"

"That's what they advertise."

The shy little-boy look stole into Domjan's eyes again. "Any reason I couldn't bunk with you, sir?"

The question brought Loren up short in the doorway. If he hadn't reached out for the polished brass handle he might have fallen over. *Is he gay?* he wondered. "I—well, I didn't get a chance to tell you before but I'm not here alone," he said. "There's a woman traveling with me."

For a moment Domjan looked stunned, as if it were unthinkable that a distinguished professor of law should share a hotel suite with someone of the opposite sex. In that moment the last shreds of fear that the sergeant was gifted with some sort of preternatural knowledge fell away from Loren and disintegrated. Not only didn't he have the slightest inkling that he'd been traveling with the note

162

Loren had taken from Jane Street, he didn't even know about Val. *Ehyeh asher ehyeh my ass*, Loren said to himself. Then Domjan contorted his features into the most ludicrous parody of a man-to-man grin Loren had ever beheld on a human face. "Any lady you'd be involved with has to be very special," he said. "Could I come up and meet her after I make my call?"

Loren checked his watch. Just past eight. Val was almost sure to be in their suite relaxing, waiting for him. Better give her some warning before he sprang an unexpected guest on her. "Phone up when you're done with the FBI," he suggested. "Suite 724." He was about to tell him to ask for the Tremaines but his imp of the perverse took too much delight in how much Domjan didn't know and he decided to maintain the status quo a few minutes longer. They parted in the main lobby with the sergeant loping off to a bank of pay phones on a wall and Loren stepping into an elevator. On seven he made the three sharp turns in the corridor and stuck his entry card into the slot of 724 with a "Just me, dear" as he crossed the threshold into soft gray darkness.

Three steps into the living room he fell over her body.

Tables and chairs were knocked over and lamps lay on the carpet like dead children and in the light from one that still shed a dim gold pool on the floor he saw the blood smears on her face and the shreds of her blouse and the way she was lying motionless and twisted while a fox-faced jut-jawed man in his thirties wearing a loose unbuttoned dark raincoat was bent over the edge of the couch gasping and rubbing between his legs with his right hand and wrapping his blood-soaked right wrist with the roll of paper towels from the suite kitchenette between his knees and in the dull gold glow he saw the bone-handled blood-spattered bread knife on the carpet at Jonathan Bloch's feet and the next second Bloch was up and howling like an animal in a steel trap and running at Loren with the knife in his hand and Loren snatched the lit table lamp from the carpet and flung it low and Bloch's legs flew out from under him as the room plunged into black. Loren dived for

163

him and caught an ankle and Bloch cursed and kicked at Loren's eyes and shattered his glasses and stumbled through the open door into the hallway. Loren tore off the ruined glasses and blindly raced after him, running by memory and instinct with arms out in front of him and careening around the first turn in the corridor and the second and the third and he was six feet behind Bloch at the long straight stretch of hallway where the elevators were and two young women were chattering and stepping out of a car as Bloch flew past them and slashed out with the bread knife and the one woman who happened to be a half step ahead of the other took the knife in her stomach and suddenly stopped chattering and the other woman screamed and a split second before Bloch could push the dead one and the screaming one aside the elevator door whisked automatically shut. Loren dived at Bloch and missed. Bloch in a low crouch flew down the corridor toward the painted steel door at the far end with EXIT in red letters in a box above the frame and hurled himself through into the fire tower. Ten feet behind him Loren caught the closing door on the rebound and clattered down the steel stairs four at a time and his feet hit the landing and he spun in a half-turn and leapt down the next flight with the tails of Bloch's raincoat billowing out four feet ahead and below him around one more half-turn and another until suddenly Bloch froze dead still at the head of a flight and was tugging at the loose raincoat sleeve that had snagged on the railing when Loren rammed himself into Bloch's back in a flying tackle and there was a sound of fabric ripping and they slammed full tilt down the next flight tangled and clawing at each other and stumbling and rolling toward the concrete wall at the next landing. They slammed into the wall with Bloch on the inside and his head and body taking the force of the impact and cushioning Loren who took Bloch from behind by the neck and pounded his face into the wall again and again and again and felt blood and something that was not blood come oozing out of Bloch and running down his hands and he kept smashing Bloch's ruined face and the top of his head against the wall until three pairs of hands forced him away from the other's shattered face and pushed him down another half flight and made him sit on the landing and he saw in a haze that the hands were attached to men in uniforms and then there were uniforms everywhere in the fire tower and some were blue and some were hospital white and he heard barked orders and running feet and slamming doors and then he heard Domjan's infinitely gentle voice in his ear saying, "No more, sir, no more" and felt Domjan's gentle arms guiding him up the half-flight to the landing where all that was left of Jonathan Bloch was rust-colored stains on the floor and the wall. He felt soft light around him and soft carpet under his feet and knew he was in a corridor and felt himself rising and knew he was in an elevator with Domjan's arms around him and felt carpet under his feet again and heard a door snicking open and saw the savage disorder of the living room of Suite 724 but it was ablaze with light from floodlamps now and Val's body had vanished into the same nothingness as Bloch's and men in plainclothes and uniforms were scattered over the room doing things Loren couldn't make out and speaking low. The next thing he knew he was in the bedroom lying limp across the foot of the double bed with Domjan sitting beside him and holding him and saying something he couldn't decipher.

This isn't real, he kept telling himself. *None of this has happened. I am not here. Bloch was not here. Val is not dead. She's alive. She's okay. None of this is real.* He opened his eyes and saw her sitting up in the bed, naked, long blond hair soft and loose, arms reaching out for him, eyes bright with desire, and he saw Kim there too beside her, Kim the way he remembered her, young and passionate and full of dreams, and he blinked and wiped the sweat of fear from his eyes and the room was empty except for himself and Domjan kneeling at his feet and unlacing his shoes.

"Did you hear me, sir?" he was asking.

"What?" Loren shook himself and then like an alcoholic in delirium tremens he couldn't stop shaking. "What?"

FRANCIS M. NEVINS

"She's okay, sir," Domjan repeated. "Your lady. I don't know her name. She's okay."

"Okay?"

"Not hurt bad. Some cuts and bruises, a chipped tooth but no permanent damage. Thank God we didn't hit one more red light after we got off the highway! Here, sir." He handed Loren a yellow pill, offered him a glass of water. "Valium. Doctor left it for you. It'll relax you, help you sleep."

"I don't want to sleep." He swallowed the pill anyway, washed it down. "Where is she? Where's . . . ?"

"She's in the hospital. Just for observation overnight. Guess you're stuck with me for a roomie after all, sir. She sure put up a hell of a scrap." He motioned with his palm toward the bedroom door and the debris beyond. "He caught her by surprise but she kept kicking him in the balls and trying to karate-chop him but he was so hopped up it didn't stop him. Slowed him down though."

"Softened him up too," Loren said. His mind flashed back to the image of Bloch slumped on the couch and massaging his crotch tenderly just as Loren came in. "I'm no Rambo. I could never have taken him alone. My God, I couldn't even see straight!"

"You and she make quite a team, sir. I wish you could have finished him in here because that poor gal who came up in the elevator at the wrong time was four months pregnant and she died in the operating room a few minutes ago. But no one else is going to have to worry about that piece of shit anymore."

"I—I killed him?"

"Better. You turned him into a vegetable."

"Good," Loren said.

"We . . . uh, well, just in case his brother or some other relative crawls out of the woodwork and tries to sue you for using excessive force on him or something, the St. Louis cops have, uh, sort of fiddled with the evidence and paperwork a bit. The record shows he inflicted most of his injuries on himself falling down all those stairs."

"Thanks," Loren said. He felt tranquillity flowing

166

through him as the Valium took hold but he didn't feel tired and knew he was so wired he'd be lucky to find three hours of sleep no matter how many pills they fed him. A paunchy fleshy-lipped man of about fifty in a rumpled brown suit and peppermint on his breath shambled into the bedroom and dropped onto his haunches beside Domjan. As they conferred in whispers, Loren looked through the open door into the front room and saw the investigation winding down, the last cops leaving. After a while he felt a tug on his arm and heard Domjan's voice.

"Sir? Don't fade on me yet, sir, we still have work to do. Corky, this is my good friend Professor Mensing. Sir, Corky's in charge of things at this end."

The chunky plainclothesman held out a sausage-fingered hand and said something Loren took to be a friendly greeting and his rank and last name, which somehow went past Loren. Hornstein? Orthwein? Then he heard Domjan again.

"Wouldn't you call that food for thought, sir?"

Loren knew he'd been fading out and shook himself. "Sorry," he said. "That Valium may have been a mistake. Mind telling me that again?"

"I've been explaining to Corky about you and me and the NYPD and the feds and the murders. And about the strong possibility that Bloch was sent over here to kill you by Garrett Anthony. Corky just got off the phone to Anthony's office five minutes ago and . . . well, you tell it, Corky."

The overweight detective popped three Altoid breath mints into his mouth. "Anthony wasn't in," he growled, "but his office manager happened to be working late. I talked with her and got his unlisted home number in Ladue. Every time I dial it I get a busy signal. That may mean he's home and on the phone or it may not mean squat 'cause his sister and mother and a full-time nurse live out there with him. Patrol car's on the way to his place now."

"Not to arrest him or anything," Domjan hastened to add. "No probable cause yet. Just to keep an eye on the house and see if he goes anywhere tonight."

"Sorry," Loren said again. "I'm afraid I'm still not with it. Why do you call that food for thought?"

"That wasn't the entree, sir. When Corky was on the phone with the office manager it suddenly occurred to me she could also give us the other lady's address."

"Other lady?" Loren had no idea what Domjan was talking about but hoped he wasn't coming across as an ignoramus. Damn Valium.

"You know, sir. The secretary Anthony took to Fulton with him when he called himself Saul Grimsby. Kay Rhodes."

Kim's new name. The sound of it drove away the torpor and he was keyed up drum-tight again.

"And this office manager's worked for the firm fifteen years," Corky broke in gruffly, "and swears up and down that no one by that name's ever had a job there."

Loren felt hope crumble inside him. So he hadn't been close to her this morning when he'd visited Anthony's office. But wait a minute, wait a minute! She had used a false name in Fulton but it need not have been a name conjured out of nowhere. It might just as easily be the name she'd been going by in St. Louis even if she'd never been Anthony's secretary. Loren stretched out an arm and pulled his extra pair of glasses from the nightstand drawer. Then he went to the bottom drawer of the bureau and hauled out the metropolitan St. Louis directory, which he opened to the R's. The Rhodes name filled most of a column but no one was listed who had the first name Kay and only one who used the initial K. He offered the book to Domjan, who handed it to Corky, who spread it on his abundant lap.

"This supposed to be a white gal?" Corky demanded.

Domjan looked blank. "She's white," Loren answered.

"Then this ain't her. This K. Rhodes lives in the 4000 block of Delmar. Midtown, slumtown, blacktown. The chick you want either doesn't live around here or she's unlisted."

Loren tossed the phone book on the bedspread and moved toward the outer door. Domjan caught up after a few steps, blocking his way. "Think you're fit to go out, sir?"

"I have to be," Loren said. "Someone I need to see."

"Anthony?"

Loren said nothing.

"Why?"

"To put him where I put his client," Loren said, and the next moment cursed himself for a lunatic.

"Sir, you can't even walk straight yet, and besides that would be illegal." With one hand on Loren's arm the sergeant beckoned to blubberlips Corky with the other and the cops exchanged nods. "I have a better idea, sir. Let's all three of us zip out to Ladue and see if Mr. Anthony got home tonight. If he did, Corky can maybe ask him a few questions."

Loren knew it was more than he had any business to expect, that they were cutting corners and bending over backward for him because Domjan and his FBI friends were telling them they should. "You're sure Val, that's the woman, you're sure she doesn't need me tonight?"

"Doctor says she'll be fine in the morning," Domjan assured him. "I'm not so sure about you and me, though, unless we get some sleep one of these nights. Ready?" They crossed the ruins of the living room and stopped at the door to the hallway.

"Try keeping me out of this," Loren said.

———————————

THEY LEFT ONE UNIFORM inside the suite for security and slipped down the fire stairs to the lobby. The clock above the registration desk read twelve minutes to ten. Corky scanned the quiet lobby and bobbed his head in what Loren took to be satisfaction. "Media's bugged out," he whispered. "Everyone rushing to get their tape on the ten o'clock news. Follow me." They took the side corridor and waited in the parking lot. When Corky waved his arm an unmarked sedan came charging up from nowhere with its headlights blinding them and screeched to a halt in the fire lane. Corky flung himself into the front seat, Loren and Domjan took the rear. "Ladue," Corky told the driver. "Rapido." The sedan squealed out onto First Street.

Loren sat back in his corner and watched the lights whirl by: auto beams, neat bright squares high in office towers, streetlamps. Domjan in his own corner stroked his chin stubble and stared at Loren curiously. Something about that look and the tautness of his posture told Loren that the sergeant in his own good time was going to say something Loren wouldn't like. The police car swung onto I-64.

"You know, sir," Domjan said then, "when Corky and I were talking with the night manager back there, we learned something I thought was a little odd. Mind explaining it for me?"

Loren tensed, made himself look Domjan in the eye. "If I can," he said casually.

"When you and the lady—Ms. Tremaine, right?—when the two of you registered yesterday, you used her name."

"That struck you as odd?" Loren asked. "What name did you want me to use, my own? The other side knows that."

"So." Domjan seemed to be smiling in the shadows of the backseat. "You thought you'd be less conspicuous if you went by Mr. Tremaine."

"Something like that."

"Any chance you might also have called yourself Judge Tremaine since you got into town?"

Loren said nothing and waited.

"Because when Corky and I were on the phone with Anthony's office manager, Corky happened to ask about Mr. Anthony's schedule today and she checked his appointment book and said he'd had lunch with a Judge Tremaine. Now wouldn't that be a funny coincidence, sir, if the guy you were after had lunch just today with a judge who had the same name you were using?"

No defense like a good offense, Loren decided. "It wasn't a coincidence," he said. "Anthony lunched with me today."

"And you made the lunch date calling yourself Judge Tremaine?"

170

Loren wondered if he was going to be arrested for imper-
sonating a member of the federal bench. For half a minute
he was on the brink of invoking his rights under the Fifth
Amendment.

"The reason I ask, sir," Domjan went on, "is that if you
did, it would tie in with something Ms. Tremaine said to
one of Corky's guys just before they put her in the ambulance. That is, something she said Bloch said to her."

Loren felt a colder fear than fear of the law bubbling up
in his chest. He bit down hard on his tongue to control
himself. The sedan whispered along the highway through
the pattern of lights.

"He came knocking on the door of your suite," Domjan
said, "and she thought it was you, that you'd lost your
entry card or something, so she made the mistake of opening and she saw him standing there looking her over like
she was meat on a hook, and then he said—no offense, sir,
I'm just quoting what she said he said—'The judge is a
good judge of cunt.' And then he went at her with the knife
and all hell came loose."

"Oh, no," Loren said. "Oh, no." He felt white-hot agony
in his belly and thought he was going to be sick. *Anthony
had seen through him, known he wasn't a judge.* Maybe
he'd been toying with Loren over lunch, trying to entice
him to the caves on his country estate. Or maybe he hadn't
become suspicious until after lunch. Either way it would
have taken him only a minute to check the roster of sitting
federal judges in any current volume of the Federal Supple-
ment that reported district court decisions and discover
that no Tremaine was among them. Then he could have
called each of the major hotels, asked if a Tremaine were
registered and, having found Loren at the Laclede Suites,
unleashed Jonathan Bloch on fresh meat. Val had almost
been killed and it was Loren's fault.

"I blame myself, sir," Domjan said. "I got you involved
in this mess. I didn't figure on you involving anyone else."

Loren almost screamed at him: *You were SUPPOSED to
figure it! You were supposed to use me as bait and keep me*

171

covered and you didn't even know I was in St. Louis till I walked in on you at the state hospital!

"You'll never know how relieved I felt when the doc said she's going to be all right," Domjan said. "I—well, I owe you a big one, sir."

Loren sat in the corner with his elbows on his knees and his chin nested in his hands and made an unearthly sound that was part weeping and part laughter.

———

THE SEDAN GLIDED through suburbs dotted with thick foliage, past PRIVATE ROAD signs and the entrances to country clubs. Light glowed discreetly from huge houses separated from the street by yards of manicured lawn. Corky in the front passenger seat spoke low into the radio mike. The driver kept making turns from one shadowed road to another and finally veered onto the grass beneath a stand of oaks. "All out," Corky croaked. They emptied quietly from the cruiser, crouched behind a hedge four feet tall. Loren smelled viburnum on the night breeze. Peering through a gap in the hedge, he caught his first glimpse of the house, a stately Tudor Revival structure with dull gold light beckoning from behind two or three windows of leaded glass on the ground floor and upstairs. Behind the house he made out the bulk of a four-car garage in the moonglow. A second car with headlights dark slithered onto the grass beside the road and two plainclothesmen stepped out. "Ladue cops," Corky whispered, and duckwalked over to touch base with them. Then the newcomers came to them and crouched in the hedge's shadow with Loren's party.

"Two patrol cars have passed by since we got the call from you," the older Ladue detective reported. "Quiet as the grave in there."

"Phone still off the hook?" Corky asked.

"Line's still busy."

"Let's rock 'n' roll," Domjan said. The six men came out from the hedge and walked in the cool May evening across the lawn to the columned front porch. Loren half expected a burst of gunfire from the windows but nothing happened. They stood three on each side of the front door. The gray-headed Ladue detective pushed his thumb against the bell. They heard no sound, not even a muffled echo. No footsteps. The detective rang again, kept his thumb on the bell. Nothing. "We'd better wait for a warrant," he said.

That was when Loren noticed the thin line of light at the edge of the doorframe. Without asking permission he leaned on it gently and felt it give under his weight. "It's not locked," he whispered.

"We've still got to wait for a warrant," the Ladue man insisted. "Goddamn it, this man's a respected attorney. He has constitutional rights and he sure as hell knows what they are."

"Either arrest me or get out of my way," Loren said softly, and pressed on the door handle and stepped inside, leaving the door wide open behind him while Domjan and Corky and the senior Ladue detective conferred in frantic hisses.

As soon as he was in the hall he heard the music. Piano music, Beethoven he thought, seeming to come from everywhere at once, its beauty filling the paneled corridor. Then he saw the intercom system, the speaker built into the wall between a Chippendale mirror and a cachepot exploding with spring flowers on a rosewood console. He made his way down the center of the hall as the music enveloped him. It wasn't recorded music. There were imperfections now and then, hesitations, wrong notes that would not be tolerated in a recorded performance. Somewhere in this house a piano was being played by a living person. *Upstairs?* His eyes traveled up the broad marble staircase at the left of the hall. *No. Search down here first.* He took the first door on the right.

A living room twenty feet square. Hardwood floor dotted with Oriental rugs. Stone fireplace, blue-white Chinese porcelain pieces on the white mantel. Camelback sofa covered in chintz, side chairs in clusters of two and three, lamp tables scattered about, a framed needlepoint coat of arms on the paneled wall. The room was empty but he still heard the music, sharp and clear as in the hall. He saw another intercom built into the paneling beside the fireplace.

An archway led into a formal dining room. Glistening mahogany table, twelve chairs, breakfront with inner lights striking gleams from the chinaware on display, huge chandelier dimly glowing. Another intercom box. More Beethoven. Loren returned through the living room to the hall.

Beyond the foot of the stairs the first door on the left was shut. He twisted the knob. Half-bath. Dark. He found and flicked the light switch and blinked at the rush of brightness. Pale-pink walls. Gold-plated fixtures. The surface and bowl of the china basin were painted in a rosebud pattern. The bowl was slightly damp and lying in it was a small ebony-handled kitchen knife. Loren saw then that some of the red-brown marks on the china were not flowers, and that the rack at the side of the basin where two hand towels should have been folded was empty.

He left the light on and the door open and went farther down the hall, followed by the loveliness of the music. The next door on the left was an inch ajar. He nudged it with his knee until the opening was wide enough to admit him, stepped over the raised threshold, groped for a light switch and found three together on a smooth square of wood. The room sprang alive. It was a home office and den but the parquet floor was littered with books flung down from the hand-rubbed cabinets that lined two walls and the tufted chesterfield was askew and a lamp table shattered and leather club chairs overturned and the phone that had stood on the walnut desk was lying off the hook six feet away and the brown leather swivel chair that should have been behind the desk was six feet beyond the phone, toppled over beside its owner's body.

Garrett Anthony lay on his stomach on the parquet with his left arm tucked under him and his right arm flung out as if he were reaching for something beyond his grasp. He still wore the faultlessly tailored suit he had worn at lunch. Loren went down on one knee and felt for the carotid artery. The chill of flesh turning cold greeted his fingertips. A trail of dried brown-red ran from beneath the body and past the outflung right arm to the baseboard. Anthony's right forefinger was stained the same color.

The haunting melody of the Moonlight Sonata flowed from nowhere through wall speakers into the room where the body lay and made Loren shiver as he read the seven letters written in the dead man's heart's blood on the parquet. The last word. The answer Garrett Anthony had hunted for so much of his life, the secret of death.

H I D E O U S

Loren lurched to his feet and ran through the chaos of the room and through the music's tingling beauty and down the long hall to the open front door where moths fluttered in the light and five detectives stood shuffling their feet.

"It's legal for you to come in now," he said.

Twelve

THE CITY AND LADUE MEN loped toward the den but Loren and Domjan detoured and took the marble stairs two at a bound. They started at the near end of the second-floor hall and yanked open one closed door after the other. The first room they saw was a neat narrow cell with a velvet portrait of Martin Luther King on a wall and a row of white uniforms in the closet. "Nurse," Domjan grunted. "Why isn't she on duty?"

The next three doors opened on a bright airy bathroom, a cedar closet and a linen closet. Here in the upstairs hall the music was faint but seemed to grow louder as they went along the corridor. The fifth door showed a bedroom five times the size of the nurse's, elegantly furnished in dark woods. Four volumes of Chesterton and a paperback copy of Sophocles' *Antigone* teetered on the edge of the table beside the fourposter bed. "Anthony's," Loren said. When they opened the sixth door they saw a flight of carpeted stairs leading up. The music was louder still at this end of the hall. They opened the last remaining door and the Moonlight Sonata poured out.

It was a two-room suite as large as the living room downstairs, with a chaise and chairs patterned in chintz. Plant stands around the room were alive with ferns and spring flowers. A Steinway baby grand stood on a Tabriz carpet. A woman in a wheelchair at the keyboard coaxed magic from the ivory with twisted ancient fingers. She didn't turn or move as they entered but kept playing without sheet music before her. *She must know the Sonata by heart,* Loren thought. He wondered if she could hear the

176

melody. As Domjan took a step forward he held the sergeant where he was with an extended hand. "It's almost over," he whispered. They huddled in the doorway like religious believers late for a ceremony. Behind the Sonata's liquid beauty Loren heard harsh sounds from outside and downstairs, vehicles braking, footsteps pounding. Domjan tiptoed out into the corridor while Loren sidled past an archway that gave him a view of the old woman's bedroom. Through a window looking down on the front yard he saw the herd of police cars with roofbar lights throwing red and white sparks into the night. An EMS van with a stripe around its middle screeched to a stop at curbside and disgorged two men in paramedics' whites who dashed across the lawn.

Domjan slithered into the room again and over to Loren's side. "Another bedroom upstairs," he reported. "A woman's. Looks like no one's used it lately. Didn't you say Anthony's sister lived here?"

Loren nodded.

"And she's gone too," the sergeant said. "I just hope to God Bloch didn't leave her and the nurse cut up out back somewhere." He kept his voice pitched low as if he were in a church. "But you know," he went on, "the more I look at this, the crazier it gets. If Bloch and Anthony had a fight downstairs and Bloch killed him, why would he clean up in the half-bath and then go right downtown and do his level best to carry out his dead boss's orders and kill you?"

"He may have had his own motive to get rid of me," Loren whispered back. "Suppose Anthony described Judge Tremaine to him and he recognized the description? Knew I was the same man he'd run into on the ferry and decided to take me out for his own safety? His brother's safety too, if you assume Clifford's seen him in the last few days and described the man Joyce picked up before he killed her."

"Weak," Domjan said. "What if . . . ?" The Sonata's final chords died away and Loren gestured the two of them forward. The sergeant dropped to one knee beside the wheelchair and touched the old lady's wrist. "Mrs. Anthony?" he said softly. Loren motioned to the dark plastic object fixed to her ear like a hardened wad of gum. "Mrs. Anthony!" Domjan thundered.

"I am Rosemary Anthony." Her voice was cracked and off-key and her face as lined and wrinkled as a mummy's. She touched a control and her wheelchair swiveled around so that her rheumy eyes were looking into theirs. Two strange men had intruded on her space in the dead of night but she showed no fear. Perhaps after ninety years or more on earth there was nothing left for her to be afraid of.

"Are you Garrett Anthony's mother?" Domjan asked.

"Garrett is my boy," she croaked. "Do you know my boy?"

Domjan cleared his throat. "I—had lunch with him just today," Loren offered.

"I'm sorry the caterer was so late," she said. "There are so many dead fish in the road and the soup is never hot enough. Were the ladyfingers to your liking? We've always grown our own."

Loren knew then that she lived in a world she shared with no one else. "They were delicious," he said. "Mrs. Anthony, do you know where the nurse is?" He spoke slowly, taking care to enunciate each word.

The old sunken eyes looked blank and forlorn. She said nothing and Loren sensed she had no idea what he was talking about but tried again. "Do you know where your daughter is?"

"I've never had a daughter," she replied. "Only my boy Garrett. Do you know my boy?"

"Garrett has a sister," Loren said. "She lives here. She has a room upstairs."

Now there was a kind of terror in her pale milk-blue eyes. "I . . . I—don't think I've ever had a daughter," she said. "Please, what is her name?"

Loren's thoughts fled back. Val, Gael, the rooftop restaurant revolving on its axis through the downtown skyline. A little more than twenty-four hours ago. If Gael had mentioned the sister's name, it hadn't registered. He pressed his lips together in a fury of concentration.

"Perhaps my boy Garrett would know," the woman broke into his trance. "Do you know my boy?"

"I don't—I don't think he can tell us," Loren said.

The old lady squinched her eyes shut in anguish and her hairy wrinkled chin began to tremble. "Oh, if only my granddaughter had stayed with us," she said. "She would know if I ever had a daughter, yes, I'm sure she would remember. She has a marvelous memory."

"Your granddaughter?" Loren echoed. "You had a granddaughter here? Living with you?"

"Why, of course I did." Her whole face was bobbing up and down and a greenish liquid ran out of the corner of one eye and along her cheek. "My boy Garrett's child. A lovely lovely child. She would sit and listen to Beethoven for hours." She smiled. A baby-pink tongue snaked out from her ruined mouth and licked at the green ooze on her cheek. "I know Beethoven's complete works for solo piano by heart," she proclaimed. "He was my music teacher when I was a girl. I know Bach's piano works too, and I believe some of Mozart."

Garrett's child? How could a child be living here? There was no sign of a child's presence in the house.

"Would you like to see her picture?" Mrs. Anthony invited.

Loren was too stunned to reply. "Yes, ma'am," Domjan answered for him. "We'd like that very much. If you'd just tell us where we can look . . ."

"Why, where does anyone keep pictures?" Her cracked meek voice was filled with wonderment at how much her visitors didn't know. "In an album!"

Loren's eyes darted around the room, locked on the tall prim piece of furniture between the front windows. He stepped over to the mahogany secretary desk and tugged at the dainty brass knob that lowered the droplid, revealing a nest of empty pigeonholes and, centered precisely on the blotter, a photograph album covered in green leather with gold trim and ROSEMARY ANTHONY lettered in gold at the bottom right edge. He bent over the desk surface and turned pages. The album bulged with photographs. Those

179

at the front were attached to the pages by curled and browning corners. The clothing and hairstyles of the men and women in the album moved closer to the present as he moved to the back pages. Once he realized that Mrs. Anthony or one of the family had arranged these pictures chronologically he turned to the end of the album. The last dozen or so pages were still unused. The face of Garrett Anthony in a posed studio portrait gazed up at him from the final page with any photo at all. On the page opposite that there were several small color shots of Anthony and his mother in this room by the piano, the lawyer's arm lightly around the ancient woman's shoulder. Loren turned back to the previous page.

For a moment his heart and breathing stopped.

There she was. Another professionally posed portrait, full-face. Smiling gravely at him.

Perhaps a few years younger but otherwise almost exactly as he had seen her during those infinitesimal seconds before Bloch and his goons had seized her in the St. George ferry terminal.

Kim.

He hid himself away in the bare quiet room on the third floor. Her room. He roamed through the space where she had lived, cool impersonal space now, the closet and dresser drawers barren, the attached bathroom austere, not so much as a box of bath powder on the shelves. Just a barely perceptible scent that had told Domjan the room had been a woman's. Anthony must have disposed of whatever she hadn't taken with her when she went on the run but he'd forgotten the photographs in the album and the traces in his mother's wandering memory. Loren sat on the bedspread with the album on his knees and stared in the dim radiance of the night-table lamp at the handful of pictures of Kim, studied them intensely as if she were somehow alive in those images, smiling at him, speaking to him.

180

Anthony's daughter. Put the shots of the two side by side and the resemblance leapt out. No wonder he'd had the strange sensation on meeting Anthony that he'd seen the man before! So at long last Kim had found at least one of the biological parents she'd been longing to find as far back as a quarter century ago. The age difference between her and Anthony would be eighteen or twenty years at most. Had she been the product of some long-forgotten encounter from Anthony's youth, decades before abortions were legal? How had she tracked her father down? How had she come to learn so much about his dirty business that she had to go into hiding and he had to send his pet killer after her? Loren could formulate only the questions, no answers. From the hair and clothing styles in the album pictures he knew she'd been living here at least ten years. Why had she been content to pass as his sister?

Before the police let him come up here he had repeated what Gael had told him about Anthony's obsession with wresting the secret from death. "He got it right," Corky had said, frowning down at the seven letters written in the lawyer's blood. Ever since Loren had trudged up the stairs to this room, the whirlwind of investigation downstairs and outside meant nothing to him. Time meant nothing. Sounds drifted up to him but he didn't take them in. Once he went to the dormer window overlooking the backyard and saw the teams of men prowling the woodland behind the house, flash beams painting wild patches of light that flitted across tree trunks and bushes. Portable floodlights burned on the rear gardens. Evidence vehicles and TV station vans sprawled at chaotic angles around the paved area by the garage building. It was like watching a movie, a documentary that bored him. He lay on her bed and studied the pictures.

Every so often Domjan would bound up the stairs with news, or a Benzedrine tablet, or just to stay in touch. There was something of the friendly cocker spaniel about the unorthodox young sergeant that was bound, Loren thought, to get in the way of his lofty career goals. Once he brought up a sterling silver tray that held four gigantic doughnuts on a paper plate and two huge styrofoam cups of coffee. Loren flashed back to the doughnuts and coffee in the bleak room in the bowels of the St. George terminal where he and Domjan had first met. "Dinner, sir," the cop smiled, setting the tray on the night table. "Better late than never, I always say. Corky knows this little guy runs a doughnut shop over in Maplewood and got him out of the sack to sort of cater for us. There are seventeen people on the case at last count, sir. Looks like we'll be here all night."

Loren tried a doughnut. It might have been a leftover from the Staten Island serving, with all the flavor of a moistened hunk of wrapping paper. He chewed mechanically and forced the bite down with atrocious coffee. "What time is it?" He'd forgotten that he was wearing a watch.

"About one-thirty, sir," Domjan said without looking. He broke a doughnut in half and bit into the gob of jelly at its core. "Like a briefing?"

"They haven't found her body?" Loren motioned toward the dormer window.

"No sign of any body or any burial yet but they can't do a really thorough search till daylight."

Let her be alive, Loren prayed again. *Let her be alive.*

"The nurse is back." Domjan wiped his fingers on a paper napkin, then reached into his jacket pocket for a notebook while he licked dry jelly from around his lips. "Came in around midnight. She says Anthony came home a little after five, which was early for him, and told her to take the evening off after she'd fed his mom her dinner. He said he'd be home all evening and would watch out for her, put her to bed and all that. Sounds to me like he was expecting a visitor and didn't want company."

"Bloch," Loren said. "One or both of them."

"No, sir. I'll get to that." Domjan's eyes dropped to the notebook. "The nurse also tells us that her evening off was supposed to be yesterday but Anthony took a phone call, oh, somewhere around seven or seven-thirty, and right after that he told her something had come up and he had to go out for the night so she'd have to stay and take care of his mother."

"That must have been Bloch calling," Loren said. "To tell him he'd just killed Mrs. Schrader and needed to be picked up and taken to a hideout."

"Concur," Domjan said. "By the way, this nurse has only been here two weeks. She says Anthony told her his sister had lived here and cared for their mother till recently but had gotten sick and had to move to a drier climate."

"She never saw Kim?"

"Never laid eyes on her. Well, so much for the nurse. She's put Mrs. Anthony to bed and is spending the night with her. Poor old lady has no idea her son's dead. Keeps talking about the fish in the road and flowers in the sky. Christ, I hope I die before I'm like that." He gulped coffee as if it were the elixir of life.

"Why did you say Anthony's visitor wasn't one of the Blochs?" Loren demanded. "Were someone else's prints on the knife?"

"Just smears. Nothing usable. No, sir, it's other evidence that takes the Blochs out of this one. First of all there's the timing." He consulted the notebook again. "Neighbor across the street says he noticed a strange car pull into the driveway a little after eight. He has no idea what make or model. The next time he looked was maybe an hour later and the car was gone by then. If that was the killer it sure couldn't have been Jonathan Bloch 'cause he was downtown in your suite by eight, duking it out with Ms. Tremaine."

"It could have been Clifford Bloch," Loren argued. "Or—well, maybe the eight o'clock visitor wasn't the killer at all but just someone who had an appointment with Anthony and found him dead and didn't want to get involved or call the police."

"Theoretically," Domjan conceded, "it could have been. But then there's the blood. You see, sir, whoever had the fight with Anthony over the knife was cut himself. Nothing too serious but bad enough so he got careless when he left the house. Didn't lock the front door properly. We think he borrowed the face towels from the half-bath as a sort of improvised bandage. The bloodstains in the basin aren't Anthony's type, and when we called the hospital where they took Jonathan Bloch we found they're not his type either."

"They could still be his brother's," Loren argued. "Siblings don't have to have the same blood type."

"Well, whoever he is, sir, with the DNA tests we can prove it to a mathematical certainty once we catch the guy."

Keep thinking it's a man, Loren screamed silently at him. *For God's sake keep thinking a man did it! Don't see what I see!* The picture in his mind made his stomach churn. *Kim did it. His daughter.* She was alive, she'd escaped from Bloch somehow and come back to St. Louis to confront her father. She had stabbed him to death and, bleeding from her own wounds, had fled into the night to die. Maybe if Loren spoke out now, the police would find her in time, save her life but lock her up, take her away from him again. On the other hand, if the picture in his mind was an illusion, then the thread of hope that she'd still been alive and well a few hours ago dissolved into nothing. He lay like a dead man on the bed Kim had slept in while the horns of nightmare gored him.

And suddenly in the pit of darkness everything came together in his mind. There was an implosion of understanding and he knew. His eyes focused inward. His thoughts raced, made connections, soared. He was somewhere else. In another world.

He felt himself being shaken and rocked on the bed as if by a lover's body and willed himself back to the real world where Domjan was bending over him with his hands locked on Loren's shoulders. "Sir? Professor Mensing? You all right, sir?"

"Oh." Loren smiled at him inanely. "It's you. Yes, I'm okay." He was desperate for food and sleep and even more desperate for Kim but he felt okay. No, not just okay: wonderful, magnificent, full of power and joy. He had seen the truth and it fit. He could never explain to Domjan how he felt or what he knew.

When the sergeant wished him good night and left the room, Loren collapsed. He fell back on the flowered bedspread and was asleep in an instant. Grayish light was seeping through the windows when he felt gentle pressure on his shoulder and jerked awake and saw Domjan looming over him again. "Time, sir," he announced. "You sure you want to come with us on this?"

"I have to," Loren said. "Don't you remember what Anthony had on the little table next to his bed?" Domjan was silent. *"Antigone,"* Loren reminded him. "And do you remember what kind of death Antigone was sentenced to?" He didn't give the sergeant time to comb through memories of college literature courses. "She was condemned to be walled up in a cave," he said, "with just enough food and water so she wouldn't starve to death right away. Wait a minute, I need to call the hospital before we go." He groped for the princess phone on the nightstand. Princess: his pet name for Kim, a quarter century ago.

"No need, sir," Domjan said. "I called just now from downstairs. She's had a restful night. They'll do a few more tests on her and let her go sometime this afternoon."

"I have to see her," Loren said. "God, how can I be in two places at the same time?"

"May I make a suggestion, sir? The other lady? The former student of yours that you and Ms. Tremaine had dinner with?"

Loren was so groggy that at first he couldn't recall her name. "Gael?" he asked then.

"From the way you talked about her, sir, I had the impression you and she were, well, old friends. Couldn't you call her now and ask her to see Ms. Tremaine in the hospital and tell her where you've gone and why?"

Loren felt a weight lifted from him, knew the bliss of a convict released from solitary confinement. "Sergeant," he asked, "if Ms. Tremaine and I ever decide to live together, would you consider quitting the force and coming to work for us? The way you solve these little domestic problems reminds me of Jeeves."

"Jeeves the butler, sir?" Domjan flushed in the gray half-light. "Those old movies with what's-his-name, the fish and chips guy? Arthur Treacher? That's a great compliment, sir, but I can't leave the PD till I make commissioner. Put in your call and let's move."

When Loren continued to sit motionless, the sergeant rummaged in the nightstand drawer for a phone directory and set it down beside the pillow. A minute later Loren was waking Gael from a sound sleep.

THE SIRENS' KEENING died away as the three police cruisers skidded to halts on the tarmac behind the state barracks. Tight-faced hollow-eyed men poured from the cars, crowded into the waiting pair of helicopters, strapped themselves into their seats. Loren and Domjan were in the first chopper to lift off. The blades spun and the motor roared, the radio beside the uniformed pilot squawked as the flying bubble veered northeast. Loren had never been in a helicopter before. He watched enchanted as midget autos and toy villages and emerald pastures grazed by microscopic cows and horses flowed beneath them. It was seven-twenty by his watch when the machines touched down in a flat green field. "Keep your head down, sir, or you'll lose it!" Domjan yelled over the din. They ducked through the hatchway and trotted toward one of the three state patrol cars fifty yards to the side. "Welcome to Mark Twain country," Domjan said as they flung themselves into the backseat. "Next stop Hannibal."

They bobbled and jounced in their seats as the convoy rocketed over two-lane roads mined with potholes. Beyond the trees and fields rose the Mississippi bluffs with the river meandering placid and brown below. The cars squealed onto a dirt road, bounced and writhed so furiously Loren felt his insides coming loose. A graveled path made an X with the dirt track, led to a long low ranch-style house a hundred yards from the intersection, its front yard jammed with more police cars. Loren's convoy kept to the poorer road. When he was on the verge of begging the driver to slow down to a crawl, the foliage that masked the view fell away and he saw their destination, the craggy face of the bluff. Highway Patrol cars, a pickup truck, a paramedic van, a generator truck and a catering bus were parked at grotesque angles wherever they could squeeze in. Loren and Domjan jogged across the reddish dirt with the rest of the newly arrived searchers, past knots of troopers in camouflage gear drinking coffee out of steel cups. Four burly teenagers unloaded portapotties from a trailer truck. It was like a chaotic parody of a military bivouac.

Loren followed Domjan to the cool dark cave mouth. The thick wooden door that had kept the cavern sealed lay smashed to kindling at one side, an assortment of axes nearby. A paunchy trooper sat in a canvas chair at the entranceway with a heap of laundered coveralls at his feet. "Suit up, gentlemen," he ordered in a lazy drawl. "Lights and commo're inside. Watch the spiders."

Wrapped in Day-Glo orange, Loren stepped into the cave in Domjan's wake. Inside the rock vestibule a pimpled young patrolman sat cross-legged on the hard earth floor in the center of a sprawl of equipment. He lit a Coleman lantern, handed it up to Domjan, tossed Loren a walkie-talkie and a flashlight. With Domjan in the lead they moved along the clammy passage, obscene shadows oozing like lava over the limestone walls. A baby bat flew at them in terror, brushing Loren's cheek. The passage narrowed so that he could barely sidle through. Cold stone caressed his face. When he thought of the spiders that might be nesting on those walls he almost fell over in fright but there was no place for him to fall. The next instant his body was wrapped in blissful open space and he could move his arms and breathe. "Jesus," Domjan whispered in awe, the Coleman lantern raised above his head. "Have you ever seen anything like it in your life?"

The passage had opened onto a room as vast as a cathedral, so high Loren saw no ceiling. Lanterns in the hands of scattered search teams spilled zones of light through the chamber, on stalactites and stalagmites shaped like thrones and pillars, their pinkish-red onyx shades glowing softly. Loren heard a liquid rush, looked to the left and gasped. That end of the cathedral room was a waterfall, dropping from the blackness overhead into a pool fifty feet below the floor that was so clear and limpid he could see creamy white onyx formations like fleece lying in its depths.

"And to think we try to build churches," Domjan said.

"Hey! You two!" A tall lean black man in peach coveralls double-timed toward them from the center of the room with flashlight raised. A spade-bearded beanpole in an old sweatshirt and jeans trotted like a footman at the edge of his companion's zone of light. The black man wore a major's insignia on his cap. "James Duke," he introduced himself. Domjan dug beneath his coveralls for the badge and shield in his trousers pocket. "You take responsibility for this civilian?" The major's deep voice echoed mournfully through the chamber.

"Yessir," Domjan said.

"Good." Duke flashed bright teeth in a grin. "These caves have no end. I need every man I can get." He explained the procedure as if he had every detail memorized, while the beanpole's jaws worked at what Loren was sure was a chaw of tobacco. "This is our staging area," Duke finished. "No one in living memory has been beyond this room until today, except whoever the late Mr. Anthony brought here. If you get lost you may never get found. Stay together. Report back by walkie-talkie at ten-minute intervals." He tossed Domjan a thick coil of clothesline, pointed to a narrow crevice in the rock wall. "That one is yours. Good luck."

Loren and Domjan crossed a gurgling stream on a fallen stalactite. At the crevice opening the sergeant knotted one end of the clothesline around an onyx pillar and the other around his waist. "Remember the Greek myth about Theseus and the minotaur in the labyrinth, sir?" he asked.

"I didn't know they'd made that into a movie, too," Loren said.

"Read it in the seminary," Domjan told him.

The passage wound and dropped, opened into chamber after chamber so full of dazzling colors and shapes of rock that Loren came close to forgetting why he was here. Water trickled unseen between layers of limestone, eating through the bluffs as it had since the morning of the planet. Loren forgot time, hunger, fatigue, but not even the magnificence of the world below the earth drove from his mind that Kim or what was left of her might be in the next cave chamber bleached by his light. He had to keep looking and he was terrified that he would be the one to find her. What did a woman starved to death look like? Images of films from Bergen-Belsen and Sobibor burned into his mind's eye. But even if she had been left here to die, even if the surest and safest way to kill her was to let her starve in these caves like Antigone and never be found, why must she be dead? Less than two weeks had gone by since she'd been seized on Staten Island. Those gunmen who'd been imprisoned by the British in northern Ireland and had starved themselves to death one by one on orders from the IRA—hadn't they survived more than a month? But they had carried out their self-imposed fast in a clean modern prison, sustained by fruit juice and water, not in a dungeon like this. He remembered that Antigone in the Greek play had not starved but hanged herself in despair. He began to call her name into the darkness at the mouth of each chamber they entered. "Kim Hale! Kim! Kim!" He shouted her name until his throat ached, and Domjan's voice joined with his, echoing in and out through the passages like a chant for the dead.

They found nothing.

When they reached the end of their rope they began to make their way back to the cathedral, taking it slow. Loren kept the flashlight beam moving in a constant circuit, to the left, up along the ceiling, to the right, along the path at their feet. At the mouth of every chamber he bent forward and aimed the light as far in as he could, bathing a wall, the ceiling, another wall and pools of water in the other-worldly brilliance.

In a shallow pool just inside the mouth of the seventh chamber on their return, he found it. The rays from the flashlight caught a face in the bottom of the pool. Gray, eyes bulging hideously. Loren cried out, stumbled forward, made himself train the beam full on the dead face. His hand shook in the cavern chill. Domjan held him steady from behind, one arm around Loren's waist, the other supporting his hand.

"Don't lose it, sir," he said. "It's not her. Look. That's a man down there."

Loren almost fell on his knees in thanksgiving. Domjan's arm kept him from slipping to the cold stone floor. "Look closely at the face, sir," the sergeant told him. "Haven't you see him before?"

The strong brutal jawline . . . Yes, yes, he'd seen it for a split second last Tuesday evening when Joyce Clarke in a sedan with him at the wheel had accosted Loren on upper Park Avenue. He'd called himself Morgan then but his real name was Clifford Bloch and less than an hour later he had used that sedan as a weapon to smash the woman to death. "It's him," Loren agreed. There was no need to say more.

Domjan took the walkie-talkie from Loren and spoke low into the mouthpiece. They marked the cavern entrance by coiling Domjan's end of the clothesline around the nearest stalagmite and followed the rope back along the ghostly passage to the cathedral chamber where Major Duke was waiting with four troopers. "Fine work, gentlemen!" he congratulated them. "Now you two wait for us outside."

Loren and Domjan crawled through the crevice that led to the vestibule and out into the warm sweet sunlight and the smells of the living earth. The brightness blinded Loren for a minute. He couldn't read the numerals on his wristwatch. The first thing he noticed when his sight came back was the catering bus and a straggling line of troopers on break, munching sweet rolls and sandwiches. Domjan left him stretched out in the shade of an elm and ambled over to buy snacks and soda for both of them. After a while Duke's slim commanding figure strode from the cave entrance. The major came over to them, dropped to the grass and sat cross-legged like a tribal chief at a pow-wow. "Get you a diet cola, sir?" Domjan offered politely.

"Maybe later," Duke said. "It's good to be back in the world, gentlemen!" He pressed a readout button on his wrist. "In case you were wondering, the time is 2:19 P.M. Have you heard the other news? No, of course not, how could you have heard? Team Seven found a lovely chamber half an hour ago, a complete office under the earth if you will. Field desk, stack chairs, portable generator for light . . . Amazing setup. Have you ever been to London, Professor?" Loren nodded that he had. "Ever seen the underground room Churchill used as his command center during the blitz?" Loren nodded that he had. "It seems Mr. Anthony saw it. There are seven reinforced steel cabinets lined up very neatly along one wall and I have sent for a locksmith to break the locks and a semi to bring everything out. Though how we are to get them through the paltry little crevice that leads into it is more than I can see at the moment. My informant Mr. Yoacum—that's truly his name, the fugitive from a hillbilly comedy you saw with me in the cathedral—Mr. Yoacum has spent seventy years in these hills and he swears there are other entrances into the caves somewhere along the bluffs. I suppose," he sighed, "I shall have to bribe him to find one. It was Yoacum by the way who found the bones."

Bones. The word struck Loren like a kick in the belly. He shook as if at an electric shock and fell back against the elm's trunk.

"Oh, no, no, no!" Duke slid across the grass to him on the seat of his fatigue trousers, put an arm around Loren's shoulders. "I'm so sorry, Professor, that was unconscionably stupid of me. These bones could not be Miss Hale's. They have been down there for generations. A pathologist will have to examine them but I have no doubt they are all that remains of some slave or Indian no one gave a damn

191

about who got lost in the caves when Mark Twain was a boy."

Loren trembled in the major's embrace. "Thank you," he kept mumbling. "Thank you, thank you."

Duke released him, his cocoa eyes boring into Loren's like awls. "I deserve no thanks," he said coldly. "Miss Hale or her body may be beneath us somewhere. If she is, do you know when she'll be found? A century and a half from now, the way Mr. Yoacum found those other bones today."

Loren jerked away from the major as if he'd been struck in the face.

"Professor Mensing," Duke said, "there are over five thousand known caves in the state of Missouri, and two hundred or more are discovered every year. Those caves are like the surface of Mars. It would take untold time and personnel to search this property exhaustively. This is a low-tax state and my resources are limited. I cannot and will not throw them down a sinkhole. Once those files are removed, we are through here."

Domjan on the grass between them raised his knees and wrapped his arms around them. "Look at it this way, sir. We know she was alive and somewhere in the 212 area code when she called you a week ago Monday morning. Maybe Jonathan Bloch forced her to make that call or maybe she got away from him after the ferry and he caught her again later. Either way, if he and his goons had her and wanted to kill her, what would they do? Bring her alive all the way back here and stick her in the caves? Hell, no! That's a thousand-mile trip. She could make another break anytime. Kill her in New York and bring her body back here? Of course not! They'd kill her in New York and dump her in New York. Sir, the odds she's underneath us alive or dead are . . ."

"Microscopically small," Major Duke finished.

Loren felt the cool earth beneath him and tried to weigh their arguments objectively and couldn't.

"Pity we can't question Mr. Bloch on the subject," Duke said.

Loren looked down at his hands that had crushed and pounded Bloch's head against the fire-stairs wall as vacantly as if they were alien creatures he had never seen before. The two policemen silently edged away and left him alone in the elm's shadow.

Nothing. All for nothing. He knew more about Kim now than he'd ever known before and he still understood so little and still had no idea if she was alive or dead and his rage last night had swept away the only person who might have told him.

No. Not the only person. Not necessarily anyway.

He sat under the elm and worked in silent fury to impose some order on what he knew. He was alone with his thoughts. Time ceased to pass. Other people didn't exist. He noticed a box lunch lying untouched beside him on the grass and vaguely recalled that Domjan or Duke or someone had tossed it down to him but for all it meant to him it might as well have dropped from the sky. After a while he got to his feet, stretched, brushed the dirt from his coveralls and trudged to the edge of the clearing where Domjan and Duke were watching the paunchy trooper use hand signals to help the driver of the semi maneuver through the trees. He took the sergeant aside and whispered in his ear. When the trailer had squeezed through the gap between a pair of gnarled oaks, Domjan approached the major and conferred in undertones. Duke nodded as if giving permission, strode to his parked command cruiser, reached through the open window for his radio mike. Domjan went back to where Loren was standing.

"He doesn't mind if I tell you, sir. They took Cliff Bloch's body out more than an hour ago, and the forensic pathologist in Hannibal phoned us a preliminary report just now. Cause of death was either drowning or arsenic poisoning depending on how you look at it. He was left in the caves with just a book of matches and a tuna salad sandwich. We found the matchbook cover in his pocket, pathologist found the grub in his innards."

"*Antigone,*" Loren said. "Remember on Anthony's nightstand?"

"The king in the play didn't poison the food he left with Antigone in the cave. Anthony did."

Loren was silent.

"I can understand why he was mad as hell," the sergeant went on. "Killing Joyce Clarke but cutting himself off from grabbing the scrapbooks from her apartment after he did it—Cliff screwed up badly."

"Or he was just unlucky," Loren suggested. "If I hadn't seen her keys in the street and used them to get into her place, he could have ditched the car, come back and broken in."

"I doubt Anthony was in the mood to hear Cliff's side of it," Domjan said. "Can you imagine the poor bastard's last couple of days, sir? Alone in those caves, running out of matches, starving by the hour, not knowing if that sandwich was okay to eat and left so he'd suffer a while longer or if it was poisoned. And finally he can't hold out any longer, he bolts down the sandwich, and then he gets to feeling those awful pains in his gut . . . Arsenic's a miserable way to die, sir. I'm not surprised he drowned himself instead."

"He deserved every bit of that pain and more," Loren said. "I won't pretend I feel sorry for him."

"Me neither." Domjan scuffed at a patch of dandelions with the toe of his shoe. "Ahhh—the pathologist says Cliff's been dead at least thirty-six hours, sir. You see what that means?"

"It means he couldn't have been in Ladue killing Anthony at eight last night," Loren said. "Which we knew already."

"And that in turn means we've gotta look elsewhere for the killer," the sergeant pointed out.

Not Kim! Loren willed him to keep his thoughts far from that direction. *For God's sake not Kim!* "Grimsby." He pronounced the name with a legal scholar's detachment. "We know Anthony was systematically getting rid of anyone who knew too much about his operation so it makes sense to suppose one of them saw what he was doing and got him first. The only one left who seems to fill the bill is Grimsby."

"Smart thinking, sir. We thought of it too. You notice Corky's not out here anymore?" Loren scanned the clearing but saw no sign of the fat plainclothesman and realized now that he hadn't seen the man since their group had boarded the two choppers behind the state police barracks. "He went into Hannibal a few hours ago to start up some action on that front. Called in to us awhile back. Seems Mr. Grimsby left St. Louis two and a half weeks ago for a vacation on his ranch. You have any idea where that is?"

"Sergeant, I've never set eyes on him," Loren replied impatiently. "How could I know where his ranch is?"

"On Kauai," Domjan told him. "The priciest of the Hawaiian islands. Five thousand miles from Ladue, give or take a few hundred. I don't know if he went out there on a genuine vacation or if he saw what Anthony was up to and wanted to get out of the line of fire but he's on Kauai now and that's as good a perfect alibi as I've ever seen outside of an old British detective novel."

"How do you know he's out there?"

"Local FBI agents rousted him for us. He was still asleep when they pounded on his door—you know, Hawaii's five hours earlier than Central Daylight Time—and the native couple that take care of the ranch swear he came out there two weeks ago yesterday and has been there ever since. Unless he has a private rocketship on his lanai or something, he's out of it as sure as the Bloch brothers."

Loren absorbed the news in silence and debated whether he should try making a case against the black nurse or Anthony's ancient mother. *Forget it,* he decided. *He's no fool. If I overdo it I make things worse.*

"Sergeant," he asked, "is Duke going to let you and the feds go through those file cabinets he found in the caves?"

"He doesn't have a choice, sir, but he's cooperating, yes."

"Then you and your team plan to stay around Hannibal a while."

195

"As long as it takes. Thank heaven I had my last exam at Fordham before this all came down!"

"I want to go back to St. Louis," Loren said. "Now if possible. I can't do anything more here and Val, Ms. Tremaine, should be getting out of the hospital soon. I have to be there for her."

"I understand, sir. Let me talk to Major Duke. You need your sleep tonight but I'll call you at the Laclede Suites at, say, eight sharp in the morning and give you an update."

"I'd appreciate that," Loren said.

FORTY MINUTES LATER he was belted into his seat in another Highway Patrol copter and whirring southeast toward St. Louis. As an unmarked sedan from the Headquarters barracks drove him into the city against the westbound late-afternoon traffic stream, he saw nothing and heard nothing and felt nothing. He stumbled out of the sedan under the Laclede Suites marquee, forgot to thank the trooper who'd driven him, and stalked through the lobby like a zombie. His mind was dead, his emotions were numb and he stank. He took an elevator to seven, found his rooms, used his entry card. The living room was all but bare, the ruined furniture taken out but not yet replaced. He couldn't have cared less. He flung his suit and shirt and underwear on the carpet and groped his way into the bathroom and shaved and stepped into the shower and let himself be engulfed in steaming water. The roar drowned out every other sound in the world. He soaped himself and rinsed and shampooed his hair and rinsed and swayed with fatigue and for a few moments he was asleep on his feet with the blast of scalding water in his ears. He dreamed he heard the shower curtain flutter. He dreamed soft hands were caressing him from behind and lips were brushing his neck and shoulders and he jerked awake and felt smooth naked flesh against his and knew it was no dream and turned within her embrace and there she was. They clung together under the hard spray and kissed and fondled and explored each other with the magic of their first time so many years and horrors ago. They said nothing. Neither could have heard the other over the drumming of the water and words were not what they needed. Before they fell intertwined among the bedsheets they did have one breathless conversation.

"You're sure you're okay?"

"Never felt better," she assured him.

"Gael saw you in the hospital?"

"She told me where you were and drove me here just now when they let me go. We came up in the elevator together and were going to grab a bite to eat and gossip some more about you but I saw your filthy clothes on the rug in there and heard the shower and I asked if she minded if we put off the girl talk till later."

"What did she say?"

"She just gave that giggly screech of hers and promised not to call us before eight." She brought his mouth against her breasts. "Darling, what are you doing?"

Loren wriggled free of her just long enough to take the bedside phone off the hook. "Making sure her alarm clock isn't fast," he said, and held her close.

HE SLIPPED OUT of her arms and the bed long before seven, found his robe and tiptoed to the east windows and watched the rising sun touch the river with fire. She came up behind him in naked silence and when he felt her he drew her against him. "Feel better now?" she asked.

"I'd take you back to bed and show you how much better I feel if my stomach wasn't growling so loud." He laughed. "I honestly can't remember if I ate at all yesterday."

"I did but hospital meals don't count," she said. "Let's pamper ourselves this morning."

They ordered from room service and moved the nightstands at either side of the bed until they were back to back at just the right distance from the pair of wingback armchairs to form an impromptu dining table. Breakfast was orange juice, a banana and strawberry compote, a huge basket of assorted muffins and croissants, and a pot of cinnamon-flavored coffee. They were on their third cups when Val brought up a serious subject.

"You never asked me how my day went before that Bloch slug almost killed me," she reminded him.

"Okay, I'll bite," he said, doing just that to the last cranberry muffin. "How did your day go before he almost killed you?"

"Not bad. I dug up a lot of the information you wanted about the two trials where he was found not guilty by reason of insanity. Spent thirty bucks photocopying transcripts and things and I'd just finished stowing it all away in a dresser drawer when he came knocking on the door and I assumed it had to be you and opened up like an idiot without checking the peephole. I suppose you'll need to read everything yourself but you specifically asked me to find out who Bloch's lawyer was, remember?"

"And?"

"The same man handled both his trials. Solo practitioner by the name of Robert Carr."

"Never heard of him."

"I checked a bit and discovered he was Saul Grimsby's brother-in-law," Val said, and licked her croissant-buttery fingertips.

Loren leapt out of his chair and paced the bedroom passionately. *Another lawyer connected with Anthony!* Maybe another junior associate in his operation, another likely suspect in his murder. Then he froze, running through his mind exactly what Val had just told him. "*Was* his brother-in-law?" he asked.

"He's dead too," Val told him. "He was killed last year in a seven-car pile-up on Interstate 270 during a thunderstorm. Makes you wonder, doesn't it, darling?"

Another Clifford Bloch special, Loren thought as his excitement level dropped like a stone. *Shit.*

He was still trying to digest the news when the bedroom phone atop a pillow began to ring and he threw a glance at the clock radio on the pillow beside it and read 0800 in ruby numerals. "Domjan," he growled, reaching for the handset. "Morning, Sergeant," he greeted the caller without waiting to hear a voice. "Sleep well?" In the moments before there was a reply he realized it might just as likely be Gael on the other end and mentally kicked himself.

"I've forgotten what the word means, sir." Relief flooded him at the sound of the sergeant's voice, which was ragged with exhaustion. "If I can only sleep forever after I die that'll be heaven enough for me. Want to know why I've been up most of the night?"

They found Kim's body, a voice not Domjan's told him without words, and he almost dropped the phone.

"You'd never believe what Anthony kept in those file cabinets," the sergeant went on. "Documentation on every dirty deal he had a hand in, everything from bribing assistant attorney generals and paying off judges to multiple murders with the Blochs or a couple of freelance hit men doing the honors. The way you put it all together when we were driving in from Fulton was right on the money. The stuff in Joyce Clarke's scrapbooks was just the tip of the iceberg. Take my word, sir, with what we've got we could have sent him and everybody else in the operation to the death house if they hadn't killed each other off and saved us the trouble."

"How about Grimsby?" Loren asked. "No one's killed him yet."

"Feds picked him up on Kauai a couple hours ago. He'll fight extradition of course; probably claim everything we found in the caves was the fruit of a poison tree and can't be used against him. But that's still not the half of it, sir. Anthony was—well, he was keeping a sort of a diary in one of those file drawers. Couple thousand pages of typescript, neat as a pin, packed full of details like a Victorian novel, but what I kept thinking of as I went through it wasn't Dickens or Trollope, it was reading the Confessions of Saint Augustine in the seminary."

"Maybe when this is all over some publisher will want to do it as a book," Loren suggested. "Call it *The Confes-*

sions of Saint Anthony." In a vagrant corner of his mind he wondered who would own the rights to such a book, and tentatively decided it would be Kim. If she was alive. If she ever came back.

"He didn't leave anything out," Domjan said. "His first meeting with Howard Clarke, how they discovered they were sort of brothers in evil under the skin and formed a law partnership and started with just getting their hands a little muddy and graduated to being covered in filth. Where they first hooked up with the Bloch brothers. Why Clarke left the firm to become a judge. How . . ."

"What was his reason?" Loren interrupted.

"He was owed favors for some political dirty tricks and he knew as a federal judge he'd have maximum power to hurt people and close to zero accountability. I tell you, just skimming this damn script I feel like I've been eating putrid corpse meat."

"Anything in it about Anthony's obsession with death?"

"Dozens of pages. That maniac really believed he was never going to die! And he's constantly quoting Chesterton and, my God, Chesterton was a *religious* writer! Ever hear of a book of his called *The Man Who Was Thursday?"*

"Just vaguely." Loren dredged through memories of the law school weekends he'd spent in the main university library, struggling to cope with old Hirschberg's bizarre paradoxes by speed-reading as much of Chesterton as possible. "I think it's a sort of metaphysical spy novel. The good organization and the bad one turn out to have the same man at the top, this Thursday."

"I don't know the book but that ties in with what Anthony wrote about it. That's where he got his inspiration for the vigilante idea. He'd been behind all these murders and other crimes and now he'd be behind this phony organization that was supposed to root out the rot in the legal system. Joyce Clarke was a pawn, he used her like a piece of toilet paper, but she took the fake vigilante notion seriously and tried to make it real. Poor schnook." At the mention of toilet paper Loren's thoughts had flashed to the note he'd found in Joyce's apartment. *My God, is it still in the tissue box in the Cressida!* "You know, sir, as I think it over, I'm convinced I was wrong what I said before. We could never in a million years have put him in the death house. His lawyer would have trotted out this manuscript and proved he was batty as a bedbug."

"What does he say in the book about Kim?" Loren demanded.

The silence roared in his ear.

"Come on, tell me!" he cried out into the mouthpiece.

Then for a long time he said nothing and just listened. Across the room Val knew from the way he sat and the look in his eyes that something inside him had died.

───────────

"HE MADE THE LAST entry in the book two months ago," Loren said. The numerals on the clock radio read 0853 and most of the time since eight sharp he'd been on the phone with Domjan. At the end of the session he had taken the instrument off the hook and gone to the bathroom and gulped three Valium with a glass of water. "We still don't know if she's alive or dead or how deeply she got involved in his operation or why she went on the run but we know a great deal about her. More than I ever wanted to know."

"Tell me," Val said gently.

"Remember how Rosemary Anthony couldn't remember if she ever had a daughter?" Val said nothing. "She had one. Anthony had a sister. He started having sex with her when she was ten. At fifteen she got pregnant. Rosemary sent her out of the state to one of those private sanitariums where girls with money went to have babies back in the forties. She gave birth to a healthy daughter but died of septicemia a few days later. Rosemary arranged for a private adoption. The baby's new parents were named Hale."

"Oh my God," Val whispered.

"Rosemary was widowed early and raised her two children alone. Now she was down to one. She handled everything so Garrett would be protected and then she pre-

sented him with her bill. Made him have sex with her. It
went on until the Korean War broke out and he was sent
over."

Val took his hand between hers and stroked the fingers
softly. He could feel the Valium deadening him.

"I don't know how Kim tracked him down but somehow
she found out he was her father. We don't know if she ever
knew his sister was her mother but there's a chance that's
why she went on the run. Domjan says there's nothing in
the manuscript about anything that happened in the past
two months. I guess he was too busy killing his former
colleagues to keep the diary current." He took his hand
from her embrace, crawled under the bedcovers into a fetal
position. "I wish I could sleep and never wake up," he said,
his voice drifting. "I can't handle . . . can't . . ."

"How can I help, love?" she said. "What do you want me
to do?"

"Stay with me," he said. She sat on the edge of the bed
and tried to blink the tears from her eyes and caressed him
through the blankets until the Valium drew him into the
caves of sleep.

Most of that day and night and most of the next he lived
in a soft twilight haze. Whatever life went on outside the
room, whatever Val did, was in a world apart. Sometime
late Friday afternoon he emerged from the cave. Stumbled
into the bathroom, took a long scalding shower, shaved,
found fresh clothes, opened the bedroom door and discovered the living room of the suite refurnished and Val in a
pale-blue pantsuit half asleep on the couch in a nest of
weekly news magazines and paperback romances. She
heard his steps on the carpet and leapt awake. "Are you all
right?" she asked.

"I'm fine now more or less," he said. "I'm going back to
New York tomorrow."

She swept the papers and magazines to the floor and
tugged him down on the cushions beside her. "Why?" she
asked.

"To see if I can end this." He saw the sudden panic in
her eyes and heard her sharp intake of breath and knew

he'd said the wrong thing. "Not my life. This nightmare. With luck I can end it tomorrow."

"I'm going with you," she insisted.

"I have to do this alone," he told her. "You committed one crime for Kim already when you had your hacker friend break into the FBI computer files. I may have to commit a bigger one for her tomorrow. I don't want you involved."

"If I can help you I don't care what the law calls it," she said.

"Besides I need you here. Has Domjan called back?"

"Three times. And I called Gael yesterday right after you went under for the first time. I told both of them you were too wiped out to come to the phone. Gael's really concerned about you. We had dinner together last night."

"I don't want either of them to know where I've gone," Loren said. "Domjan especially. When he calls again— don't come flat out and say this, after all you hardly know the man, but give him the impression you're afraid I've flipped out over all this and Gael and I have gone off for a weekend in each other's arms. Think you can pull it off?"

"Easy as pie," she assured him, and grinned impishly. "About ten percent of me has a sneaking suspicion that's actually where you're going to be, darling, except I know you've been out like a light for the past thirty-six hours and there's no way you could have arranged it."

"I could have called her while you were on the way to meet her for dinner," he argued playfully.

"In a pig's eye you could have," she informed him. "First of all, I know you were in no shape to call anyone because I've been with you since yesterday morning and every time you got up to go to the bathroom and chugalug more Valium I heard every move you made. Second of all, Gael and I didn't eat out, we ordered from room service right here."

"Outgunned again," he sighed, and concluded it was prudent to change the subject. "Are you in the mood for a real restaurant meal tonight, maybe some jazz later?"

"The W. C. Handy type or the other?"

He knew she knew the original meaning of the word as well as he did. "How about both kinds?" he suggested.

ELECTRIC EYES slid back the glass doors and he marched into the Saturday-morning drowsiness of Lambert International Airport. The airline ticket he'd purchased at the Laclede Suites travel desk was stuffed in his breast pocket and his attaché case held all the luggage he needed. He took an escalator to the lower level, passed under the lifesize model of Lindbergh's Spirit of St. Louis suspended like a mobile from the ceiling, went through the security checkpoint and marched down a long sterile concourse carpeted in orange and blue. Ten seconds after he'd dropped into a scooped-out plastic seat in the waiting area next to Gate 36, a voice brimming with artificial joy came squawking over the PA system to thank the passengers for choosing the mighty airline that they had and to inform them that their flight was ready for boarding. Loren followed the jetway corridor into the plane, snapped his seat belt into place and, to the extent possible in coach class, stretched his legs.

The two-hour flight was smooth as a sheet of glass. Part of the time he dozed and part he spent thinking about Kim. What if she was found alive and well but in legal trouble? How would he defend her? It wasn't hard to devise a plausible account of her going on the run that would obviate the need to admit she'd ever been involved in Anthony's crimes. The man was walking evil. He'd slept with his sister and his mother. Might he not have made a move on his daughter too? Wouldn't that have sent any normal woman on the run, made her do and say what Kim had done and said?

He decided that any reasonable jury would buy the story but he still had no idea if it was true and wondered if he ever would.

THE AUDITORIUM of Vanderbilt Hall overflowed with guests. The administration and faculty of NYU School of Law were seated on the stage in four long rows, looking down on nearly two hundred graduating students and their spouses and parents and friends who filled the chairs and rear aisle and spilled out the padded double doors into the corridor. The law school had awarded something like four hundred J.D. degrees and three hundred advanced degrees at the general graduation ceremony that morning while Loren had been in the air. The evening program was an honors convocation, admittance by invitation only, reserved for the best and brightest, for those who had graduated cum laude or served on the Law Review or earned some special prize or distinction. The dean took the podium and introduced Justice Blackmun of the U.S. Supreme Court, who delivered an address on the social responsibilities of the privileged. Loren hovered at the edge of the open doorway and caught glimpses of the ceremony through the shifting screen of bodies that thronged the rear aisle.

Yes. There he was. The end was in sight.

The associate dean began to call names. Family members with cameras scurried up the two center aisles to strategic spots from which they could record for posterity the moment when a son or daughter or sister or brother or spouse or significant other was summoned from a front-row seat to go up on stage and be congratulated. Loren recognized the names of some who had been in his classes or seminar. *And what will all these new lawyers do now?* he wondered. Join the old ones whose outrages fed the public disgust at the profession? He kept to his place outside the doorway until the convocation was dismissed and a tidal wave of relatives and friends surged forward to kiss and embrace and hug their honored loved ones. When the doors and the rear space were clear, he began working his way up the left center aisle.

He had covered half the distance to the stage when he saw his quarry shake hands with Blackmun and move slowly to the side and down the steps at the front edge of the stage. He was heading out by the right center aisle, and Loren was trapped in the left center aisle amid a mob of men and women pressing remorselessly forward.

He elbowed his way into one of the center rows of seats and past some of the spectators in the row and trampled on toes without apology until he found his path blocked by three stout old men standing together and gossiping and couldn't get past them and vaulted over the tops of two vacant seats into the next row. He came out into the right center aisle twenty seconds too late. The target was beyond him and only a few feet from the corridor doors. He plunged along the aisle in his quarry's wake and reached the exit to the street just as the other was leaving the building and came up in a frenzied dash from behind and felt the other wince as he seized his left arm.

"That where the knife got you, Tex?" he asked.

For a moment Okamoto stood in the doorway rigid as an obelisk but then he seemed to go limp and the tension vanished from his bright dark eyes and Loren knew that Tex knew it was over.

"These boots were made for walkin'." Okamoto glanced down at the cowboy footwear by which Loren had picked him out on the stage. "Let's mosey, okay?" Like comrades from a forgotten war they strolled arm in arm to the corner of West Fourth Street and crossed to the edge of Washington Square Park to an empty stone bench and a table inlaid with a chessboard. They sat on the cold stone and the streetlight glow dyed their faces amber.

"Where did I slip up, pardner?" he asked.

"It all clicked," Loren explained, "when I saw the scene around Anthony's body for what it was. You were cut fighting over the knife but he was cut worse. You left him to bleed to death, found the half-bath and took care of your wound as best you could. Then you went back to the study to make sure he was dead and you discovered that after you'd left him on the floor and before he died he'd managed to write part of your name in his blood. Your real name, H I D E O, and maybe the beginning of the first letter of Okamoto. You gave him a business card when he came to the door, right? That's how he knew your name."

"Old habits die hard." Okamoto shook his head in disbelief at his own stupidity.

"What were you going to do about it? You didn't know how much time you had but you did know Anthony's mother was upstairs. Was she playing Beethoven all through your fight with him? Suppose she'd heard the noise and called 911? The study phone was off the hook but she could have had a private number in her room. You're a quick thinker, Tex. Every good law professor has to be. You knew from Joyce Clarke about his obsession with death and what it would be like to die. That gave you the answer. *You altered his message naming you, so it read like a message about the nature of death.* All you had to do was moisten his finger with a bit more of his blood, turn the beginning of his second O into a U and add an S. Then you left."

"On the money so far, hoss." Okamoto offered Loren a polite formal bow he had never learned in Texas.

"Once I saw that much," Loren continued, "so much else fell into place. Like the way it began a week ago Sunday morning when Kim phoned me begging for help. Well, anyone could have found out I was visiting at NYU this year. *But how could she have known the phone number at the apartment I'd borrowed?* It wasn't in my name! Someone who knew the number must have given it to her. *And you knew the number, Tex.* You called me there the night you invited me to the Yale Club for dinner with Judge Ostrander."

"Well, I sure wasn't the only one who knew." Okamoto spoke dispassionately, like a lawyer arguing a position he didn't believe in, or a person playing a game to keep from being bored.

"*But you were the only one in the world besides Ostrander and myself who knew I was walking him uptown to his co-op after dinner!* Remember how you excused yourself outside the Club and headed for Grand Central to catch a cab home? Less than an hour later, the minute I'm leaving Ostrander's building on Park and Eighty-eighth, Joyce Clarke and Clifford Bloch happen to be driving south on Park and stumble into me! I don't care how much coincidence there is in the world, Tex, that was too much for me. Someone must have told them where I'd be. And no one could have done that but you."

"Too subtle," Okamoto chided him gently. "No jury would buy that unless they'd grown up reading a lot of old-fashioned detective stories, and maybe not even then."

"Oh, but there's more," Loren said. "When I thought back to what Joyce told me, I realized she'd said something that confirmed the conclusion I'd already reached on other grounds. While she was trying to recruit me into her hare-brained vigilante scheme, she said I couldn't hide behind my professor title, *that others didn't*. I didn't catch it at the time but later I saw she had to be referring to you."

Okamoto said nothing but turned away from Loren and looked across West Fourth to the laughing, chattering young law graduates and their families in the shadow of Vanderbilt Hall. "Guess my professor title's up shit creek now," he said quietly. "You know, I had a hunch I'd be picked up tonight. Must have left a mile-wide trail in St. Louis. Flew under my own name, rented a car under my own name, left some of my blood in the house . . ."

"You believed you'd be arrested but you came here anyway?"

"Where am I going to run? I have a fourteen-year-old daughter who's been in a persistent vegetative state since she was five. What was I going to do, abandon her?"

Loren remembered Tex's cryptic mention of a daughter during one unguarded moment in the faculty lounge a week ago Monday. "Tell me," he said.

Okamoto took out tobacco and his cherrywood pipe. "I'd rather do this with a bourbon in my hand but what the hell. I'd gone through a rough divorce. She got custody of our daughter and married again and moved to the Chicago area when she and her new husband both got good jobs out there. One foggy morning she was on the Dan Ryan Expressway, taking the kid to pre-school before she clocked in at the ad agency. Her car and nine or ten others got into a wreck in the fog. Three people were killed. She was one, the president of some corporation was another. A bunch of people were maimed for life. One of them was my kid. She had a cerebral contusion and her brain was without oxygen for ten minutes before the paramedics reached her. That's irreversible damage, hoss. She is a spastic quadriplegic. She can't eat or drink. She's kept alive by tubes . . . Her new father couldn't take it and bugged out of the picture. That left me. I had her flown back to New York in an ambulance plane and she's been here ever since, in a hospital uptown. I see her every couple of days. I know she'll never get better but I . . . I suppose I keep hoping for a medical miracle. I just can't ask the doctors to pull the plug." He sat motionless on the stone bench and stared at the chessboard.

Loren dimly sensed the shape of the next chapter before Tex told it. "Then you met Joyce Clarke," he said.

"I ran into her in a bar on a snowy night, oh, say, a year and a half ago. She was just so damn lonely and pathetic. I wasn't interested in her sexually, she was built too much like the sovereign state of Texas for my taste, but we sort of drifted into being casual buddies. Then after a few months she started dropping hints about a vigilante organization to wipe out the filth in the legal system. I played along with her. In time she let me have a peek or three at her scrapbooks. Have you seen them?"

"One," Loren said.

"A lot of the stuff in them had to do with the obscene garbage lawyers and judges get away with, but what she called the justice book, the stories about some of them getting killed in so-called accidents or by natural causes— well, the accident that left my child a vegetable was in there, and so were a passel of other multi-car pile-ups. I began to realize that there was a connection between Joyce Clarke and some fucking bastard who'd destroy a dozen people to kill one target." His pipe bowl glowed as he drew on the stem. "I stayed friendly with her and after a while she opened up to me about her scumbag father and his former law partner Garrett Anthony, and she claimed it was Anthony got her to recruit Ruth Schrader to blow her old man to hell. I could see Anthony'd been twisting her mind like a pretzel and in time I saw he was responsible for, oh God, so much evil and—well, I decided to do something about him."

"Of course you didn't try to open Joyce's eyes to the truth," Loren said.

"She was no more curable than my kid. Any fool could see that. No, I just bided my time. I've got more patience in me than most Texans. And then two and a half weeks ago she called me and asked me to come over to her place right away and she had a woman staying with her. Beautiful woman about forty or so, petite, terrified . . ."

"You saw Kim at Joyce's place? What did she tell you?"

"Nothing specific. Just that she was in deep trouble and couldn't go to the cops. They neither of them mentioned Anthony or St. Louis even. Then the next day I called Joyce and she said Miss Hale was gone. Wouldn't say where, wouldn't say why. I still don't know if she gave Anthony the tip or if he figured on his own Miss Hale would go to see Joyce. My God, he was her father and he sent a psycho killer to . . ." Tex's eyes shut. In the streetlight Loren saw tears shining as they trickled along his cheeks.

"Hold it," he said. "Backtrack a bit for me. When Joyce had you come over to meet Kim, you gave her my number. There's no other way she could have called me at home. You mean you didn't know . . ."

"The only reason I thought of you was because you've had a bunch of investigative experience. How could I have known the two of you'd been lovers back in the sixties?" Okamoto's eyes were wide now and bright with emotion as Loren had never seen them before. "The way she looked when I mentioned your name and said you were on the faculty with me . . . If I could see my daughter look at me that way just once . . . Oh, fuck it." He withdrew into a shell of silence. Loren counted thirty before he broke into his colleague's pain.

"A week ago Monday," he said, "we had lunch at the Old Corral and I told you what happened to me on the ferry. That was when you put it together, right? You knew I must have heard from Kim."

"Had to be. And the way you described the hombre that conked you in the terminal put me in mind of that picture of Jonathan Bloch in Joyce's scrapbook."

"So what did you do about it?"

"Called Joyce when she got home from work. Told her what I knew and that she'd damn well come visit me pronto and explain. She didn't come herself but she sent her flunky. Called himself Morgan but he sure God looked like Jonathan Bloch's picture and your description of the skunk on the ferry."

"That was Jonathan's brother," Loren told him. "The auto stunt specialist. Don't you remember reading about him in the scrapbooks?" Okamoto shook his head no. "He was the one who killed your ex-wife and left your kid ruined."

Okamoto howled, a single cry so horrible that stragglers from the ceremony on the other side of West Fourth craned their necks to see what possessed the two men at the chess table and then, being New Yorkers, hastily moved away.

"He's dead now," Loren said. "A good rough death. Anthony left him to starve in a cave with just some arsenic sandwiches to eat when he couldn't take it any longer." Okamoto let out a soft breath. "I have to know what he told you when he paid you that visit."

"He said they'd had to put Miss Hale out of the way because she knew too much about the vigilantes. That may have been bullshit, I don't know. But he swore up and down that she made a getaway a few hours after they'd grabbed her at the ferry slip. He said they were still hunting for her but hadn't cut her trail."

"Did you believe him?"

"My God, man, how could I tell? He might have tracked

her down before our talk or after, killed her, dumped her somewhere. Or maybe she got away clean."

"And you didn't call me or the police," Loren said. "I can never forgive you for that, Tex."

Okamoto's eyes burned in agony that made Loren flinch. "How could I risk involving myself and leaving my child in the lurch just on the chance he was lying to me? Would that have helped the woman if he'd killed her already?"

"It might have saved her if he hadn't killed her yet."

"I did what a lawyer does," Okamoto said. "Compromised. I set up a meet between you and Ostrander, sort of nudged you in the right direction. Then I called Joyce and put the idea in her head she ought to pick you up on Park Avenue and invite you into her outfit. I was hoping you'd follow the trail from her to Anthony and St. Louis and . . ." He shook his head in bewilderment. "I don't know what I was trying to accomplish. Save Miss Hale's life maybe. Ease my conscience. I swear I didn't know Joyce would be killed next."

"Was that Anthony's orders or Bloch's own idea?"

"I don't know," Okamoto said. Loren felt a cold hollow spot growing inside him like a cancer as he realized how much of the truth no one would ever know.

"Anyway," Tex continued, "I let things fester till last Tuesday and then I flew to St. Louis for a showdown with Anthony. You got it right, I gave him one of my cards when he answered the door. He knew who I was 'cause Joyce had told him she'd been recruiting me but he had no idea on earth what he'd done to my life and my daughter's life. We were in his study when he pulled that toad-sticker on me. He said there was another law prof from NYU in St. Louis and I knew it was you. Said you were using a phony handle but he'd recognized you from Bloch's description of what went down on the ferry and had sent him to your hotel to finish you off. Afterward the two of them were going to truck me out to his private caves and leave me to starve. You saw I wasn't surprised when you brought up those caves and starving to death a couple minutes ago. Now you know why. Anyway, that's not the way I plan to die. I went for him and we had a slambang free-for-all and—well, in the end I got the knife."

"And then things happened the way I laid them out before?"

"Right on the money. You are one righteous detective, amigo."

"But once again you didn't bother to call me or the police."

Okamoto leaned forward with palms extended in supplication. "This you've got to believe. I would have warned you Bloch was after your scalp but I didn't know where you were staying or what name you were using! All I could do was fly back here and pray he didn't find you. I didn't sleep a wink that night. Wednesday morning I went to the newsstand on Sixth Avenue that carries all the major papers in the world and I bought a St. Louis *Post-Dispatch* and saw that Bloch had got what was coming to him. And—then I just hung around waiting to be caught. Saying a few goodbyes. I don't give a shit what the law does to me as long as my kid's looked after. Will . . . you see to her for me, pardner?"

"If it comes to that, I will." Loren reached out a hand which Okamoto clasped in his own. "Maybe the police will find you on their own but I don't aim to help them."

They sat under the streetlight in the late-spring chill in a long deep silence encircled by the night sounds of the city. They might have been two sitting statues. The spell was broken by Okamoto's sardonic chuckle.

"Hell of a pair of law professors we make, hoss," he said, and put away his pipe.

Thirteen

THE WHEEL HAD SPUN HIM back to where it had started. Waterside Plaza. Sunday morning before dawn. Horns hooting and sirens wailing from invisible streets. Shimmer of moonlight on boats gliding down the lonely river. He was in the same bed alone and holding the same phone to his ear but with a different woman listening. Not Kim. Not Kim. He seemed to have been talking forever. He knew there was a chance that Domjan and the FBI still had the apartment bugged but he was too spent to care.

"I'm going out with him tomorrow to see his daughter. As long as he knows she'll be cared for I'm afraid he may kill himself if he thinks he's going to be arrested for murder. I don't know how much I can do for her if that happens. I've got the money from my father's estate, I can pay the hospital bills but . . ."

"Suppose her father's put away for a long time," Val said, "or does something to himself. Would you adopt her?"

Loren sat with his back propped against the pillows and wondered if he had the strength to adopt a child who would never know him or smile at him or put her arms around him, who would spend the rest of her days in a hospital cage pierced by tubes and would die in her youth without once having lived.

"I might like an Asian daughter," Val said quietly, "if a big Caucasian bear with glasses came with the package."

The words seared him like a white-hot poker through his ear. He winced and bit his lip hard and looked around the dark empty room with a hunted animal's desperation and said nothing.

"I'm sorry, darling." It was as if she could see him, read his mood from the silence. "I know you have to be sure about Kim first."

"But what if I'm never sure? When I think about it my mind tells me she's dead. Bloch lied to Tex. They found her and killed her somewhere around New York. What's left of her will be found next week or next year or in the twenty-second century. But some crazy instinct tells me different. Tells me she's still alive and needs me."

"Wouldn't she have come forward by now if she were?" Val asked the question with infinite gentleness.

"She could be too terrified," Loren argued.

"Domjan called again last night. He told me they've kept a blackout on the whole story till now but he and the FBI and Major Duke will be holding a joint press conference Sunday morning. Once the media come out with everything, won't she know she's safe?"

"Safe from Anthony and the Bloch brothers," Loren said. "Not necessarily from the law. We still don't know how deeply she was involved in her father's operations. She visited Mrs. Schrader in Fulton posing as his secretary. She signed in as Kay Rhodes but either she or Anthony told Mrs. Schrader her real name was Kim because that's the name she called her by in the note she smuggled out to Joyce Clarke. Joyce had to know her by her real name too, or Mrs. Schrader wouldn't have used it in the note. Kim must have been involved at least to that extent and maybe a lot more. She may have good reason to keep in hiding. Or suppose she's where the news won't reach her, or she's hurt and can't come forward? I can't go home yet. I have to stay here and see if anything happens."

"How long will it take?"

"I don't know," he said.

"Darling, will you ever be able to let her go? Come back to here and now? To me?"

"I don't know," he said. "I want you, I need you so much

215

but I just don't know." He kept his voice low, tried to keep the anguish inside him.

"How long am I supposed to wait for you?"

On the river the horn of a night boat hooted.

That was in the spring of 1987. He never found her.